A TORMENTED MAN (SPECIAL FORCES OPERATION ALPHA)

AN APPALACHIAN STAR NOVEL

BOOK SIX

DEANNDRA HALL

Dear Readers,

Welcome to the Special Forces: Operation Alpha Fan-Fiction world!

If you are new to this amazing world, in a nutshell the author wrote a story using one or more of my characters in it. Sometimes that character has a major role in the story, and other times they are only mentioned briefly. This is perfectly legal and allowable because they are going through Aces Press to publish the story.

This book is entirely the work of the author who wrote it. While I might have assisted with brainstorming and other ideas about which of my characters to use, I didn't have any part in the process or writing or editing the story.

I'm proud and excited that so many authors loved my characters enough that they wanted to write them into their own story. Thank you for supporting them, and me!

READ ON!

Xoxo

Susan Stoker

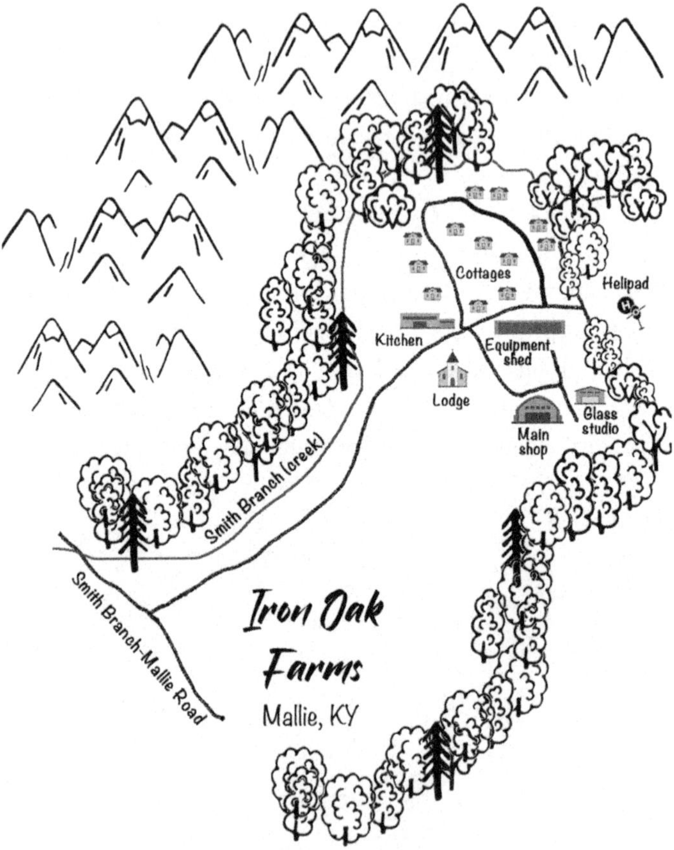
Cottages
Helipad
Kitchen
Equipment shed
Lodge
Main shop
Glass studio
Smith Branch (creek)
Smith Branch-Mallie Road
Iron Oak Farms
Mallie, KY

AUTHOR'S NOTE

The map of Mallie, Kentucky, is not an accurate depiction of the area, although Mallie does indeed exist. It is roughly 24 miles from Hazard, Kentucky; 13 miles from Hindman, Kentucky; and 20 miles from Whitesburg, Kentucky. It's also approximately 81 miles from Fallport, Virginia, the home of Susan Stoker's Eagle Point Search and Rescue.

CHAPTER 1

PADDY

AFTER I TALKED TO REBOOT ON HIS PORCH, I WENT BACK TO the kitchen, but there was nobody there. On the off chance that they might still be up, I headed to the lodge. The lights were on in the great room, and I figured it was a possibility anyway.

Luckily for me, Tony, Nikki, Laura, and Vic are up, along with Steve and Kelly McCoy, and Patch and Penny are with them. But they're all having a drink together, and I feel like I've stepped in at the wrong moment. "Oh, sorry. I'll—"

"No, no, Paddy! Come have a drink with us!" Tony calls out, and the rest join him in calling me back, so I step inside.

Vic's already on his feet. "Whaddya want? Beer? Bourbon?"

"Just a beer will be fine. Thanks," I say as he hands it to me.

"What are you doing in here at this hour?" Steve asks.

"I was hoping to talk to … Nikki." My heart is pounding out of my chest.

I'm just sure one of them is going to say it's time for pleasure, not business, but instead, Nikki pats the cushion beside her on the sofa and says, "Come on over here and have a seat, hon. What's on your mind?"

I sit, but I'm afraid to scoot back into the cushions, for fear that'll be too familiar or something. "Um, I wanted to talk to you about … You know that scholarship you …" Maybe this was a mistake. Maybe I should just crack a joke and change the subject.

"Oh, for school? Yeah. You want to apply?"

"Oh, um, well, I just wondered if anybody had applied for it. That's all." She'll say yes. I'm sure of it. Somebody's bound to want it.

"No. Do you want to? Oh, please, tell me you do!" She looks very excited, and I'm surprised at that.

"Well, I … If nobody else has applied, I thought …"

Tony leans in, his elbows on his thighs. "Paddy, if you want the scholarship, I think I can speak for Nikki and tell you that it's yours. She's been hoping for weeks that somebody would say something and show some interest."

"Yeah, I'd about given up. I was beginning to think nobody would want it. Do you? Want it, I mean?" Nikki asks, and her eyes are lit up like I've never seen.

Get your shit together, O'Brien, I tell myself. *Say the words*. "Yes. I do."

To my surprise, Nikki hops up from the sofa and does a little dance. "Oh my god, I'm so excited! This is so great!" Then she spins and hugs me. And in the next second …

She's crying.

Now I'm really confused until Tony says, "Babe, you're confusing the hell outta him. Come here." She turns me loose, then shifts and buries her face in Tony's shoulder, sobbing.

"I'm sorry. I mean, I don't … If you don't want to—"

"No, no. Nothing like that." When she sits up and faces me, her face is a mess of tears, and then I notice that Laura and Kelly both are crying too. "I did this in memory of my kids, and I'd just about decided nobody cared. So thank you. You have no idea what this means to me."

Don't say the wrong thing, I chide myself. "Well, I hope I can live up to your expectations and make you proud, and help everybody remember them."

She smiles and pats my hands. "I'm sure you will. I'm sorry. It just hit me out of the blue. I just don't want their lives to be for nothing, you know?"

"They weren't, Nik," Vic says and reaches to take her hand. "They made the world a better place while they were with you. They'll keep doing it because of this. It's a great thing you're doing here," he says with a gentle smile.

"So generous," Penny says, her eyes misty.

"I just want to help. That's all. What good is money if you don't help somebody with it? It's no good. So this is my way of helping." She sniffs and wipes her nose with the tissue Laura hands to her. "So, what do you want to do? What's your goal?"

"I'd like to get EMT certified."

"Yes!" Patch barks. "Hallelujah! I'm not even getting the scholarship and one of *my* wishes is coming true!"

"That's so awesome, Paddy! Yes! You're definitely getting the scholarship. Steve," Nikki says, turning to the family attorney and friend, "do you have the paperwork for him to fill out?"

"Yeah, I can get that in a few minutes. I've got my laptop with me, so I can print it off and we can finish that up in no time. Congratulations, Paddy," Steve says and gives me a warm smile.

"It's getting late, and I'm sure you guys don't want to be bothered with me. Can I fill it out tomorrow?"

Steve nods. "Sure. Kelly and I are going into Hazard to have brunch with a friend, but we'll be back here to go back with everybody else and I'll pick it up then."

"Great! Thanks." It was just this easy. I can't believe it. I'm going to be an EMT!

I finish my beer and look around. "Well, I guess I'm gonna hit the hay. All this excitement today has worn me out."

One by one, everybody else stands. "Yeah, it's been a long day—a good one, but a long one," Tony says and stretches. "I think I'm headed to bed. Babe, you comin'?"

"Yep. Right behind you. Night, guys. See you in the morning." Nikki takes Tony's hand and I watch as he leads her down the hallway and into the room they're occupying.

"Lights out for us too. Come on, big guy," Laura says and takes Vic's hand.

As she leads him down the hallway, he turns back and grins. "Can't say no to somebody this beautiful, now can you?"

Steve's laughing. "Ball buster!"

"I heard that!" Laura calls back, laughing.

"We're gone too," Steve says as he takes Kelly's hand. "I'll get those forms to you in the morning and I can pick them up when I come back. After you fill them out, have Tony and Nikki look at them to see if there's anything else they want to know."

"I'll do that. Thanks, Steve." He gives me a backhanded wave as they wander down the hallway, and the bedroom door closes behind them.

"Well, well, well. It's a surprise, but a good one," Patch says and slaps my shoulder. "This is really awesome. Once you get the paperwork all filled out, you can get some info from the school and we'll figure out schedules and all that shit. Right now, I'm headed to bed, but congratulations, brother. This is great." He hugs me, and then Penny gives me a hug.

"I'm proud of you, Paddy," she whispers as she turns loose and steps back.

"Thanks. I hope I can make everybody proud."

"You will, brother," Patch says and smiles. "I have no doubt of it. See you in the morning." I wait as he and Penny stroll out the door, then I grab another beer before I head to my cottage.

Looks like there's going to be another EMT at Iron Oak Farms. I'm going back to school!

IT'S KIND OF EARLY FOR ME TO BE UP ON A SUNDAY MORNING, but I'm a little excited. I check and, sure enough, there's plenty of breakfast food in the refrigerator. I'm about to pull something out to heat up when the kitchen door opens and a polished-as-ever Vic Walters strolls in with four huge boxes. "Hope you like donuts," he says as he plops the boxes down on the counter.

"Love 'em, but you didn't have to do that," I say. Then I add, "But thank you for doing it."

He chuckles. "You can't imagine how great it is to wake up without a three-year-old staring into your face."

"Actually, I can," I answer, thinking about my boys.

"Yeah? You got kids?"

"Yeah, but I haven't seen them since before I went to prison."

"You should change that. Kids are such a blessing. I didn't think I'd ever have any, and now I have a houseful. Wasn't an easy road, but I got there."

"Yeah? I figured you and Laura had been married a long time," I say, trying to figure out which donut I want first.

"Nope. Not that long. Sophie and Christopher are adopted. And I'm twelve years older than Laura."

"Would never have guessed *that*." It's not a lie. He looks younger than her, at least to me. "Been married before?"

"Nope. Never. Long, hard history with women. Started being pimped out by my dad when I was twelve, and ended with working as a service Dom in Steve's club until I met Laura."

I'm pretty sure I'm having some kind of hallucination. "Wha … What did you say?"

He grins without looking at me. "Yeah. I was a service Dom in Steve's club."

"Steve has a club?"

"Yeah. Kink club in Lexington."

Holy shit. I don't know what to say or think. "Wow. I had no idea."

"Yeah. Lemme tell ya, you won't meet a kinkier family than the Walters. Our oldest brother is a Dominant who lives with his submissive. I think they're getting married."

I snicker. "But not Tony and Nikki."

Vic laughs. "Oh, you got that one totally wrong! She's the kinkiest little thing in the state."

"Nikki?" Have I just slipped into an alternate dimension?

"Hell yeah. She taught my brother a thing or two."

"And they haven't been married that long either?"

"Nope. Both of them were married for a long, long time.

Her husband was killed, but you knew that already. His ex-wife was crazy as a loon. She finally got herself killed by a husband. Third or fourth. We never were really clear on that one. Nope, my brother was a sweet, innocent thing, and Nikki turned him wrong side out and upside down. Taught him things he never would've known otherwise. Good little Catholic mama's boy. I'm not knocking it. He's a great guy, but boy, was he sexually starved. He's turned out to be a really, really powerful daddy Dom. He runs the household, and she knows she's taken care of and safe. That seems to be all she ever really wanted. Well, that and a fun foursome, but he totally doesn't share. Period."

Something tells me this is exactly the guy I need to talk to. "So can I ask you something?"

Vic shrugs. "Sure. Ask away. We're really open in our family about sex … and pretty much everything else."

"I'm trying to figure out how to meet a woman."

I'd already started a pot of coffee, and Vic pours both of us a cup, then steps over to the table, sets them down, and picks up his plate of donuts before he takes a seat. I do the same. "So, you go to a church around here?"

"Nope. Don't believe in that stuff."

"Gotcha. What about internet sites?"

"I don't even know how to go about finding somebody online who would share my … proclivities."

"There's a fetish website, but it's pretty swampy. So if you don't mind my asking, what are you looking for? Something really, really unusual? Because that's going to be difficult."

"I wouldn't say unusual. At least not that unusual. I mean, I like women who are smart and independent, funny, outgoing. And I don't want a submissive. I'm not interested in somebody who wants to *serve* me. At all. I just …" I might as well come out and say it. "I'm only interested in a woman being submissive in the bedroom."

He's chewing, but that comes to an abrupt halt, and he sits there for a few seconds, like he's mulling something over. Then he says, "Steve hasn't left yet, has he?"

"I don't think so."

"I need to talk to him before he leaves."

Holy shit. Did I just do something to jeopardize my scholarship? "Look, if it's about what we were talking about, I—"

"Yeah, it's about what we were talking about, and I think I may have your answer, but I need to talk to Steve."

"Oh. I thought you were going to say I couldn't have the scholarship because—"

"First, that's none of my business, and second, why would I think you should be penalized for your own needs? And for being honest with somebody about it? I respect you, man. You're a problem solver. That's great. And I—"

"Coffee? Is there coffee somewhere?" a voice asks, and I turn to see Steve standing there.

Vic nods and points. "Yeah. We've got a whole pot over here. And I need to talk to you before you leave. You're going to have brunch with Natalie, right?"

"Yeah."

"Tell her I said hello."

"Will do. Paddy, I'll get that scholarship form printed out for you, but I had to have some brain fuel first," Steve says, holding up his cup and heading back toward the door in his lounge pants and tee.

"Hey, you should probably take a cup to that little subbie of yours if you want to live to see brunch," Vic says and grabs a cup to fill.

When he hands it off to Steve, the attorney laughs. "Yeah,

you're right. If I come back with a cup and none for her, there'll be trouble for sure. See you guys in a bit."

The door closes behind him, and Vic turns to me. "Your problem may be sorted out by the end of the day."

I'd like to say, *Fat chance of that*, but if there's anything I've learned about the Walters family, it's that if they say something, they mean it. I just can't imagine how he's going to solve *that* problem.

But wouldn't it be nice if he could?

Natalie

"Oh my god, I've missed you guys!" I'm hugging Kelly, and then Steve, and then Kelly, and then Steve, and then … They can't possibly know how excited I am to see them. I feel so cut off here.

"We've missed you too! Let's all sit down so we can talk. Come on." Kelly leads the way and in a couple of seconds, we're seated in a big, comfy booth. "You look great! How's the job?"

"I like it. Of course, I'd like it a lot more if I was back in Lexington, but it's still great. The move was definitely worth it."

"Met anybody yet?" she asks, a twinkle in her eye.

"Nah. There's nobody here. I mean, yeah, there are people here, but I don't know how to meet them, and I sure don't know how to meet the kind of guy I need. I've just given up."

"Don't give up. Never give up. Any interesting cases lately?" Steve asks.

"Not really. Just garden-variety stuff."

Steve's laugh is sarcastic. "There are no garden-variety cases on the federal level."

"Actually, there are. Occasionally, we get a really juicy one thrown in, but not normally. There is a rumor of one coming down the pike, but I don't know if it'll be here or not."

"Which one is that?" Steve asks.

"Nope. Not saying. Don't want to jinx it." He laughs. "You know that'll happen!"

"Yeah, yeah. I'm just glad I'm not practicing anymore. Listening to the constant lying was getting to me."

"I hear ya. So you're visiting out at that farm. Iron Oak? What's that like?"

"Nice place. Nice people. You should check it out sometime," Kelly says and glances over at Steve.

I don't miss that look she gives him. "Oh? Is there something I should know?"

Steve's gaze is intense. "Actually, let's order our food and then we can talk."

After the first two bites of the most delicious quiche I've ever tasted, Steve says, "So how would you like to meet someone who's exactly the kind of guy you want?"

"And what kind of guy would that be?"

"Don't be ridiculous, Natalie. You and I have talked about this dozens of times, even before Kelly and I met. I know where your head is. And I think I know a guy whose head is in the exact same space."

"Oh, yeah? Really? And where's that?"

"Wants a woman who's smart, funny, as independent as she wants to be, but wants somebody who'll let him take control in the bedroom."

Now he's got my attention. "Uh-huh. And where might this guy be?"

"In Mallie."

The snort that I let loose is involuntary. "A man in Mallie? I wasn't aware that they even had a post office."

"Oh, they most certainly do have a post office, and they have some pretty manly men there too."

"And gorgeous. Did he mention gorgeous? Because they're gorgeous," Kelly adds.

"No, I didn't mention gorgeous because I don't know what constitutes a gorgeous man, Sunshine," he tells her, and she grins from ear to ear.

"Well, they are. Gorgeous," she reiterates, still grinning. "Look in the mirror and you'll see what I mean." She winks at him and for the first time I can ever remember, I almost think that big, bad Dom I've known for so many years just might melt.

Back to reality. "Okay, there's a catch. There's always a catch. What is it?"

Steve takes a deep breath, blows it out, and says, "He's an ex-con."

"Oh, no. No, no, no. You know I can't—"

"Hold up! Minimum security lockup for nine years, served his sentence with no problems or infractions, non-violent crime … Matter of fact, I don't think he should've been locked up. But a judge and jury didn't agree with my opinion, so it doesn't matter. Thing is, he's—"

"Sex crime?" I blurt out.

"No! Nothing like that. But it's a long, sad story."

"Drugs?"

"No. Nothing like that either. It was an accident that wound up ruled involuntary manslaughter. They tried to label it negligent homicide, but they couldn't make that stick."

"I see." And I'm not being flippant. I really do see, and from what he's saying, there shouldn't be a problem.

Steve leans in. "Are you the least bit interested?"

If I turn this down, I may never find anybody. What if this guy *is* the right one for me? "Sure. Yeah."

"Okay. I'll be seeing him later, and I'll ask him to give you a call. His name is Paddy. No. That's his nickname. Sunshine, what's—"

Kelly rolls her eyes. "Dennis. His real name is Dennis."

"Yeah. Dennis. So do you want to hear from him?"

What have you got to lose? I ask myself. "Sure."

"Okay. I'll give him your number and tell him to give you a call if he's interested. Now, tell me what happened with Judge Osborne. I hear he was doing some pretty kinky shit in chambers."

I launch into the story as best I can. There are some things I can't divulge, because the ethics board has already called me to ask what I know. But a chance to gossip about those stodgy old farts who think they're better than everybody else?

Fuck yeah.

PADDY

I'M OUT IN BACK OF REBOOT'S COTTAGE, LOOKING AT THE boat and trying to figure out what to attack first, when my cell phone rings. It's an unfamiliar number. "Hello?"

"Hey, it's Steve. Come on over to the lodge. I'll take your paperwork."

"Great! Be right there." I hit END and slap Reboot on the shoulder. "I've gotta go to the lodge and give Steve my scholarship paperwork."

"You're applying? Good luck!" he answers.

"Not luck. Nikki assured me I've already got it. Just had to fill out all the appropriate forms," I say as I wipe my hands on a rag and turn to leave.

"Oh, well, congratulations! That's awesome. What are you hoping to do?"

As I walk away, I turn and walk backwards so I can grin at him. "Do you feel superior being the only EMT on the team, or would you like to have a second?"

"WOO-HOOO!" he shouts, grinning. "That's *awesome*! Congrats, man! You'll do great!"

"Thanks! I'll come back when I'm finished." I break out into a jog and head to the lodge, stopping at my cottage for just a second to pick up the paperwork.

I find the four Walters and the two McCoys sitting there with Patch and Penny again as I step inside. "Got it?" Steve asks as he turns.

"Yep. Sure do." I hand it to him as he reaches for it, then take a seat on the sofa beside Nikki. When I'm sitting, she reaches over and gives me a one-armed hug, so I turn and hug her back. Damn, it's just like getting hugged by my mom!

Steve flips through the paperwork, then hands it to Nikki. "Everything seems to be in order. All you guys have to do is sign it all around and Paddy here will be college bound. Patch, can you call Hollywood? Is he around? We need a notary."

"Sure."

As Patch makes the call, Nikki and I look through the paperwork, and she asks me some questions, making little notes in the margins as we go. A minute later, Hollywood appears, darts down the hallway, comes back with his stamp, and shows us where to sign before he signs it himself and presses the seal into it. When we're finished, he hands it back to Nikki. "Here you go. It's official. Congratulations, brother," he says and shakes my hand, then hugs me. Everybody's happy for me.

"All done. We should probably go pack," Tony says, then smiles at me and shakes my hand. "Congratulations, Paddy. I'm so happy Nikki could do this for you."

"Thank you. Thank you so much. I really appreciate it."

"Thank her. She loves everybody. I'm especially grateful that she loves me."

Nikki stands, but before she walks away, she leans over and hugs me tightly. "I'm so proud of you, honey. You're going to do great. Keep me posted and let me know if there's anything I can help you with."

"I will. Thank you. I really …" A lump forms in my throat and I can't speak.

"I know. We love you guys too. You're family to us now. Get enrolled, and if there's any paperwork they need, let me know."

"Thanks. Love you guys too."

"I guess we should go pack too," Laura says and stands, but Vic doesn't rise. "You coming, babe?"

"Actually, Steve, Kelly, and I have something we need to talk to Paddy about, if that's okay. Can you handle it by yourself?"

"Sure. Go ahead." She leans over and gives him a kiss on the cheek, and he grabs her and lays one right on her lips. Look, I'm as straight as they come, but if he kissed me like that, I'd definitely be happy about it.

"Can't believe the fucking honeymoon isn't over yet," Steve mutters.

Kelly swats at him and laughs. "Oh, hush, you! We're the same and you know it!"

"Quiet, subbie! Gah, I get no respect." Then he leans over and kisses her on the cheek. "There. Better?"

Kelly giggles. "Much!"

"Okay, now that the tomfoolery is over … Paddy, I hope you're not upset, but Vic told me about your conversation last night."

I shake my head. "No. I had a feeling he was going to talk to you, and that's fine."

"Remember when I asked Steve if they were going to see Natalie today?" Vic asks, and I nod.

"Well, there was a reason for that. Here." Steve hands me a business card. "Give her a call. She's expecting to hear from you. Actually, she's *hoping* to hear from you."

The card is upside down, so I turn it over and almost choke. "A … federal judge? What? No. That … No."

"What? You're prejudiced against federal judges?" Steve asks with a chuckle.

"No. It's just that … She's not going to want to …"

"She already knows your former situation, and it's fine. You were minimum security, non-violent, lessened charge, no sexual implications. She knows all of that, and she still wants to hear from you."

"You told her? I mean, about …" It's too hard to finish the sentence.

So Steve does it for me. "That you want to be in control in the bedroom? Yes. That's what she's been looking for, at least for the twelve years I've known her."

"You've known her twelve years?"

"Oh, yeah. Scened with her a couple of times, but that wasn't really what she wanted. She doesn't want to be somebody's submissive. Yeah, she'd like to have a partner, a relationship, but she's not interested in being a submissive. She just has a demanding, high-powered job where she always has to be in control, where she's in control of passing sentence on other people's lives, and in her personal life, she'd like to at least be able to enjoy herself and let somebody else take over."

I sit there for a few seconds and then I mumble, "Well, that makes perfect sense to me."

Steve nods. "So call her. She's hoping you will. Honestly, I know Natalie and I know you, and I think you'll be perfect together."

"By the way," Vic interrupts, "I know her too, and I think Steve's right. You'd make a great couple."

"Wow, um, okay. I'll call her this evening." I stare at the card and commit it to memory.

Judge Natalie Anderson

United States District Court

Eastern District of Kentucky

The address and phone number of the office in Lexington are on the card, so what is she doing here? "Wait. She's here? This says Lexington."

"They have courtrooms in London and Pikeville. They needed somebody who could travel between, and she decided that Hazard was a good spot. Good spot for that purpose, but a lousy spot to meet anybody, especially men. You're the first hope she's had in a long, long time." Steve's smile is gentle. "Natalie's a good person—wonderful person, in fact. She could use a little happiness in her life. I could be wrong, but I think you could too."

Somewhere in my mind, a little voice whispers, *Oh, Steve, you have no idea.*

CHAPTER 2

Paddy

I MANAGED TO GET THE TOP OF THE ENGINE CASE OFF, AND it's a mess in there, but nothing I can't fix. Most of what's below is gears and shafts, and those will be pretty easy to deal with. In the meantime, Hollywood and Bear have figured out how to move the boat from the trailer so they can work on the trailer. Reboot and I will be working on the engine, and Patch and Priest said they'd work on the aesthetics. Bulldog volunteered to pull the seats, take the measurements for the carpet, and drive all of it over to the upholstery guy Tinsley told us about. Ghost is looking at the wiring harness on the trailer, and once we get the engine in good-enough shape, he'll look at the wiring there too. He's already warned Reboot that we'll probably have to take the dash out to fix all of the wiring, but having the seats out is perfect for starting all of that. At one point, I swear Reboot was going to break down and cry. Between having Mavis with him and knowing we're all helping him with this boat, the guy is so damn happy he looks like he's going to have a stroke.

By the time dinner rolls around, all of us need showers and clean clothes because we're filthy. Audrey doesn't cook on Sunday evenings, so I decide that I want pizza, but nobody else seems to. Something flits through my mind, and I reach into my pocket, then step outside the kitchen and pull out my phone. Dusk makes it hard to read the numbers, so I hope I got them right. It rings twice and a female voice says, "Hello?"

"Hi. I'm trying to reach Natalie?"

"Oh! This is Natalie."

"Hi, Natalie. This is Dennis O'Brien. Steve gave me your card and—"

"Yes! I'm glad to hear from you! I was hoping you'd call."

This is promising. I may ruin it in five minutes, but what the hell? I don't have her now, and you can't lose something you don't have. "Good! So, um, I've been working on something all day and just managed to get cleaned up. Nobody here wants pizza, but I do, and I wondered … I mean, I know it's short notice and all, and I don't usually do this, but … I didn't know if you'd be interested in—"

"Meeting you for pizza? I'd love to! That would be great. I mean, I'm not dressed up or anything, but I need a meal, and if you can stand being around me without me putting in much effort—"

"I'm sure you look fine. That would be great. I'll come to Hazard. That's not a problem. But where? Where's a good pizza place?"

"Monty's Pizza down on Fourth Street is great. If we get there in time, we won't have to compete with the church people."

"Okay. It'll take me about thirty minutes to get there, so how about you go in a little while and get us a table and I'll meet you there?"

"Sounds great! I'm looking forward to it. See you shortly. Bye."

"Oh, wait! You still there?"

"Yeah."

"How will I know you?"

"Mmmm … Oh! I'm wearing a pink shirt with a Tweety Bird on it. How's that?"

I chuckle. "Perfect. I think I can find you unless it's 'wear your Tweety Bird shirt day' in Hazard!"

"That would be just my luck! See you in a little while. And Dennis?"

"Yeah?"

"Thanks for calling."

"Thank you for being willing to meet me on short notice. See you in a few." I hear the phone go silent and I'm suddenly thrilled at how easy that was. Then panic sets in.

What does she look like? I'm instantly ashamed of myself. What difference does it make? Steve, Kelly, and Vic all seem to think a lot of her, so she's a good person. No matter what she looks like, I should give her a chance. I'm the last person in the world who has a right to be picky about a woman's looks. I don't want to be hooked up with a beautiful bitch. That's no good.

I check with everybody inside, and Patch tells me to go ahead and take his truck because if they go somewhere, it'll be in the SUVs. I grab the keys from the key hooks behind the kitchen door and head out.

It's not quite dark yet, and stupid me forgot to map the pizza place, but she said Fourth Street, so it should be easy to find. Monty's Pizza. Sure enough, I roll up on it with zero trouble. There's a parking lot adjacent, so I park, hop out, and head inside.

I'm instantly in love with this place. It's a typical seventies pizza joint—dark red and black patterned carpet, dark furniture, and a huge jukebox over in the corner. There's beer on tap, and the place smells heavenly. It's pretty busy, and I'm looking around, trying to spot her, when I see someone waving at me from a booth in the back corner.

I get within ten feet of her and almost run to the door. The woman is absolutely, positively breathtaking. Her smile, her eyes, her hair … I don't know what her figure looks like yet, but that face is the face of an angel. When I'm five feet away, I stop. "Natalie?"

"Yep! Sit down! Good to meet you!" I slide in and she gives me a smile that I swear is melting the salt and pepper shakers. "Have any trouble finding the place?"

"No. It's really obvious and, oh my god, I fell in love when I stepped inside. How cool is this?"

"Yeah, it's like stepping back in time, right? I love it. And their pizza … It's incredible. You'll love it. Hungry?"

"Starving."

"So you said you'd been working on something all day," she says. She actually remembered what I said! That's promising.

"Yeah. One of the guys got a boat from his girlfriend, an old one, and we're helping him fix it up."

"Big job?"

I chuckle. "Honestly? Huge. My grandfather owned a marina—my dad owns it now—and I worked on boats the whole time I was growing up. This thing is a disaster, but I'm determined to whip it into shape."

"Your friend is lucky."

"I'm just glad I can help him. Otherwise, it might be

beyond his budget, but this way, he'll just be paying for parts, and I might even be able to get some of those used."

"Hi, y'all! Welcome to Monty's! What can I get you started off with to drink?" a girl who looks like a little kid asks. We give her our drink orders and she disappears.

"She'll be back in a minute, so I guess we should decide what we're getting. I mean, if we want to share a pizza, or want individual stuff, or what," Natalie says, picking up the menu. "What do you want to do?"

"I'll gladly share a pizza with you if we can decide on what to put on it."

"I like everything," she announces.

"I do too, but I'm fond of meat."

Her grin is huge. "Ooooo, their Meat Fanatic pizza is delicious."

"Sounds good to me! Want a salad to go with it?" I ask.

"Sure! That would be great."

This is my test. I'm going to see what happens when I order. Sure enough, the server is already back. "What'll it be?" I look to Natalie.

And she nods.

That's a great sign. "Okay, so we'll have a salad apiece and a medium Meat Fanatic pizza. Or do you want leftovers to take to work with you tomorrow?" I ask her.

"Oh, that would be great."

"Okay, so make it a large. You like hand-tossed?" I ask her.

"You read my mind."

"Okay. Hand-tossed it is."

"Sounds great. I'll put that in and it'll be about fifteen minutes." I watch her walk away, her ponytail bobbing, then smile at Natalie.

"They get younger all the time, don't they?" she asks with a tiny grin.

"Yeah, they seem to. Before you have to ask, I'm forty-four."

"And I'm forty-one."

"I wasn't going to ask!" I say with a chuckle.

Natalie laughs. "So I saved you the wondering!"

"You did! Are you wondering about anything?"

She nods and her eyelids flutter. "I hate to ask, but yeah. I'm wondering what happened that you were sentenced in federal court."

God, I hate talking about this, but I know I have to. "So I owned a tower company with my best friend. Every time we climbed, we had to do safety checks, and we did them for each other. I mean, you can't technically do your own safety check. So this one day, we climbed up. I was above. We were about eighty feet up, and his harness broke. I mean, just broke. And he fell all the way down. Didn't hit anything on the way down, just fell."

Her eyes are wide. "Oh. My. God."

"Yeah. You can't possibly …" I stop. God, this is excruciating. It's not just what happened. It was the pain of losing Michael. We'd been best friends since we were little, and I miss him every fucking day. Every day. "I called nine-one-one immediately, told them what had happened, that I was still aloft, and that I'd be climbing down but I needed someone there immediately. When I finally got to the ground, they still weren't there. I had to deal with the … scene … by myself."

To my total surprise, her eyes well. "Oh, god, I'm so sorry. That must've been horrifying for you."

"I thought when I got to the ground, I'd take his pulse, maybe try to make him comfortable … There was none of that. Nothing." That's the moment I notice that my hands have started to shake. "It was like something from a really horrible movie. I can't—"

Hands press onto mine to stop the shaking, and they're warm and soft. "Don't. Just tell me about your trial and sentencing. I didn't mean to make you relive all of that. I'm sorry."

"It's okay. Sometimes it seems like a really weird, horrible dream, you know? It was strange, like time stood still, and I couldn't quite take it all in. It wasn't until later that it hit me hard, and I wanted to go to prison. I wanted to go somewhere, anywhere, that I might be able to forget."

"I can understand that. Steve said they charged you with negligent homicide but couldn't make it stick."

"Yeah." That gives me a chance to take a deep breath. "I told them that I did the check, but we couldn't find the forms. He did mine, and we couldn't find that one either. I looked and looked and never found them. I don't know what happened to them. But when they realized they couldn't find the one he did for me either, they dropped it to involuntary manslaughter. That's how I wound up in minimum security. That never would've happened if it hadn't been for OSHA. They descended on the office like a bunch of vultures. They were the ones that pushed for me to be sent to prison."

She pats my hands, then sits back in the bench. "Yeah, figures. They sometimes stick their noses in where they don't belong. I understand following the law, but if you had documentation from other checks—"

"We did. There was a document for every equipment check, and they cross-referenced those with the billing statements we sent to customers. Every one of them were accounted for—except those two. It was a pretty compelling argument for my attorney to use. In the end, it helped, but it didn't get me completely off."

"And you did how long?"

"Nine years."

"Yeow. That seems excessive to me."

"My attorney was mad at me. Told me to plead guilty, but I wouldn't. Because I wasn't. He said the jury would be sympathetic to the widow, and they were. I was too. She and I were like siblings. After the trial she sued me for everything I had and I lost the company, which I guess didn't matter, seeing as how I was going to prison."

"Were you married?"

"Yeah. Lisa served me with papers the day after I went to prison."

"So much for 'til death do us part."

"Yeah."

"You have kids?"

I stop. That's where my heart hurts, the place that just can't heal. "I told her not to bring them to the prison and I gave her full custody. I didn't want them seeing me there, knowing their dad was a convict."

"But they're your kids!" she says, her eyes wide again.

"I know. And I love them. But they were three and five when I went in. They're thirteen and fifteen now. I'm no good to them. Her new husband raised them, so they have a dad."

"And she won't let you see them?"

I shake my head. Here's where the humiliation begins. "It's not that. She keeps telling me she wants me to come see them or to bring them to see me, but I keep saying no. Why upend their lives? Why confuse and hurt them? That doesn't seem right."

"Okay, here's your salads," the server says and interrupts.

"Thanks." Maybe I can steer the conversation in a

different direction. As soon as she walks away, I ask, "What about you? Have you been married?"

She shakes her head and that auburn hair sways. "Nope. Gotten pretty close a time or two, but never took the plunge."

The lettuce is crispy, and I hold a forkful of it in midair to ask, "Mind if I ask why?"

Her hand comes up to cover her mouth—she's already managed a forkful—and when she swallows, she says, "For the reason Steve told you." I guess she can tell I'm confused. "One wanted to defer to me in everything because it made his life easier, and the other wanted to completely take over my life and tell me what to do right down to what to wear. That's not happening," she says and wipes her lips with her napkin.

"Yeah, that's bullshit," I agree after I've swallowed my bite of salad. "So why do you think you … like what you like?"

"My job is super stressful, and I have to be in control every minute. The courtroom is my responsibility. Paperwork is my responsibility. Managing the jury—my responsibility. Then I come home and I'm alone, so all of that is my responsibility too. It's exhausting. So having an area of my life that brings me pleasure is crucial, but knowing I don't have to be responsible for it and I'll still be … satisfied … is perfect." She forks up another bite, then holds it and smiles. "What about you?"

"Oh, I dunno. I wasn't popular in school. I didn't date a lot in college. I—"

"What's your degree in?"

"Electrical engineering."

"Sorry. Just happened to think about it."

"Yeah, that's fine. So I didn't date a lot in college. I actually met Lisa through Michael after we started the business.

She let me take over, but there was no adventure. No play. No incorporating … Well, you know what I mean."

"I think I do. So I'm guessing you're forty-four and there are things you still haven't tried that you'd like to?"

"Hell, yeah. Absolutely. But it wasn't going to happen with Lisa."

The smile she gives me almost causes me to explode in flames. "Well, maybe she did you a favor by divorcing you."

I just grin. "Maybe."

Her fork stops midair again and she says something that shocks the shit out of me. "I was a little worried, but Kelly said you were gorgeous. She was right. You really are. I'm sitting here with the handsomest guy in the place, and I'm happy to be a woman." Her mouth opens and she pops the fork in. I've never wanted to see my cock in somebody's mouth so badly in my life.

"I was a little worried too, but it didn't matter. I just knew Steve, Kelly, and Vic said you were a great person, so I—"

"You know Vic?" she says, her eyes lighting up.

"Yep. And his wife too."

"Lucky woman. Damn, he's got to be the finest man I've ever seen in my life. I mean, sorry, but it's true."

"He seems to have that effect on every woman in his universe, and honestly, some of the men too. I'm straight as an arrow and I'd do him in a heartbeat," I say, laughing.

"Oh, is that right?"

Now I'm laughing. "Yeah. That's right!"

"Could I get in on that?" she asks, laughing along with me.

"I'd sure let you!"

"Good. We've got a bargaining chip!" We're both still laughing, and I realize something.

I'm having fun. She's fun to be around. Not only is she a

great conversationalist, but she's also compassionate. She asks questions, but not in a threatening or judgmental way. It means she's interested in me and wants to know more about me. Have I asked her enough questions about herself? "So your people … Are they from around here?"

"I didn't—"

"Oh, right. I'm stupid. You're not from here."

She giggles, and it's adorable. "You're not stupid! I grew up in Shelbyville. My dad's a professor of law at the University of Kentucky and my mom's an English professor. And I have a brother who's a doctor in the army. Neurologist."

"Shelbyville?"

"Yeah. Outside Louisville."

"Do you know the rest of the Walters family?"

Her eyes fly open wide. "Yeah! Of course! My dad and Tony play golf sometimes. Vic's brother."

"Yeah! So Nikki has this scholarship fund in memory of her kids—"

"Tony's wife. I've met her. She's really sweet."

"Yeah. And it's for the guys at the farm. I applied and I got it. I'm going back to school."

"Oh my god, that's awesome! So what are you going to do?"

"I'm getting my EMT certification."

"You want to become an EMT? What do you do now? I mean, I know you live at that farm, but I don't know what you guys farm."

"No, no. Nothing like that." As we get our pizza and start to eat, I explain to her about the farm, what we do, about the team and what my role is, all of it. "So having my EMT certification will let me be of more use to the team. I mean, these are my brothers. I'd do anything for them, and they'd do the same for me."

"Where are your people?"

"Point Pleasant, West Virginia. Right across the river from Gallipolis, Ohio."

She grins. "Wait. The Mothman!"

That makes me laugh out loud. "You know about the Mothman?"

"Of course! I loved the movie! And the lore. It's pretty incredible."

"Yeah, because it's all bullshit. But it's fun bullshit."

"Yeah, but the Silver Bridge—"

"Damn, woman, you *do* know about it!" I'm still laughing.

"Of course! I've read about it. So have you ever seen him? It?"

"No. Of course not. Somebody was smokin' some powerful shit when they thought they saw that." She starts to laugh again. "Come on. Do you really believe that?"

"Weird stuff happens, Dennis. You know it does!"

"Yeah, yeah. Lots of weird stuff. Like right now, two strangers, sitting in a restaurant, eating pizza, and laughing about the Mothman. Who would ever dream of *that*?" We're both still laughing.

"So," she starts again, trying to tamp down her laughter, "siblings?"

"Yeah. Two sisters."

"Don't tell me … You were the baby of the family," she says with a sneer.

"Yep. Dad works at the marina and Mom teaches school. Elementary school. My oldest sister is a teacher too, middle school, and my middle sister is a stay-at-home mom. Her husband is a chemist at a chemical plant in Gallipolis."

"Nice! Sounds like a sweet family."

"Nobody special. Just an average blue-collar, working family."

"Nothing wrong with that. When I was growing up, I wanted to be a farmer who owned an orange orchard. We went to Florida and visited an orchard while we were there, and I thought that was the greatest thing I'd ever seen. When Dad told me I'd have to move to Florida to be an orange farmer, I cried for a week because I didn't want to leave my mom and dad behind. Now they'll probably retire to Florida when they both leave their careers. There is no justice in this world," she mutters with a grin and I let out a little laugh.

"You're sure right about that."

We just keep talking, and the longer we talk, the more I like her. It's a pleasant way to spend the evening, and I'm so glad I took the chance and called her. As the pizza disappears and the conversation wanes, I finally say aloud, "I'm so glad I decided to call you."

"Me too. This has been so much fun."

"Want a box for the rest?"

"Yes, please."

The server shows up in a few minutes. "Do you guys need refills?"

"Thanks, but I don't think so?" I look to Natalie, and she shakes her head. "But we need a box, and I need the check."

"Yes, sir. Be right back."

As soon as she's out of sight, Natalie says, "I'll go in halfsies."

"Not necessary. I asked you out, so I'm buying. I wanted pizza and none of those dumbasses wanted to eat pizza with me, so I called you. I'm glad they didn't want to eat with me. You're a lot more fun, and you're a damn sight prettier than any of them!"

That laugh—it's like music. "Well, thank you! I'll tell them that when I get to meet them."

"You do that!" We keep chatting as the server takes my payment, then load up the pizza into the box and get up to leave.

When we step out, it's dark. "Where are you parked?"

She points three spaces from the truck. "Right there."

"Okay. Just didn't want you walking to your car alone."

"Thanks. That's kind of you." There's an awkward pause, and then she says, "I really, really enjoyed this, Dennis, and I really enjoyed meeting you."

"Same here. This has been a lot of fun. And I'd really like to see you again."

"I feel the same."

"Okay. See what your schedule looks like and we'll put something together. Do you mind if I call or text you in the meantime? Just to stay in touch?"

With one step, she's standing right in front of me, her breasts touching my chest, and she looks up at me. "I'll be hurt if you don't." There's no hesitation on my part, no question. I just bend down slightly and press my lips to hers. I feel something, and realize her hand has sought out mine, clasping it ever so gently. It's this really sweet moment when time stops and for just that few seconds, we're the only two people in the whole world, simply me and this beautiful woman I've just met but want desperately to know better.

When I straighten and break the kiss, I look down at her. "I hope that was okay."

Her smile is gentle and calm. "I would've been hurt if you hadn't kissed me." Our hands are still clasped, and she steps back a pace and turns loose. "Night, Dennis."

"Night, Natalie. Be careful going home."

"You too. Let me know when you get there so I know you're safe."

Somebody cares. Somebody wants to know I'm safe. I mean, if I didn't show up at work tomorrow morning, the guys would come looking for me, but this woman wants to make sure I make it home okay. That means something to me, sappy as it sounds. "I'll do it. See you soon."

"Absolutely. See you soon." I watch as she slips behind the wheel of her little Honda CRV and straps in, and she honks and waves as she pulls out of the parking lot, leaving me standing there watching her go, my heart full.

I didn't want her to go. I didn't want the night to end.

Boy, am I ever screwed.

Natalie

I really don't think my car's tires are touching the ground. I'm floating so high that I've taken it with me. Oh my god, Dennis is amazing. Perfect gentleman, smart, funny, and damn it, Kelly didn't do him justice. From those hazel eyes to that mop of dark brown hair, he's downright beautiful. I've never been a beard person, but his is neatly trimmed and not long, and it looks so fucking manly that I could cry. Where has this guy been all my life?

And then I remember—well, for the last nine years, he's been in a prison somewhere. Question answered.

But his answers to my questions satisfied my curiosity. I'll talk to the chair of the ethics board, but I really don't think this is going to be a problem. They may frown a little, but there's nothing ethically wrong with me seeing him, and that's all that matters.

I've been home for almost thirty minutes when my phone rings. "Hello?"

"Hey, I made it. I'm safe and sound and in my cottage."

"Cottage?"

"Yeah. The farm was an old Church of God campground. We have a large building that's the kitchen and dining hall and an even bigger one that's our lodge, but we've all got our own cottages. They were here on the property, and the Walters redid them for us."

"Oh! So you've got your own space! It's not like you're in a dorm or bunkhouse or something."

"No. Absolutely not. Little living room area, bedroom, laundry, kitchen area. They're really nice. So no, I have complete privacy when I come in here and close my door."

"Nice! I'd like to see it sometime."

"I'd like for you to see it sometime," he says with a chuckle.

"Well, now that we've got that out of the way, I should go and get ready for bed so I look halfway decent for court tomorrow morning."

"You'll look beautiful, I'm sure. You have cases to hear in the morning?"

"No. Monday is arraignments in London. Tuesday is arraignments in Pikeville. Then the trials trickle down from there."

"Gotcha. Makes sense. Well, get some sleep and I'll talk to you tomorrow, I bet."

"Okay." *Go for broke*, a little voice says in my mind. "Can I tell you something?"

"Sure."

Summoning up my courage, I struggle but manage to say, "I really didn't want to leave you behind at the restaurant."

"I know. I didn't want to see you go either."

Oh my god. He feels it too! I think I'm going to cry. "Good. So call or text tomorrow. Goodnight, Dennis."

"Night, sweet pea." And the phone goes dead.

He called me sweet pea. He didn't want it to end either. Holy hell. I look at the clock, and it's really not that late, so I go through my contacts. My call is answered with a sweet feminine voice that says, "Hey, girl."

"Hey yourself. Guess where I just got home from?"

"I dunno. Where?"

Giddy. That's how I feel. "A date with Dennis!"

There's a squeal from the other end of the phone, and I hear a male voice ask, "What the hell are you shrieking about?"

"It's Natalie! And she went out with Dennis!"

"Why is she calling you? She should be attending to him," I hear Steve growl.

"It was not a booty call, Steve!" I bellow into the phone, and I know he can hear me.

"Good god, you work slow," he yells back, and I'm laughing so hard that I can barely breathe.

"He says—"

"Yeah, I heard him," I tell Kelly, still laughing. "Look, I'm not twenty anymore. I want more than dick."

"You want more than dick? You mean you want two dicks?" Kelly asks loudly, laughing the whole time.

"She wants two dicks? Typical woman. Never satisfied," Steve says in the background.

"Oh, you shush, Sir. If she'd had a dick like yours, she wouldn't say that."

"She *did* have my dick a long time ago," Steve tells her.

Kelly's still laughing. "You had his dick?"

"Yeah, but that was a long, long time ago, and it must've been unremarkable, because I really don't remember it that well." That makes her scream with laughter.

"She says she doesn't remember it that well so it must've been unremarkable," she tells him.

"Early onset Alzheimer's. That's the only possible explanation. Otherwise, she'd never forget." There's no way I'd tell him, but I do remember vividly. That one night was the best fuck of my life, especially since I knew it would never be anything but a fuck. He's hung like a horse and try as I might to not do so, I've measured every man I've ever met by Steve's monster cock. Never met another one like it, but a girl can dream. I'd envy Kelly, but the son of a bitch is bound to be nearly impossible to live with.

Don't misunderstand. I love Steve. We're good friends. But damn, he's one abrasive, sarcastic motherfucker.

"Anyway, even with my advanced dementia, I remember enough about tonight to know it was fun," I say to a still-laughing Kelly.

"So are you going to see him again?"

"I sure as hell hope so. I really like him, Kelly. I mean, really, really like him."

"Does he like you?"

"He just called me."

"You just got home and he already called you?"

"I mean, I asked him to so I knew he was safe, but yeah. And he admitted that he didn't want the date to end."

"Oooo, girl, you've got a live one!"

"I hope so. I just wanted you to know that your matchmaking paid off."

"Did you talk about the sex issue?"

"Yes. We were both very up front about it, and we both

know exactly where we stand. I think we're sympatico in that area too."

"Good. Best to be clear about that kind of stuff from the very beginning."

I let out a chuckle. "Although he said he's as straight as they come, but if Vic wanted to do him, Dennis would take him up on it."

"Wouldn't we all, baby, wouldn't we all? Mmmm-hmmmmm. Wish I'd been at the club before he left."

"And now they're talking about Vic," I hear Steve say from the background.

"Damn, he's smarter than I thought. Okay. Sorry to call so late, but I figured you'd be thrilled."

"I am. Thanks for calling. And I enjoyed spending time with you this morning."

"Same here. Tell the old fucker back there that I won't be in need of his services ever again, so he can quit daydreaming about me," I say, laughing.

"I'll tell him! Night, girl."

"Night."

I'm still chuckling as I hang up and plug the phone in to charge. I can laugh all I want, but I know the truth.

If this goes how I hope it will, I'm going to owe them big time. And I know Steve well enough to know that he won't let me forget that.

CHAPTER 3

Paddy

I head to the kitchen to hang up the key to the truck, then wander to the lodge. When I open the door, I'm shocked to find pretty much everybody there. "Hey! Get your pizza fix?" Hollywood calls out.

"Yep." I grab a beer, open it, toss the cap in the trash, and sit down on a barstool near the sofa.

"You've been gone a long time. Where did you go to get pizza? Louisville?" Patch asks with a smirk.

"Nope. Hazard."

"Why didn't you just drive up to the convenience store and get some?" Priest asks.

"Because." They all turn and stare at me. "I had a date."

They look so confused that I start to laugh. "You had a *date*? With a *woman*?" Bear asks.

"No, a heifer down at Buster's farm. Of course, a woman."

"Who?" Ghost asks, and the whole bunch of them leans toward me, including the women.

"Her name is Natalie and she's beautiful."

"And where did you meet the beautiful Natalie?" Bulldog asks in his usual sarcastic way.

"Through Steve, Kelly, and Vic."

"Wait. So this is real. You're not making it up. Natalie's real, and the date's real, and—"

I cut Reboot off. "Yes. It's real. Am I that ugly and socially unacceptable?"

"No! It's just that we didn't even know you were looking to meet anybody, that's all," Hollywood says, trying to cover their asses.

"I wasn't. But I was talking to Vic, and he knew Kelly and Steve were going to Hazard to meet Natalie for brunch, and he talked to Steve, and he and Kelly talked to Natalie, and there you have it. I met her at the pizza place and we really hit it off. Matter of fact, I just talked to her a couple of minutes ago. She wanted me to call her and let her know that I made it home okay."

"Whoa, she *cares*," Priest says.

"Yes. She does. She's just nice that way."

"So what does this beautiful Natalie do for a living?" Patch asks.

Oh, I can't wait to see their faces on this one. "She's a federal judge in the Eastern District of Kentucky."

Nobody says a word. It takes everything I have to keep from exploding with laughter. "You're joking, right?" Bulldog finally asks.

"Nope. Not joking at all. That's how Steve knew her—she was in Louisville first. Worked as a judge magistrate. When they wanted her to move up into the judicial seat, they told her they wanted her to cover London and Pikeville, so Hazard seemed like a good central location. And here she is."

"Holy shit. A federal judge. Does she know about you? About us?" Bear asks.

"Yep, and she says it doesn't matter. I was non-violent, non-sex offender, minimum security, no infractions, finished my sentence. No issues. No reason why she can't see me."

"Well, how 'bout that? Congratulations! I hope this works out if you really like her," Patch says, and his smile tells me that he's being genuine.

"Thanks. I really, really do. I'm hoping we can see each other during the week, but if not, there's always the weekend."

"Don't drop the ball on this one, brother. She sounds like a catch," Ghost says with a grin.

"Wait until you see her. You won't believe it. I walked in and was like, wow, she's really something."

"All this talk of girlfriends and dates and all that makes me want to take my favorite date to bed. Come on, babe. Tomorrow's a new day," Patch says and stands, then reaches for Penny's hand.

"Oooo, sounds promising! See you guys tomorrow," Penny says and lets him lead her out the door.

"Same for us. I've got a blade to finish tomorrow. Night, everybody," Reboot says and rises. "You comin', sweetie?"

"Yup. Night, everybody." There's a chorus of well wishes as Mavis steps up beside Reboot and they head out.

"Think I'm going too. It's been a long day." I toss my bottle in the trash and look around at the guys and women left in the room. "I really appreciate you guys being supportive."

"You know we will be. We just want to see you happy." Then Ghost cuts his eyes toward Izzy. "A *federal judge*. He's lost his fuckin' mind." She starts to laugh.

I know I'm grinning like a fool, but I can't help it. "Yeah. I've lost my mind. See you guys in the morning. Night." I can hear them tossing back the same toward me as I wander out into the darkness and head toward my cottage, wishing I had just one more slice of that pizza. Damn, that was good.

I get out my work clothes for the next day, empty my pockets onto the dresser, and get undressed. Once I slide under the covers, I tell my phone's onboard assistant to set my alarm and I reach over and turn off the light. My eyes close, and I get a big surprise.

All I can see is Natalie, her smile, her hair, those eyes. I can hear her voice, hear that sweet laughter, and I'm so fucking hard that I can't think. In my mind, I imagine her saying, *I like to be dominated in the bedroom. I want a man who'll take over and take charge. Make me come a dozen times. Fuck me hard. I want him to use me however he wants, whenever he wants, for as long as he wants.* Damn, I'm stroking away and it's just not good enough. I want her. The memory of her tits pressing against me as she leaned into me before I kissed her … I want to palm them, to stroke my thumbs over her nipples, to listen to her breath hitch. Oh, god, I want to dip my fingers into her, feel how wet and hot she is for me, listen to her moan, put my lips to her …

Damn it, why didn't I put on a condom? Now I've got a fucking mess to clean up. *Oh, well, it was worth it,* I'm thinking as I get some tissues and start mopping. Shit, based on the quantity, I'd say I should probably do this more often. Maybe before long I won't have to.

My sheets are really soft and comfortable, and I snuggle in. But just before I drift away, it's the same thing, the thing that happens every night. I'm right on the verge of sleep, and there he is. That voice, the one I've known all my life, says, "It's okay, Dennis. It wasn't your fault. I've forgiven you.

You have to forgive yourself." Michael, every night, torturing me with his easy smile and his calm voice. I remember that day like it was today, the way he plummeted downward without a sound. He never screamed, never yelled, never shrieked. He just fell, silently, like a movie in slow motion. One minute he was there, and the next minute, he was gone.

Maybe someday I'll get one night's sleep without that clip playing over in my mind, but obviously, tonight isn't that night.

Natalie

It's gonna be a long day. I step into my chambers, look over the docket one more time, slip on my robe, and pick up my folio. The clerk prepares it for me before every arraignment, and today's is actually pretty thin. That's how I like 'em.

When my door opens, I hear Darrell Blanchard, one of my bailiffs in London, say, "All rise. Court is now in session, Honorable Natalie Anderson presiding." I enter to everyone in the courtroom standing, and to my surprise, there are about forty people there this morning. Even more unusual is their attire. They're fairly well-dressed. What's this about?

I sit down and say, "Please be seated," into the microphone. They do. "Before we start, I know the bailiff has already said these things, but there are no recording devices in this courtroom. The proceedings are already being recorded. There is no headwear. By headwear, I mean hats and caps except as deemed necessary by a religious belief system. All defendants will be respectful and answer questions truthfully. Now that that's out of the way, bailiff, please call the first defendant."

"The court calls Carlos Montoya. Please rise and proceed to the podium." A man in an orange jumpsuit stands with another man in a suit and they step toward the podium.

"Mr. Montoya, this is your arraignment. According to the paperwork I have here, you have ninety counts of possession with intent to distribute illegal narcotics as described in the Kentucky Revised Statutes. I'm not reading the citings, as your attorney can do that with you. It also says you have three counts of assault with a deadly weapon on an officer of the law, and … you're accused of shooting a Kentucky State Police helicopter and causing it to crash, causing bodily harm to the two officers aboard. You're a busy man. Mr. Collins," I say to the attorney. "I assume you've advised your client of his rights."

"I have, Your Honor."

"And how do you plead, Mr. Montoya?"

The dark-haired man answers, "Not guilty, Your Honor."

"Very well. I also see that you have a lengthy history of breaking the law in the United States and you're not even a citizen. Based on the charges, and the fact that you're obviously a flight risk, I'm setting your bail at two million dollars."

Collins pipes up. "Your Honor, my client is no flight risk. The United States has been his home—"

"Illegally. Let's get that point straight," I say as I interrupt.

"Yes, but it's been his home for eight years, so I doubt he's a flight—"

"Eight years during which he's racked up an impressive list of crimes that have gotten several people seriously hurt. This time, sir, he's accused of injuring two Kentucky State

Police troopers. That leads me to believe that his behavior is escalating, and for that reason, I believe two million dollars is reasonable." I'd like to say twenty million, but that would just be overkill. "Mr. Asher, you have a say in this."

"As the Commonwealth Attorney prosecuting this case, I'd actually prefer that all bail be denied and the defendant be remanded to custody."

"Your Honor," Mr. Collins begins.

"Actually, Mr. Collins, before you say anything, I think maybe you should listen to Mr. Asher. Being in prison might be the only thing that keeps your client from, oh, say, trying to murder the governor? Or shooting up a local mall? Because he's increasingly violent, and there's no telling where he's going to strike next. Based on the arrest warrant, he colluded with a local radical group to cook and sell methamphetamine and distribute it far and wide. And by wide, I mean out past our jurisdiction, which is why he's a flight risk. Bail is denied. Defendant is remanded."

"*Coño*," Montoya mutters.

"Señor Montoya, *te advierto que estuve doce horas de clase aprendiendo español. Otro arrebato irrespetuoso como ese le costará un cargo de desacato. ¿Lo entiendes?*" I have no problem with giving this asshole a contempt charge for calling me a twat.

"*Si*, Your Honor," he spits in my direction.

"Okay then. Bailiff, remove the prisoner." My other bailiff, Cliff Hannity, takes him from the courtroom. "Next."

"The court calls Adolfo Cansala. Please rise and proceed to the podium." Yet another man in an orange jumpsuit stands with Mr. Collins and they step toward the podium.

"Mr. Cansala, this is your arraignment. According to the paperwork I have here, you … Uh-huh. It appears you and Mr. Montoya must be really good friends, because your charges are identical to his. I'm assuming you were in the same place at the same time with the same guy, am I right?" I stare at the defendant, but there's no reaction. "Mr. Collins, I assume you've advised your client of his rights."

"I have, Your Honor."

"And how do you plead, Mr. Cansala?"

"Not guilty, Your Honor."

"Then I'm going to streamline this and we're going to come to the exact same conclusions we did with Mr. Montoya because I'm looking at the charges against Mr. Cansala and his history, and it's pretty much identical. No bail and remanded."

"But Your Honor—"

"Mr. Asher, would you like to say anything?" I ask.

"Nothing except thank you, Your Honor."

"You're welcome. Bailiff, please take the defendant back to the jail."

As Cliff leads him away, the man turns and grins at me. "*Bonitas tetas.*"

Under my breath, I whisper, "Well, you're just a delight, aren'tcha?" I roll my eyes as the door closes behind them.

I hear a few more, but those two are interesting. What's even more interesting are the swarthy men sitting at the back of the courtroom, whispering to each other. When we've gone through the docket and court is adjourned, I call out, "Bailiffs, in chambers, please."

I've barely made it through the door and unzipped my robe when Cliff and Darrell step into the room. "Door," I say and point at it, and Cliff closes it. "So, who were the guys in the back of the courtroom. Any ideas?"

They both shake their heads. "They sure weren't reporters," Darrell says.

"No. They weren't. I mean, it's an open courtroom, but

does it strike you as odd that on a morning when I've got two Latino defendants, there are a group of Latino men in the back of the courtroom?"

"It's not a coincidence," Cliff answers.

"Yeah. I don't think so either. There's a camera trained that direction too, right?"

"Yes, ma'am," Darrell says quickly.

"Please ask the sheriff's office to run them through facial recognition and see if they get any hits. I'd really like to know who they are, at least the two who looked the most affluent."

Darrell nods. "Yes, ma'am."

"Okay. I'm going back to my office for a little while and then I'm going home. Please tell Sheriff Copeland that I appreciate you being here. You both do a good job."

"Thank you, ma'am," Cliff says.

Darrell nods. "Yeah. Thanks, ma'am."

"You're welcome. Have a good evening." They file out, and I head out the back door of chambers and down the hallway. My office is little more than a cubbyhole. The clerk's office in front of it is actually larger, but that's where the filing cabinets and such are, so that's fine.

I make notes of today's proceedings, but I'll get the transcripts from the court reporter too, so there'll be a record of everything. But some of the notes I make are about the men in the courtroom. Who were they? And why did their presence stand out to me?

After about an hour, I say goodbye to the clerk, Alinda, and head to my car. It's in the parking lot, so it's not far, but I feel like hurrying today. For some reason, I feel like I'm being watched. As soon as I'm in the car, I feel comfortable looking around behind its tinted windows. I don't see anybody anywhere, but that doesn't mean they're not there.

These are high-profile cases, and I've looked at the docket. There are twelve more arraignments to be made in this particular incident, and I wonder if the men I saw this morning will be at all of them.

It's only an hour home, so I drive down the Hal Rogers Parkway toward Hazard. It's still early, so I use speech-to-text to send a message.

Hey, on my way home. You have a busy day?

He must be doing something because he's not answering, but about five minutes later, I hear a ping and check.

Almost finished up and then I can go home. Been in Hazard most of the day at the community college.

He's in Hazard?

Are you still there?

Three wavy dots, and then another bubble.

Yeah. I've still got to go back to my advisor's office but then I'll be finished.

Oh, this is perfect.

Want to meet me for dinner when you're finished?

He answers me almost immediately.

Sure! Let me know when you're in town and we'll pick a spot.

Oh, yay! I get to see him tonight! This is awesome.

Sounds good. Can't wait.

I add a heart emoji to it before I send it. Then I wait.

Me either. See you soon, sweet pea.

Nobody knows how happy this makes me. He's given me a pet name! I can't believe how well we get along, but I should've known Steve was a good judge of character. I guess I'll see him soon enough.

Now to concentrate on my driving or I'll never make it there!

Paddy

Dear god. This has taken all fucking day. I feel bad for not being at work, but Patch told me to go ahead and get it all squared away. I start next week, so it's a good thing I did this when I did or I would've had to wait for the next class rotation. Their vocational school doesn't go by semesters, just four-month blocks, and I would've waited four more months to get started.

When I finally step out of the advisor's office, I check my watch. She texted me forty-five minutes ago, so if she's not in town, she's close. Time to find out what's going on.

Hey, I'm finished. Where are you?

Three dots and then an answer.

About fifteen minutes from town.

Hmmm. Okay, now what?

Where am I going?

Just when I think she's given up, my phone rings. "Hello?"

"This is easier. I can do it hands-free. So there's a fish place down by the discount store. On the other side of it from Mallie. You may never have been down there. It's about a block. Just go to the discount store and keep going. You'll see it—Whale of a Tail Fish 'n More."

"Okay. I'll go on down there and get us a table. See you when you get there. Drive safely."

"Will do. Bye."

"Bye, sweet pea."

Her directions are flawless, and in a couple of minutes, I'm sitting at a table in a place that has tried very hard to have a nautical theme. It's cute in a cheesy way. The "table" is a big, round board hanging from the ceiling by a huge rope that splits into four, comes down and through holes in the tabletop, and is knotted underneath. There's another spot over in the other room that has porch swings on either side of the table hanging from the ceiling. That's cute—weird, but cute.

I'm only there about ten minutes before she comes in, and she looks amazing. She's wearing a two-piece business suit, skirt and all, and some low pumps. And she sure looks different from last night, with her makeup on and hair all done, and some really business-like jewelry. "Been here long?" she asks breathlessly as she sits down.

"Nah. Just long enough to order my drink. She'll be right here. Have a good day?"

"Yeah. Intense, but good. Got called a twat by a Latino guy," she says and chuckles. "Oh, and another one told me I had nice tits."

I laugh. "That's lovely. Great guys. Real charmers. And they're right. About the tits, I mean. I wouldn't know about the twat, but the tits are nice," I say, still laughing.

"Well, thank you! I appreciate that." When she laughs, she's even more beautiful, if that's possible, and I'm glad I can do that for her, make her day brighter.

"Now, what's good?"

We eat and talk and time flies. She's super easy to talk to, funny, and smart, and I have a great time just chatting. When she laughs, her eyes sparkle, and they're beautiful, a deep blue that's almost sapphire. We hold hands on top of the table a couple of times, and it feels so natural, not forced. I called Audrey and told her I was eating in town, so they know not to expect me, but at a little after seven thirty I finally say, "I really probably need to go. I've been gone all day, and Patch is going to think I've run away!"

The sparkle leaves her eyes immediately. "You have to go?"

"I probably should."

She gives me a sly little grin. "I was going to ask if you wanted to come to my place."

"I should probably get back."

The grin widens. "I was actually going to ask if you wanted to spend the night."

"I'd have to get up and go home, and that's not how I want our first time to be."

She tilts her head ever so slightly and squinches her nose. "Why would you have to go home?"

"Because I can't stay in Hazard. I have to be there."

I can see there's something she's not understanding. "I don't get it. It's not a prison camp."

Oh, boy. This is *not* good. "No, babe, it's not. But I live there and work there, and I'm on call for the search and rescue team."

"All the time?"

"Yeah, pretty much."

"But it's volunteer. It's not like you're getting paid to do it."

Okay. Looks like I'm going to have to go all out with this one. "They give me a place to live, food to eat, someone to cook and clean, and a salary, plus all kinds of benefits—health insurance, dental, vision. There's nothing I need that I don't have because of them. In return, I work in the shop and I'm on call for the team. That's what I committed to."

Her jaw is set, and I have a bad feeling about this. "So basically, you're just back in prison, and somebody else is taking care of everything, just like in prison."

"No. Nothing like that. That cottage, the food, the cleaning, all of that, it's part of my compensation package. And the team is my way of giving back to the community. A lot of places wouldn't want us around, but they're glad to have us there. We care about the people there, and they're thankful for us. And that's important to me."

"More important than a relationship."

Wow. Just … wow. Now I'm getting pissed. "Lady, you put people like me *in* prison, but you've obviously never been there yourself! If you had, you wouldn't have the audacity to say that to me! So here's a reality check for you. When I got out of prison, I had nothing. Nothing. No business, no job, no money, no clothes, and no way to get any of those things. They put me in a halfway house because I had nowhere to go. I was on the verge of having to call my parents and ask them if I could stay with them, and they would've had to come and get me! I didn't even have a way to get there! When Patch called me, it was like an answered prayer. I get to learn something of value, get to serve my community, and because of Nikki, I get to go back to school. And I could take all this shit I'm learning and leave if I wanted, go anywhere, start a business and work for myself, but I won't, because this is my *family*. They wanted me when nobody else did. That means something to me. I can't just walk in and out of their lives."

Her tone is accusatory when she asks, "So you can't go on vacations or anything?"

This is fucking unbelievable. "Yes. I can go on vacations. I can go for weekends. But I need to talk to Patch about it first, because when one of us is going to be gone, he alerts Knott County Search and Rescue that we're going to be shorthanded, so if they need us, they know we're not going to be a full team. And I'm the hoist operator for the bird, for god's sake. I'm training Priest to do it, but I'm the only one right now. I need to be there."

She rolls her eyes. "So yeah. It's like prison."

It takes everything I have to tamp down the fury I feel right now. She's not listening. I guess prison's no big deal to her. She should have to go there for a week or two to figure this out, but that'll never happen. My teeth are gritted when I answer, "No. It's more like the military. When you're in the military, you have to ask for leave. You can't just do whatever you want. You have work and responsibilities. And you're compensated with pay and housing and clothing and food, just like I am. It's pretty much the exact same thing. When I came there, I didn't just come there—I made a commitment to Patch, to the business end, to the guys, to the community, that I'd be there for them. And in return, they're there for me. I know they have my back, and I know I can count on them. I'm sorry if you don't understand that, if you won't understand that, but that's how it is." I catch the eye of the server and motion her over. "Could you bring me the check, please? I need to go."

She folds her arms across her chest and squares her shoulders. "So that's it?"

Wow. Talk about entitlement. Where the hell does she get off demanding that *I* come up with the answer? Nope. Not with this guy. "I think that's totally up to you. That's my life. I stepped out of that car that day on the lawn of the farm and I felt like I was home. I'm sorry if you can't understand that. I would think you'd want a man who can make that kind of commitment, but I guess I was wrong." I sign my name, pick up my card, and stand. "I had high hopes, but I can't abandon the life I've managed to carve out of the rubble of what I had left for a woman I've just met who refuses to try to understand what I've been through. I'm really sorry, but I need to get back. It's been nice." I just turn and head to the door without looking back. I've been disappointed a lot of times in my life, but I don't think I've ever been as disappointed as I am right at this moment. It would've been better if I'd never met her than to meet her, think there was a possibility of having something with her, and find out she's not willing to meet me halfway.

My hand is on the handle of the truck door when I hear her voice. "Dennis, wait!" It occurs to me to pretend that I don't hear her, but I can't, so I spin and lean against the door.

She's jogging toward me in those little heels, and when she gets to me, she stops, panting from the exertion. I just stand there as she gulps in air. "Well?"

"Look, I don't understand, but I want to, okay? I really do. I'm just … I'm trying to figure out how we're ever going to have a relationship if we can't even spend a night together."

"Who said we can't spend a night together? You can come to my place anytime you want. You can stay there overnight, get up the next morning, shower, dress, eat breakfast, all the things you do at home."

Her brow furrows and she looks up at me from beneath it. "I could?"

"Of *course* you could. I told you last night, I have my own cottage. It's a house, not an apartment building. They're not connected. It's mine, and it's private. No, we can't go out and screw on the lawn because there are seven other cottages there, all occupied, but they're a hundred feet or more apart. It's not that we can't be together. It's just that I can't stay in Hazard because I'm needed there in case we get called out."

"Oh." I can see she's working on this in her mind. "So it's not like …gated. A place where no one is allowed in."

"No! It's not a prison camp with a fourteen-foot chain-link fence and razor wire! It's our home and our place of business! People can come and go as they please. Of course, we watch for trespassers. We don't want people just coming out there to mess around. We've got thousands of dollars of equipment in our shop, and Bear has even more in his."

"What does he do?"

"He's a glass artist."

Her eyes light up again. "Stained glass?"

"No. Blown glass. Hot-fired glass. All kinds. Nikki says it's the most beautiful stuff she's ever seen, and she's been all over Europe, so I think she probably knows good work when she sees it. She's bought a lot of it as gifts. So we can't just have people traipsing around all over the place, doing whatever. But we have visitors all the time. Audrey always makes so much food that an army could show up and we could feed them. So yes—you can come to my place anytime. If you were there, I wouldn't have to get up and leave you. Well, that's unless the alarm went off, and then I'd have to get up and leave, but that's a different story."

She's quiet for a minute and I wonder what's going on in that busy head of hers until she finally says, "I'm sorry. I didn't really understand, but I'm trying to. And yeah, I'd love to come to your place. Sometime. Anytime."

"Okay." *Make a decision, O'Brien,* I hear my whiney inner baby-man say. It takes everything I have to say, "Apology accepted."

"Thank you. And if I offended you, I'm sorry. This is really confusing to me."

"Once you visit there, you'll figure it out. But I really do need to get back. I've got a lot to talk to Patch about. School will be three nights a week for fourteen weeks, three hours a night, and we're going to have to figure all of this out, but we will."

"So you'll be in Hazard three nights a week?"

I nod and smile. "Yeah, so I'm thinking that means that

either we could grab a bite beforehand, or we could eat afterward. I think that would be doable. But listen, that's only temporary. Fourteen weeks. And then things will be easier. And at least for a week or two, I think we need to play this cool until we see if it's going to work. If you want to come out, we'll eat somewhere and stay in my cottage. I don't think it would be fair for you to start being invested in relationships with all of them and them with you, and then we find out we're just not going down the right path. That would be bad for everybody involved. Does that make sense?"

"Makes perfect sense. But I'm looking forward to the time when I can meet them all."

"I am too. You'll love everybody. It really is a family, Natalie. You'll see. Now, I need to get going. But I want to see you again as soon as I can, okay?"

"And I want to see you. Talk to you soon? Call me when you get there so I know you're safe?"

I smile down at her. "Do you have any idea how much I love that?"

"Yeah? That I care?"

"Yes. That you care." I give her a quick kiss, but before I can pull away, she wraps her arms around my neck and pulls in closer. The quick kiss catches fire, combusts, and I can feel my toes curling from the heat. When she finally steps back, I chuckle. "Whew. That was some kiss!"

"There's more where that came from, big boy," she says with a wink and heads to her car. "Drive carefully."

"Will do. You too. Talk to you in a bit."

"Yep. Bye."

"Bye, sweet pea." I watch that ass sway as she walks across the parking lot and almost come undone. Fuck, I wanted to go home with her! That would've been awesome.

Take it slow, I hear my inner sensible guy say, and I know he's right.

The drive home is uneventful and, sure enough, Patch is in the lodge when I get there. I grab a beer and say, "We need to talk. Got a minute?"

"Sure. Need to go to the office?"

"Nah. Everybody needs to hear this." Everybody's not in here, but Priest and Bear are, so that's a few anyway. "Class starts next week. Three nights, Monday, Wednesday, and Thursday, three hours a night, six to nine. It takes an hour to get there and an hour back, so I'd have to leave here before five and I won't get back until after ten. And that's if I don't take a few minutes to have a little something to eat before or after."

"What if you knock off those afternoons at four, get cleaned up, and go on? You can get something to eat in Hazard," he offers.

"Okay. I can start earlier in the morning to keep on top of things."

"You don't have to, but that sounds good."

"Thanks." This is easier than I thought it would be.

Then he asks, "How are you and Natalie getting along?"

"Um, had a bit of a hiccup tonight, but I think we got it straightened out."

"How so?"

"She wanted me to come over and spend the night with her tonight, and I had to explain to her why I couldn't. She said it was like I was still in prison. I finally managed to get through to her by explaining to her that it's more like the military, that for my compensation, which isn't all monetary, I make a commitment. And I take that commitment seriously."

"Right. And she understood?"

"Yeah, I think so. Shit! I forgot to call her and tell her I'm okay." I grab my phone and send a quick text.

Sorry. Talking to Patch, but I'm home. I'll give you a call when we're finished.

I get one back immediately.

Okay.

"She's keeping up with you!" Priest says with a laugh.

I grin. "She says she wants to know I made it home safely. I think it's kinda nice. Makes me feel like she cares."

"I think she genuinely does," Patch says and smiles. "So why don't you stay with her on the nights you have class?"

I stop and stare at him. "I could do that?"

"Sure. Yeah, it'll be hard on us if we get called out, but that's fine. We'll make do. It just makes more sense than you driving back at ten at night, and you can get up and drive back in the morning. At least you'll be rested when you make the drive."

"True. That would be great. I mean, we're not at that stage yet, but we will be soon, I think. I'll talk to her about it. But thanks for working with me on this," I say and stand. "I'm beat. I should probably go get some rest."

Patch stands and in a split second, he hugs me. It's like being hugged by my dad, and I hug him back. We stand there for a couple of seconds, and then he turns loose and moves back. "I'm getting an EMT out of this deal, and you're getting another skill that can help you if you ever want to leave here."

"But I never want—"

"You might someday," he argues, "and this will be one more possibility to make yourself a living. Can't hurt. Now go talk to Natalie and see if you can stay with her. I mean, I know you don't want to, but …" he says, laughing.

"Oh, trust me, I want to!"

"When do we get to meet the beautiful Natalie?" Bear asks.

"I told her I think we need to take it slow, make sure this is going to work before we get invested in each other's lives that way, and she agreed. So soon, but not for a week or so."

"That's smart," Priest adds.

"Yeah. I thought so." I drop my beer bottle in the trash on the way by, and when I get to the door, I turn and look at the three of them. "Thanks, guys. I appreciate all of you. I couldn't ask for a better family."

"And we couldn't ask for a better brother. Good luck," Patch says as he throws his feet up onto the coffee table and settles into the corner of the sofa.

When I get back to the cottage, I hit her number from my previous contacts and she answers on the first ring. "Hi!"

"Hi. Well, that was painless."

"Yeah? What were you talking about?"

"My school schedule and everything. I'll be going on Monday, Wednesday, and Thursday from six to nine. And he surprised me."

"How so?"

"Asked if I'd want to spend the night with you on those nights."

I hear her gasp before she says, "Seriously?"

"Yeah. He said they'd make do, and he'd like that better than me driving back at ten at night. At least that way I could drive back in the morning when I was fresh."

"Yes! I think that's a great idea! So could you come tomorrow night and spend the night?"

"No. I think that would be pushing his generosity, but there's nothing that says you can't come here. We eat at five, so I could fix plates for us and you could come straight to my cottage. That's … if you want."

"I want! Yes! Please! It'll be fun. I can't wait. Tomorrow is arraignment day in Pikeville, so I'll drive home, pick up my stuff, and come there. It'll probably be six? Something like that?"

"Sounds good. I'll shoot you the address so you can find us."

"Okay. Anything you want me to bring?"

"Yeah. Those nice tits."

She laughs. "Okay! I'll pack them in my bag."

"You do that! I'll talk to you tomorrow, babe. You tell me when you're headed this way so I'll know you're coming."

"Will do. And Dennis?"

"Yeah?"

"I'm really, *really* looking forward to this."

"Me too. Talk to you tomorrow evening. Night, sweet pea."

"Night."

I toss the phone down on the bed and drop back onto the softness of the mattress. I'm getting laid tomorrow night! How awesome is that? I swear to god, if the horn goes off while we're having sex, I'm ignoring the damn thing. It's been too long.

Nothing's going to screw this up. Nothing.

CHAPTER 4

Natalie

Last night was … intense. It's all I think about on the way to work. It took hours after I got home to process everything that had been said. I understand what Dennis is saying, but I still don't have to like it. I just have to respect it. It's true that what he's doing sounds like being in the military, but it makes me think of prison too. Coming from his situation, I can see how that would be attractive to him, and I can't blame him for that at all. But he kept mentioning family, and I haven't gotten to experience the Iron Oak family yet. I'll be glad when I can.

Today is arraignment day in Pikeville, and I know there won't be anything nearly as interesting as yesterday's proceedings. The faces of those men in the back of the courtroom are still haunting me, and I can't forget about them. My head is a busy place this morning. I'm finding myself not remembering miles of the trip while I'm driving because I'm so deep in thought, back and forth between Dennis and the previous day in the courtroom. By the time I get there, I'm totally flustered, and I've got to concentrate.

We go through the first four on the docket—two meth manufacturing and distribution cases by two brothers, one theft by unlawful taking for an ex-husband who took the ex-wife's car without her consent, and a guy who stole a cow out of a field, killed it, and took its head and legs back to the field. When we're finished with that one, I notice a pointed stare focused on me. What's that about? "Bailiff?"

"Permission to approach, Your Honor?" he asks, and I nod.

Pete Monroe has been one of my bailiffs ever since I came here. "What's up, Pete?"

"Got a call from the sheriff. You need to check your text messages."

"Uh, okay." I don't usually do that in the courtroom, but I reach up under my robe, pull out my phone, and look. Sure enough, there's a text message there.

Judge Anderson, this is Sheriff Copeland. Call me ASAP. Thank you.

That worries me a little. "Court will be in short recess. We'll reconvene in fifteen minutes." As I rise, I look toward Pete and motion toward my door, so I know he'll follow me.

By the time I get seated, Pete's there, along with the other bailiff, Ashton Harvey, and as they come to the door, I point to it. Ashton closes it, and I nod toward the sofa. "I want both of you to sit in on this so I have somebody to help me remember what's said if I get upset."

They both nod. "Sure, ma'am. No problem," Ashton assures me.

I press my contact and the phone rings. "Laurel County Sheriff's Office."

It takes me a second to put the phone on speaker, and then

I say, "Hello, this is Judge Natalie Anderson from Eastern District. I had a text to call Sheriff Copeland immediately."

"Yes, Your Honor. Hold just a second." There's a little obnoxious music, and then a voice says, "Judge Anderson?"

"Yes, sir. I got your message. What's up?"

"Those men in the back of the courtroom yesterday? We identified them. They're both members of the cartel Montoya and Cansala are part of."

"All in the country illegally?"

"Yeah. As soon as we realized who they were, we started looking for them and we can't find them anywhere, so they're holed up somewhere nearby. We just don't know where."

"What do you think they're up to?"

"If I had to say, I'd say they're going to perpetrate some nastiness to derail the trials."

"And how will they do that?"

There's silence for a couple of seconds before he says, "If I were you, I wouldn't be anywhere alone, and I'd watch my back."

That's what I was afraid he was going to say. "Honestly, I got the feeling that someone was watching me yesterday after the arraignments."

"They most likely were. They most likely *are*. I won't lie to you—I'm a little concerned for your safety. These guys are bad business."

"What do you suggest I do?"

"I think your first act should be to call your superiors and see if they can assign an FBI officer to you as a security detail."

A sour chuckle comes from my throat. "Don't you think that's a little drastic?"

"Actually, no. I don't think it's enough, but it's a start."

Wow. This has really shaken him. Maybe I should take it

a bit more seriously. "Okay. I'll do that. Thanks, sir. I really appreciate it."

"I can tell you this. On the days district is in session down here, I'll be assigning extra officers until this whole thing with these yahoos is over. There are several of them left, although if I had to guess, they won't care about anybody except the members of the cartel. Those white supremacist idiots they were using aren't of any value to them now that the operation has been shut down. All they care about are their men."

"Gotcha. I can see how that could be. I'll talk to the sheriff here in Pikeville too."

"I think that's an excellent idea. Please, be careful. These cartel guys are bad news."

"I will, I promise. Thanks, sheriff. I appreciate it."

"You're quite welcome. Let me know if there's anything I can do."

"I will. Thanks again. Bye." When I've hit END, I just sit there in stunned silence.

"Ma'am, you okay?" Pete asks.

"Yeah. I just can't believe that I've stepped into something with a cartel involved in Kentucky."

"They're everywhere, ma'am," Ashton assures me. "Literally everywhere. The more unlikely the place, the likelier they are to be there."

"I guess that's probably true. That's how they operate but, damn, why me?"

Pete shrugs. "Why not you? Could be anybody. Just happens to be you."

He's right, and I know it. I was just the unlucky one this time. "Could you guys talk to Sheriff Lasher about this for me?"

Pete nods. "Sure. No problem. I'll ask her to assign additional deputies over here if she can."

"Thanks. Okay. Guess I'd better get back into courtroom mode. Thanks, guys. I just wanted somebody to sit in with me on this because I knew whatever it was, it wouldn't be good news."

"No problem, ma'am. If there's anything we can do, just let us know. We'll be happy to do it," Ashton says, then does something very uncharacteristic of bailiffs. He reaches for my hand, and when I take his, he drops his other hand on top of it and squeezes. "You've proven yourself to be very fair and dedicated to the judicial process here. Everyone respects you, and we enjoy working in your courtroom. Every time I'm here, I learn something I didn't know before about the law. It's interesting and kinda fun. Well, until we get hold of an asshole!" he says and laughs, dropping our hands.

"Yeah, we get our fair share of those, don't we?" I ask, laughing.

"I swear, if one more 'sovereign citizen' turns up in this courtroom, I'm moving to Canada!" Pete says, laughing along with me.

"I hear ya! Oh, lord, we get some doozies! Well, let's get back to work, but thanks, guys. You both do an excellent job, and I'm lucky to have you."

"Thank you, ma'am," Pete says and stands.

Ashton rises too. "Yes. Thank you so much, ma'am. We're here to serve."

The rest of the workday is totally uneventful. When I leave the building, I don't have that feeling that I'm being watched, so I guess that's good. Doesn't mean I'm not. It just doesn't feel like I am. By the time I get to the house, it's a good bit after five, and I text as soon as I step through the doorway.

Just got home. I'll pack a little bag and be there in about an hour, if that's okay.

I've gotten my bag out and unzipped it when I hear a *PING!* and check my phone.

More than okay. Can't wait to see you. Tonight's offering is pot roast, mashed potatoes with gravy, green bean casserole, and yeast dinner rolls, and it smells amazing. I'm getting in the shower and then I'll fill us some plates. Might even get a container of extra so we can have seconds. LOL

The pain I'm feeling is coming from my cheeks because I'm smiling so widely that they hurt.

Sounds delicious. Sorry you're having to eat late.

Three wavy dots, and then a message.

It's worth it to eat with you. See you soon. Please let me know when you're on your way.

I send back a thumbs-up. As soon as my stuff is packed, I take a quick rinse-off shower, put on fresh perfume, and find pretty underwear and a bra, then slip into a pair of comfy jeans and a sweatshirt. I put my business suit in a garment bag so I can hang it, stuff my pumps into the bag with my robe, night clothes, and fresh underclothes, and head to the car.

Now is when I start feeling like I'm being watched, and it's disconcerting. As soon as I'm in the car and locked in, I glance around. There are cars parked up and down my street—not everybody has a driveway—and most of the cars have slightly tinted windows like mine. Once I've pulled out, I watch behind me, but I don't see a car pull out from anywhere, and no one falls in behind me, so I feel pretty safe.

The drive is nice. It's not that far, about thirty minutes, and the countryside here is pretty. I drive along, admiring the little farms and the majesty of the mountains all around us. The road is a bit twisty and curvy, but it looks like they followed a natural path, so it's not too bad. My GPS is telling me where to go, and before too long, I'm driving through Hindman. As towns go, it's not much of one, and Dennis said Mallie is even less of one, more like a wide spot in the road, but it's still cute. I make one turn, and the road starts to become far more rural. Trees line both sides, as well as broken-down wire fences, with the occasional house thrown in. Here and there are old trailers. We're not talking manufactured housing here; we're talking trailers, and it's obvious some of them are being lived in. Others are half off their foundations, windows broken out and doors missing. I keep driving until I finally see the sign.

Iron Oak Farms

Appalachian STAR Team

The phone number is at the bottom of the sign, and I wonder whose it is. The first building is huge. Wait—he said it was a church campground. I guess that was the church maybe? The second one is just as big, but low to the ground. Kitchen, I suppose. And then there are a bunch of small cottages. It occurs to me that I don't know which one is his. A guy is walking my direction, and when I get close, I put my window down. His smile is wide, and he greets me with, "Hey there! You must be Natalie! I'm Reboot. Lookin' for Paddy?"

"Um, Dennis?"

"Yeah, that's him. Cottage over there with the green door," he says, turning and pointing.

"Thanks. Nice to meet you."

"And you too. Take care. See you around." With that, he keeps ambling toward the long, low building, and when I look in my rearview mirror, I see a dark-haired woman step out the door and greet him with a kiss. That was sweet.

I stop in front of the little cottage and before I can get out, the door opens and Dennis appears in the doorway. When I've climbed out, he grins. "Have any trouble finding the place?"

"Nope. GPS brought me right to it."

"Good! Need help?"

"Yeah. Can you get my garment bag out?"

"Sure." As I grab my bag, he pulls the garment bag from its hook and heads toward the cottage. "Work clothes?"

"Yep."

When I step inside, I'm shocked. It's a cute little place with a comfy sofa and recliner, a nice little kitchen, and a pretty table and chairs. "You can put your stuff in here," he says and disappears through a doorway.

The bedroom has a king bed, and then I realize that on the wall it shares with the living room, there's an electric fireplace that can be seen from both sides. Very cool. "This is really nice."

"Thanks. I like it. There's room in the closet, there's an empty drawer on the top right of the dresser, and there's space in the bathroom for that kind of stuff. Just make yourself at home. I'll go unwrap our dinner and get it set out. Want a soda or tea?"

"I'll take the tea, please."

"Okay. Dinner coming right up."

This is incredible. He helped me bring my stuff in. He made room in his closet, dresser, and bathroom for my things. He's got dinner in the kitchen, waiting for me. A girl could get used to this.

By the time I get finished putting my things away, it's all on the table. "Oh, this smells delicious."

"I'm telling you, Audrey is a great cook. We have something new all the time, and she has these standards too, but they're better than anything I've ever eaten. Hollywood did good when he brought her into our lives."

"I think so! I met a guy named Reboot in the drive?"

"Yeah. Derek. He's got a girlfriend, Mavis. They haven't been together long, but she's our webmistress. She takes care of our email, ads on social media, all kinds of stuff. Has an office in Penny's house."

"Penny is Patch's girlfriend?"

"Wife. Yeah, she has her grandmother's house down the road here—you passed it on the way in—and she has an office there. Mavis's office is there too. It works out really well."

"I bet." I let him hold my chair for me and help me scoot up, and then he joins me. "This place is really cute," I tell him as I take my first bite. He wasn't kidding—it's absolutely scrumptious.

"Thanks. They're going to redo the last four and double their size so people with kids can have bigger cottages. You know, like Bulldog and Tinsley."

"What's the story there?"

"Long and difficult, but she's pregnant and they're expecting a little boy. We just had a big baby shower for them this weekend."

I grin. "And that's why Steve and Kelly were in the area."

"Exactly."

What takes place next is the loveliest evening I've had in a long time. We laugh and talk, and when we're finished, or I should say after our second helping of pot roast, we rinse the dishes and put them in the compact-sized dish-washer, and then we sit down to watch TV. We don't get a lot of TV watched because about twenty minutes in, we start making out, and let me tell you, this guy knows how to kiss a woman. I totally lose myself in those kisses.

They're some kind of delicious. We take a break, we get a drink, we sit and talk, and then we go right back to making out.

At nine thirty, he says, "You've got to get up early to drive to … is it London tomorrow?"

"Yeah."

"Then we should probably go to bed and get some sleep."

I snicker. "Is that what you want to do? Sleep?"

He lets out a laugh. "Well, yeah, afterward!"

My grin is silly, I'm sure, but I can't help it. "Ah! That's more like it!"

"But listen … There are some things I think we need to talk about. First off, I've only been with one woman since I got out, and that was one time. That's it. I was careful, but I'll gladly be tested if you want."

"I trust you. I haven't been with anybody in over a year, so I'm not too concerned."

He nods. "Me either. Are you on the pill?"

"Yeah."

"Okay. I'll still opt for condoms. I just think that's the best policy unless and until we decide if this is going to be permanent." I nod my agreement. "I think the first two or three times we're together, we need to not worry about the power exchange. I'm not some power Dom. When we step into the bedroom, you'll do what I want, but I won't expect you to do things you really don't want to do. We need to learn each other's likes and needs before we start getting serious about that stuff. That's if you want a relationship. If all you really want is sex, then that doesn't matter. And if that's the case, I need to know up front."

Holy shit. Have I completely misread this? "Um, I thought you wanted a relationship. That's how you've acted."

"I do. I just want to know if we're on the same page."

Whew. I thought I'd really stepped in it! "Yeah. I definitely do. I really like you."

"I feel the same about you. So we're looking to forge a relationship, not to just have mind-blowing sex, right?"

I nod with a grin. "Right." *But mind-blowing sex is still good!* my horny inner teenager announces in my head.

"Good. So let's just try to enjoy ourselves, but if you're not getting what you need, you need to tell me. I do *not* want you unsatisfied because I can't read your mind, okay?"

"Yes. I agree."

"Okay. You take the first turn in the bathroom. I'll go in when you're finished. While you're in there, I'm going to pick up and clean up in here. I've got stuff for breakfast, so we're all set."

"Sounds good." I struggle to my feet after sitting for so long, then head for the bathroom. There's not much I need to do in there, but I do want to freshen up. Do I want to put on my night clothes? I don't think so. Once I'm finished in the bathroom, I just step back into the bedroom, toss my clothes on the chair, and slide under the covers in nothing but a smile.

Only a couple of minutes pass and Dennis strolls into the room. "Well, making yourself at home, I see," he says with a grin.

"Yep. Figured that's what you wanted."

"Enjoy that bed. I love that thing."

"Yeah. It's really comfy. It would be even comfier with you in it," I say, sliding my hand back and forth across the comforter.

"Then I'll be out in just a minute." I can hear him in there brushing his teeth. A few seconds later, the toilet flushes, and then the water is running. He washes his hands after he takes a piss—I like it.

He wanders out of the bathroom naked and I'm surprised,

not just that he'd already feel so comfortable undressed in front of me, but his cock … Let's just say I don't think I'm going away unsatisfied. Instead of coming straight to the bed, he steps to the dresser, lights a couple of candles, and then turns on the fireplace. Its gentle glow is sweet, but not as sweet as the way he looks at me when he turns around. "Lexie, turn off bedroom lamp," he says, and the lamp clicks off. "Do you like music or no?"

"I don't care."

"No music then. Just your gasps and sighs. That'll be fine with me."

"What about your gasps and sighs?" I ask, grinning.

"I'm a very reserved gasper and sigher. Probably won't hear them." He settles under the covers beside me and presses a palm to my cheek. "You're beautiful, Natalie. I can't believe I'm here with you."

"I can't believe I'm here with you either. There's not one damn thing about you that's not sexy."

His eyes pop open wide. "Seriously? Nobody's ever said that to me before."

"You must've been with women who didn't talk during sex, because you're so fucking sexy that my heart is racing right now."

"Really?" He reaches out and presses his hand to my chest just above my left breast. "I don't feel it."

"It's lower. A good bit lower."

To my delight, he slides his hand down my torso, cups my left breast, and drags the pad of his thumb back and forth across my nipple. "Oh, yeah. I can feel it now. It's really thumping."

I'm about to say something else when his lips touch mine, and the feeling that passes through me is positively electric. No one has made me feel this way in a long, long time, and I want it so badly that I'd almost kill for it. There's no time to even think before his tongue slips between my lips and dances along my own, luring me into a simmering boil. I haven't been this turned on in forever. Even though my eyes are closed, I see him in my mind, those big hands and hazel eyes, the thickness of his dark hair, and the broadness of his chest with its dusting of dark hair that winds downward toward its terminus. When he ends the kiss, I open my eyes and find myself staring right into his, and I have no words. What I saw in my mind's eye can't compare to the man right here, holding me in his arms. An attorney at a loss for words is unheard of, but I am. Before I can come up with anything, he whispers, "Do you have any idea how soft and lovely you are?"

The feeling that stirs in my chest is overwhelming. "No one's ever told me that before."

"I find that hard to believe." I can feel his hand trailing down my side, and when it reaches my hip, it takes a dive. As soon as he touches my mound, I suck in a breath. "You're about to become mine. If that's not what you want, you should say so now."

"It's absolutely what I want." I know what's about to happen, but I want it so badly that I can barely wait. A split second later, I feel his finger part my folds and I know what's next. He dips it into my wetness and trails upward, and I try hard to prepare myself for what I know is coming.

And I can't. Three strokes. That's all he gets, and I feel my body tighten, every muscle screaming. What happens next is what happens every time—the chill spreads over me, my legs stiffen, and I let out a long, low hiss as my hips begin to buck. My eyes are closed so I can't see his response, and that's a good thing. Even so, he keeps going, and I'm a wild thing, arms and legs spasming, belly jerking and shaking.

When he finally stops, I feel myself sinking into the mattress, finally absolved of all the tension his touch brought to me.

"Fuck, that was quick," he whispers.

I fish in my climax-addled brain for something to say. "Do you know how long it's been for me?" I ask, my voice as pithy as I can manage to make it.

"Yeah, but I barely touched you! I think I got four strokes in and—"

"Actually, it was three." That's when I finally force my eyes open and look at him.

His jaw is hanging, his mouth partially open. "I'm just … What just happened here? I mean, one minute, I was sliding my hand down and the next minute …"

"I needed it."

"Uh, yeah. I'd say."

"The desperate woman," I mumble to myself.

"No. I wasn't thinking that."

"Yeah? What were you thinking?"

A little shrug lifts his shoulders. "I'm just happy you enjoyed it. It's been a long time for me too, and I was hoping I hadn't forgotten how that works."

"Yeah?"

"Of course. Is it usually this easy to get you to climax?"

I think about it for a few seconds before I say, "I guess. It's not something that I have trouble with, if that's what you mean. It's never been an issue. I always figured most guys would like to not have to spend forty-five minutes trying to get a woman to have an orgasm. You know, when she's thinking about something else, or gets interrupted, or whatever happens to women who have trouble having orgasms. I don't know. I never have. Had trouble, that is."

"So you can have an orgasm in under two minutes. It lasted for a little bit, didn't it?"

"Yeah."

"Yeah, and that's something. Question is, when that one's gone, do you have any luck having another one?"

Nobody's ever asked me that before. "Uh, yeah. Every time."

"So I could give you another one right now?"

I side-eye him. "Yeah." Something passes across his face, something I can't read. "What?"

He gives me a wicked grin. "Mmmm."

"What?"

"Orgasm torture."

"Oh, you wouldn't …"

"Wouldn't I? You want a man who takes charge? You're probably going to regret letting that pussy out of the bag." I don't get a chance to say another word before he presses me down into the mattress and grins down at me. "You'd better get ready, sweet pea." His hand drifts downward again as he declares, "I'm getting ready to drive you crazy."

The orgasm is fast and sharp, snapping the breath right out of my lungs. My back bows and my legs vibrate. I can hear myself making a weird sound, but I can't concentrate on it. I can't concentrate on anything. My world snaps back into focus and I'm panting. "Oh, that was fun. Let's do it again," he says.

"Gimme a second," I whisper.

"That's all you get." A couple of the muscles in my belly are still fluttering when he starts again.

"Oh, fuck, Dennis!" I mutter, squirming just a little. It rises almost immediately, and the clenching in my pussy is painful as the climax takes me. "Damn! Oh, damn! Please!"

He stops and smiles. "Oh, wow. That was crazy."

Now I'm panting for real. "Oh, shit. Please, let's not—"

"Oh, we absolutely are. Might as well get ready."

"Dennis, please, I—"

"You're gonna come again, sweet pea. That's just how it is." His hand slides down, and I feel his finger claim my tiny little nub. "Uh-huh. There it is. Oh, baby, such a hard little thing."

Everything slides away—the room, his face, the scent of the candle. Bright lights pulse behind my eyelids, and I think I'm levitating off the mattress. I can't breathe. It's so powerful and rhythmic that my whole body feels like it's undulating, writhing on its own, and he's not stopping. I want to tell him to stop, that I can't take it, that it's too much, but I can't speak, just bounce along on the pulsing of everything between my legs.

And then it stops. There's an aching that I can't stand, a burning sensation deep inside, and I feel the heat of his body as he leans down and whispers in my ear, "Now I'm going to fuck you properly."

The muscles in my pussy are clenched so tightly that I cry out when he bores into me, and I hear him growl, "Holy shit, girl, you're so fucking tight that I don't know how long I can hold out."

"Now you know how I feel," I mutter under my breath.

"Yeah, well, get ready." He pulls back just a little, and then moves forward.

Oh, god. I've never been fucked like this before. He's hard and plenty big enough, but he's like a machine, his strokes steady and strong, the head of his cock grinding against my G-spot, and I'm aching in a way that's totally different from the previous orgasms. It's been a long, long time since I've felt even nearly this wound up. A symphony movement—that's what it's like, with him as the maestro and my body as the instrument. He's gripping my hips, but then his hands drift upward and I feel him pinch both of my nipples—hard.

"Damn, girl, you're so fucking gorgeous. Look at these, ripe and pink and hard. You like a little pain? Just a little?" he asks as he pinches my buds, then twists them and pulls outward. The pain is sharp and heads straight to my clit like a spear.

"Oh, yeah. Oh, god, yeah, please. Oh, god, Dennis, fuck me hard. Please, fuck me so fucking hard, please? Please?"

"My choice. But I do think I want to give you a little more. I think it's time." I'm not sure what he means until he speeds up, slips his hands under my hips, and lifts them just a little.

My whole body shakes, and I can feel the pulsing of the muscles deep inside me around his hardness. Without even realizing it, I let go with a long, low cry, something wild and unholy, and my hands are scrambling to reach out to him. When my fingers stroke down his chest and pass over his nipples, I slide them back up and pinch both. "Ohhhh, you shouldn't have done that, bad girl," he whispers, then leans in and kisses me.

His strokes turn into hunching, hard and fast, and my mind heads somewhere else. Time is lost, and I can't hear anything around me for the buzzing in my head. Then out of nowhere, I hear him groan, a deep, dark sound, and he stills on top of me, then drops to lie flat on me, his arms wrapped around me, cupping my ass.

I can't breathe or think. His hardness is still buried inside me, and I don't want him to ever pull it out. What has happened here … There are no words to explain it. A hunger has awakened inside me, one I didn't know existed, and I want him to fuck me again, hard and fast. A lot of things cycle through my mind, dirty things, things I've never thought about having a man do to me, and I want him to do them. And yes—*to* me, not with me. I want him to tell me what he's going to do to me and then do it twice as long and hard as I ever dreamed. It's like some kind of sex-starved beast has been awakened inside me and just won't go back to sleep.

But my leg is aching. The room is silent when I whisper, "Dennis?"

"Yeah, babe?"

"My leg's going to sleep."

"Oh!" In a split second, he rolls off me, but I feel the loss of his warmth and weight instantly. He reaches for me, and when I scoot toward him, he wraps both arms around me and draws me into him. I'm overwhelmed by his maleness, by the comfort I feel as he holds me, by the power of whatever this is that's pulling us together. "Better?" he whispers and kisses my temple.

"Much." As I snuggle into him, I feel him reach up and stroke my hair. "That was amazing."

"*You're* amazing. You know how they talk about 'getting lucky?' That's what I did tonight. I got lucky enough to be here with you. I got lucky enough to meet you." He's quiet for just a few seconds before he asks, "Was it all okay? I didn't push you too far?"

"No. Not at all."

"I just need to know what you're comfortable with and what you need."

There's got to be a way to say it without *saying it*. "Um, you could've been more aggressive if you'd like."

The gears are practically visible in his brain as they click and roll, and then he asks, "Aggressive? Define aggressive."

Shit. He's not reading between the lines. "You know, um, aggressive. Forceful."

His eyes narrow until he's looking at me through slits. "Forceful. Okay, are you into bondage?"

Maybe he *is* reading between the lines. "Light bondage?"

I could be offended at his little chuckle, but I'm not. "Is that a question?"

"No. I mean, I like light bondage. And … other stuff."

"Other stuff. Like what other stuff?"

"Are you gonna make me spell it out?"

Uh-oh. Those eyebrows spike upwards, and I know the answer before he speaks. "Yep. I expect us to talk about these things like grownups. So what are we talking about? Sash from your robe? Handcuffs? Nipple clamps? Butt plugs?"

"Butt plugs?" That makes me giggle.

There's not a hint of a smile when he says, "You be straight with me or I'll buy the biggest one I can find and shove it right up in there."

There's a tiny stabbing sensation in my chest. "Are you mad at me?"

"No. I'm not mad. Look, Natalie, every conversation we've had up to this point has been open and honest, and having sex shouldn't change that. You shouldn't feel more vulnerable around me because of it; you should feel less vulnerable. I'm not asking you these things to make fun of you or use it against you. I'm concerned with your satisfaction, and I'm smart enough to know that if you're satisfied, I will be too. You're not sixteen, and neither am I. We should be able to talk about this and be serious about it, because it *is* serious. It's about a relationship." Then he stops, and the spark disappears from his eyes. "Unless this isn't about a relationship. It's about fucking around and being friends with benefits."

"No! No, that's not what I want at all!" The previous little stab is nothing compared to the ache setting up in my chest.

"I really … care about you. Earlier was … probably the best sexual experience I've ever had. I want to spend time with you, really get to know you, be in a relationship with you. I can see myself … falling for you."

To my surprise, he sits up, takes my hands, and helps me to sitting. The sheet falls down around my waist, and I reflexively reach for it, then stop myself. Why am I trying to hide my breasts from him? I've walked through a kink club in nothing but a thong. What's wrong with me? I'm drowning in self-doubt until his hand rises and he strokes his knuckles down my cheek. "Babe, it's easy to be open and free with somebody when you don't care if you never see them again. It's harder when it's somebody you want to forge a relationship with. But trust me, I'm a safe person for you to talk to. I want to be your soft spot when you need a place to land."

I can't even respond. I just lean in, my cheek on his collarbone, and he wraps his arms around me. Mine close around his ribcage and I want to sit here like this all night. I'm so taken with this guy. "Then to answer your question," I whisper, "it's totally up to you. I told you I want you to take the lead, and I do. If you want to spice things up, I'll try anything. I've done a lot of that stuff in the past, but it's not totally necessary to me. What's necessary to me is that I'm with somebody who really cares about me."

"Then you've got everything necessary," he whispers back and kisses the back of my neck. I've never been in this cottage until tonight, but I have a really weird feeling that I'm home.

And I'm really, really happy about it.

CHAPTER 5

Paddy

Holding this woman in my arms … I can't imagine what I did right to make this happen, but my god, I'm happy. Even though I'd like to lie awake all night and stare at her, I drift off and when my alarm goes off, she's still lying beside me, her back pressed into my chest as I spoon her. I really, really don't want to get up.

Instead, I slip on some clothes, go over to the kitchen, fill a couple of plates, and carry them back. By the time I step into the cottage, Natalie's sitting on the sofa in my bathrobe, and I can't believe how much better it looks on her than it does on me. "Hey, want some breakfast?"

"Sure. Then I've gotta get a shower and get going." As we sit down, I think about how great it would be if every morning was just like this, the two of us sitting at the table, eating and chatting. Out of the blue, she blurts out, "I wish you'd think about seeing your kids."

That stops me dead. "Where did that come from?"

Her fingers are delicate as she pulls little pieces of bacon off the strip. "I dunno. I was just thinking about it. I think you should. Wouldn't you like to see them?"

"Yes and no. Yes, I'd love to see them for me. No, I don't want to see them for them. They don't even remember me."

"I bet the oldest one does. What's his name again?"

"Borden. And Tegan." I hesitate for a few seconds before I say, "I really don't think it's a good idea."

"I think it's a great idea. You're out here, nice place for kids to play and explore, the guys all around to provide good role models, the women who wouldn't mind being surrogate moms. And one of the guys has a son out here, right?"

"Hollywood's son … Well, Audrey's son, but Hollywood's adopting him. As far as they're concerned, they're father and son. He's a little boy though. Patch has a son, but he doesn't live here, although I have a funny feeling he's going to wind up here. He's in Hawaii going to college right now."

"Speaking of college … When do you start?"

"Next week. Don't have much time to get ready."

"Wow! Yeah, you really don't." I see her glance over into the living room area. "Oh, shit. I've gotta get going. Do you need the shower?"

"Nah. I shower after work. We get all hot and sweaty, so there's really no point. Matter of fact, I've gotta get over to the shop. You okay here by yourself?"

"Sure. No problem. So when …" And she stops.

"When what?"

"When do we see each other again?"

"I dunno, but I'd love to call you every evening if that's okay. And I definitely want to see you this weekend. Maybe sooner if we can manage it."

Her smile lights up her whole face. "Absolutely." Sadness

slaps at me as she stands from the table. "So I'm gonna go get in the shower, I guess. Do I need to take the dishes back to the kitchen?"

"Nah. I'll put them in the dishwasher this afternoon when I get in and then I'll take them back. There are plenty over there already." As she passes me, she drops her hand on my shoulder and drags it until it drops off on her way out of the room. Once the shower has started, I go into the bedroom, pull on some old jeans and a tee, my socks, and my boots, and then I rap lightly on the bathroom door.

"Yeah?"

The mirror is completely fogged up when I stick my head in. "I'm going. Just lock it and pull it closed behind you."

"Okay," she calls back.

"And Natalie?"

"Yeah?"

Do I dare say it? "I'll miss you until I see you again."

"I'll miss you too, sweetie. Have a good day."

"You too. Drive carefully." After I've closed the bathroom door again, I stride across the room and head toward the door, but I turn just before I step out.

Her handbag is beside the sofa and her jacket is draped across the back of the recliner, and I commit the view to memory. She's been here, at my table, on my sofa, in my bed. She's part of my life now, and I hope she becomes a huge part.

Halfway across the lawn to the shop, Reboot catches up to me. "Have a good evening?"

"Yeah. Really good evening."

"Gonna keep seeing each other?"

"Yep. As much as we can."

"I hope this works out for you."

"I do too." Thoughts of last night cycle through my head

as we walk along, and I'm overwhelmed with the memories of her touch, her smile, and her body under mine. Just thinking about her makes me want her so badly that I can hardly stand it.

We have a lot of things to work on, but there's one thing for sure. Sexual compatibility isn't one of them.

EARLIER THIS MORNING, I LEFT LISA A VOICEMAIL AND ASKED her to call me. I've been thinking about something, and Natalie encouraged it, so I figured I'd see what happens.

We're finishing up lunch when my phone rings, and I look at the screen before I answer. "Hey! Thanks for calling me back."

I hear her chuckle. "I always call you back."

"Yeah. You do, and I appreciate it."

"So you said you have something important to talk to me about."

"Yep." I take a couple of seconds to gather my courage before I say, "I've been thinking a lot lately, and I wondered if you'd come and bring the boys with you. There's room for you to stay here in the lodge, so it wouldn't cost you anything."

"Wouldn't matter if it did. I'd come anyway. Dennis, you can't know how happy I am that you've decided to do this."

"Can I ask what you've told them about me?"

A sigh of exasperation comes through the phone. "Dennis, I've told you this over and over. I've told them all about you, and how you didn't do anything wrong. Our family photos are still here and there in the house. Our wedding photo is still hanging in the hallway."

"Wow. How does Luke feel about that?"

"Luke is fine with it. We talked about it before we got married, and I told him I didn't want you erased from their lives. What happened to you was grossly unfair. You lost everything."

"You took most of it from me."

"And that's unfair to me."

Ouch. She's right. "Yeah, sorry."

"All they had was me. I had to survive, and I couldn't. I lost everything too. And I was angry and bitter for a long time, but I've come to terms with that. It was you I directed all of that toward at first, but later on, I realized that you were a victim just like we were. We all were."

"Have you seen Leslie lately?"

"From time to time I'll run into her, but she still treats me like I did something to her."

"I'm sorry."

"It's not your fault. None of this is your fault. It just … is. There's nothing we can do to change that. But we can change the way the boys see you."

"I thought you said you told them everything."

"I did but, honey, they see you as some kind of imaginary figure. You're lore. You're a story I've told them over and over. They need to meet *you*, see *you*, the real person."

"What about Mom and Dad?"

"You know they go to your parents' house for holidays. Sheila and Teresa and their husbands and kids all come, so they know their cousins. And everybody talks about you while they're there, but they still don't see you as *real*."

"I get it. And we can fix that."

"Good. So next weekend? Do you want us to come on Saturday?"

"Yeah. I don't have class on Friday night, so you can come that evening if you want. It's about, what, three hours?

You can spend the night on Friday and Saturday nights and go back on Sunday."

I'd forgotten I hadn't told her about it when she asks, "Class?"

"Yeah. We'll talk about it when you get here."

I fully expect I'll tell her about Natalie too, unless something changes between now and then. And I don't think it will.

Except that it'll get better.

NATALIE

I BARELY MAKE IT INTO THE COURTHOUSE BEFORE I RUN smack into Darrell and Cliff. "You need to come with us," Darrell says and takes my arm.

"Oh, am I under arrest?" I ask, my tone intentionally mocking.

But there's not one hint of mirth on his face when he frowns and says, "Not funny." I'm surprised when he opens the door to the family restroom and ushers me in, waits for Cliff to step in, and closes the door behind us.

Now I'm confused. "What the hell is going on?"

Cliff's eyes bore into me. "Those guys? They're here."

"What guys?"

"The Latino guys? From court the other day?"

Now I'm confused. "Why?"

"Good question," Darrell says. "We don't know. We called Sheriff Copeland when we realized they were here, and he's getting some extra deputies over here. Did you call your chief district judge and ask for FBI protection?"

"No. But it's beginning to look like I need to do that."

Cliff nods. "I really think you should. The sheriff called the state's attorney to see what they know about these guys. I can't talk about that because you're hearing the case, but just know that it's not good. Really, really not good."

"We've worked together for a good while now," Darrell says, and his eyes lock with mine. "Make that call, Natalie. If something happens to you because you didn't, we'll never forgive ourselves." They never call me by my name, so I know he means business.

"I will. I promise. Right now, I've got to get to my chambers to look at the docket and see if Alinda's got anything I need to take care of before we go into session. But I promise, I'll call." I've got more than one reason to talk to Judge Martelle, and it looks like today is the day.

Jury selection. How can I adequately describe how much I hate jury selection? It's like the very, very last thing I want to do, and yet it has to be done. And sure enough, those two guys are sitting in the back of the courtroom. Worse yet, they barely move the whole time. It's like they're staring at me, not at what's going on in the courtroom. Weirdest thing ever, and very unsettling.

When we've got two juries seated, one for a repeat offender DUI and another for armed robbery, I break for lunch. I've got another one to go, a destruction of public property case, and then a meeting with the attorneys regarding Montoya and Cansala's cases. One of the things I insist on doing is going over questions that will be asked during jury selection. I don't want anyone's time wasted on stupid stuff that's not relevant to the case, and what some of these attorneys come up with is ridiculous. Instead of going out, Darrell has gone to a sandwich shop and gotten lunch for me. I know what he's doing. He's trying to keep me in the courthouse where they can keep an eye on me and, frankly, I'm okay with that.

After lunch, it takes very little time to seat the third jury, and then I call Collins and Asher into chambers. All I do is hold out my hand. "I want to see them." Each of them hands me a sheet of paper.

The usual. *Do you know these men? Do you know their families? Have you had any contact with them? Are you or any member of your family affiliated with the Kentucky State Police? Do you have any knowledge you'd consider private about this case? Do you have anyone in your family who flies a helicopter, either privately for business or for the military?*

And, of course, Collins has some pointed ones. *How do you feel about people of other colors and ethnicities? Do you have any preconceived beliefs about Mexicans? Do you like Mexican food?* What the hell does that have to do with anything? *Does it make you angry when people speak Spanish in your presence in stores or other settings?* Wow. Prejudice much? But I guess they're valid questions, even though they make me sick, and even sicker thinking about some of the answers the potential jurors will give.

Thing is, I can't find a thing in their questions that I'd object to, so I hand the papers back. "These are fine. Disgusting, but fine." Asher gives me a disturbed grimace, and I know he's figured out what I'm talking about. He's one of the best prosecutors I've ever seen, and Collins has his work cut out for him. I desperately want to ask him about the two men who've been sitting in the back of the courtroom, but I can't.

Once the attorneys are gone, I pull out the filings to see what the trial is really all about. There's a list of witnesses, and also a list of documents sent in as evidence, plus things filed from discovery. When I'm finished with that, I work on some paperwork, make a couple of calls, send a couple of texts, and tell Alinda that I'll see her on Friday for jury selection on the Montoya and Cansala cases. It's not quite four, so I figure I'll call Dennis on my way home, and I head out the back door.

The parking lot is quiet and I'm fifteen feet from my car when I hear a voice say, "Hey-hey, *bonitas tetas.*"

My briefcase is in my left hand, and that's where my Taser is. There's no way I can get to it. My best chance is to face them and let them know I'm not afraid, which is going to be very hard with my knees visibly knocking. "I'll thank you to not speak to me in such an inappropriate way," I bark back, trying to sound as tough as possible.

"Ah-ha-ha-ha. You a tough one, huh? Who you think you are, little bird?" the taller of the two asks.

"I'm a federal judge for the Eastern District of Kentucky. And who are you?"

"Let's just say a … um … how you say, businessman? I already got my business interrupted, and I don't want no more interruptions, *tú entiendes*?"

"And exactly how did I interrupt your business?" I'm trying to figure out how to keep him talking long enough to slowly shuffle toward my car.

"You didn't," the shorter and younger man answers. "*Los federales* did that."

Basically, he just admitted to me who he is and what his interest is in the case. "Then I'm not sure what your point is in talking to me."

"We can go back to business if we have friends to help us, and they can't help us if they're *en la cárcel*. So if they go home, we're back in business! Everybody's happy!" the tall one says.

"I don't have any control over that. A jury decides that and—"

"Judge Anderson? Could I speak with you for a moment?" I hear a voice call out, and I look up to find Quentin Asher making his way down the back steps, the door closing behind him. But I know Quentin, and I'm positive that if he looked through the glass before he opened the door, he hit the panic button on his way out.

"I'm sorry. You gentlemen will have to excuse me. I need to talk to Mr. Asher and—"

"Oh, we would welcome an opportunity to speak with him too," the younger man adds.

Thankfully, the door opens again, and Darrell and Cliff power down the stairs, hands on the grips of their weapons. "This is a private parking lot for employees from within the building only, and you're trespassing. I'm going to have to ask you gentlemen to leave," Darrell announces as they make their way toward us.

The older, taller man touches his forehead with a two-finger salute. "We did not know this. Our apologies. I'm sure we'll see each other again very soon." They turn and head to their car, but not before the younger one has turned one more time to leer at me. The four of us watch as they wheel out of the parking lot.

No one speaks until they're out of sight. "Holy shit, Natalie, what did we tell you about staying where somebody could see you?" Cliff hisses toward me.

I sigh loudly. "Somebody *could* see me. Just turned out to be the wrong somebodies." I pivot slightly and lay a hand on Quentin's forearm. "Thanks for realizing what was going on."

"I *didn't* realize. I was standing at the far end of the hallway, talking on the phone, when I saw you come out, and then saw them follow you. You'd better be glad I was standing there. Otherwise, no one would've seen you and you would've been on your own."

"Do you really think they would've done anything to me?"

"We don't know what they're capable of. Have you made that call to Judge Martelle?" Cliff asks.

"Not yet."

"Then please, for the love of god, do it tomorrow. Don't wait. Now, get in your car. I'm following you to the county line," Darrell announces, but before I can turn, he gives me a hard stare. "By the way, what were they saying to you?"

"That my friends the *federales* interrupted their business, and they need their friends back to start their business back up." I turn toward my car, then call back, "You following me or what?"

I can hear Darrell heading toward his cruiser. "Yes. I am."

And from behind me, I hear Cliff say to Quentin, "You'd better put these cocksuckers away."

"I'm going to do everything I can to do that. Just keep her safe, please," the commonwealth attorney says.

I'm alert and aware enough to realize when I get to the county line that there's no one following us, just the two cars out in the darkness. I see Darrell pull off, and I'm alone, but there are no headlights anywhere. That's when it hits me.

I have to find a way to tell Dennis about all of this. It could wreck things before they start, because he's not going to want to put himself and his friends in these guys' crosshairs, and that might be exactly where they wind up with me.

But he deserves to know.

PADDY

. . .

I'M STARTING TO GET REALLY, REALLY NERVOUS. I START school next week. That's a big step for me, the guy who'd already been out of college for years when he went away to prison. But every time I think about how nervous I am and how sure I am that I'm going to botch it all, I see Nikki's smiling, tear-streaked face in my mind, and I remember her telling me how happy she is that somebody will be taking advantage of the scholarship fund she started to help memorialize her kids. I can't let her down, and I won't. I've already made myself that promise. I want her to be proud of me—I want them all to be proud of me.

I've talked to Natalie every night this week, and we've had good conversations. It's Friday, and she spent all day in London overseeing jury selection for some trials they've got going on soon. I have no idea what they are, but she said she'd explain to me when we see each other, which is tonight. I've got some news for her too, and I can't wait to tell her.

Plus we got more news today. According to Ghost, the trials for the guys who shot Izzy's bird down are gearing up, and that's a good thing. I want those bastards put away for good.

I'm in the shower when I hear someone in the cottage and call out, "Is that you?"

"Yeah! It's me!"

"I'll be out in just a minute." Good. She's already here, because I've got a surprise for her.

I step into the bedroom with a towel wrapped around my waist to find her sitting on the foot of the bed. "Hey, you!" she sings out, so I step right up in front of her and bend down to kiss her on the forehead.

"Hey, sweet pea. Have a good day?"

She shrugs. "Eh. Good enough, I guess. Nothing great. Just glad it's over. You're running a little late."

"Yeah. Had a sheath to finish, so I decided I'd just go ahead and finish it rather than put it off until Monday. I've got some things to work on with Priest on Monday, so my slate is clean and I won't have my own work waiting on me." My clothes are already laid out, so I drop the towel and start dressing. "You hungry?"

"Starving. What's for dinner tonight?"

It's my turn to shrug. "Dunno. Figured we'll find out when we get there."

Her brow furrows. "Get there? We going out?"

"No. I meant the kitchen."

"But we agreed—"

I step in front of her and press a fingertip to her lips to shush her. "Listen, I've thought about this a lot. As far as I'm concerned, we're in a secure relationship. What about you? How do you feel?"

She nods. "I feel the same."

"Then let's just eat in the kitchen."

That gets a side-eye from her. "Are you sure about that?"

"I am. Are you?"

Her answer is quick and decisive. "I am if you are."

"Good. Because I'm starving too, and there's no sense in carrying food across the lawn. Let me finish getting dressed and we'll go."

We walk across the green space hand-in-hand, and I'm thinking about all we've talked about this week. We're about halfway there when Priest joins us. "Natalie, this is Priest. Priest, this is Natalie Anderson."

He extends a hand, which she takes, and I can see the surprise in his eyes at her firm grip. "Nice to meet you, Natalie. We've heard a lot about you."

"Oh, god, I hope I can live it down," she says, laughing.

"I'm sure you can! It's all been good."

She's still laughing. "Well, that's a relief. Or maybe I should say, thanks for lying for him?"

"Yeah, well, I do what I can!" Priest says, joining in on the laughter.

"Mind if I tag along?" a voice asks, and I turn to find Reboot right behind me.

"Nah. Come on. I think you guys have met already," I say to my friend.

"We have! Good to see you, Natalie."

"And you too, Reboot."

He grins. "Coming to dinner with us?"

"Yeah. This guy thinks I'm ready," she says and throws a thumb toward me.

"You may lose her tonight. I'm not sure she can hack it," Reboot says.

I shake my head. "Nope. I'm pretty sure she can hold her own."

Natalie's still laughing. "I'm gonna give it my best shot!"

When Priest opens the door, the smells and sounds of the kitchen smack us all. He holds the door so Natalie can step in, and she stands just inside, looking all around. "I don't know what I expected, but this isn't it."

"What do you mean?"

"It's so … homey. I think I expected something that looked like a school cafeteria or something."

"Nope. Tony, Vic, and Patch worked on this, and they designed it to look as much like a family kitchen as it could and still have all the commercial appliances."

She's smiling as she looks around. "Well, they did a great job."

"Hey! You must be Natalie! I'm Patch," our leader says and rushes to greet her. "It's so good to have you here!"

"It's great to be here."

"Good. I'll introduce you to my wife, Penny, when she gets here. Mavis, Reboot's girlfriend, will be along in a minute too. Let me introduce you to Audrey and Hollywood." I watch as my boss whisks my girlfriend away and starts introducing her around.

My girlfriend. I have a girlfriend. Son of a bitch … I have a girlfriend.

A voice pierces my thoughts. "Hey! I'm Tinsley! Good to meet ya!"

"And you too," I hear Natalie say. "You're the reason Steve and Kelly were here last weekend."

"I am. Well, me and this little muffin in here," she says and rests her hands on her little baby belly.

"I hear it's a boy," Natalie says.

"It is." Tinsley points across the room where Bulldog is pouring tea in glasses. "That-un over there is mine. But don't tell him I said that. He thinks I'm his. He's just a little mixed up. He'll get with the program pretty soon," she says with a laugh.

Natalie snickers. "I bet he will! Diaper duty will do that to a man."

Tinsley lets out a little laugh. "So I hear. We're gonna find out the hard way."

"Who do we have here?"

I turn to find Ghost standing there. "This is Natalie. Natalie, this is Ghost." Izzy steps up beside him and smiles. "And this is his girlfriend, Izzy."

"Izzy! That's an interesting nickname," Natalie says and extends her hand.

I watch as Izzy takes it and just holds it. "I know, right? It's short for Isolde."

It's like everything stops as Natalie's smile disappears. "Isolde Bruce?"

"Yeah. How did you—"

"No." Natalie's hand falls and she starts to back away, her eyes wide with … what is it? Horror? Anger? Fear? "No, I can't be here, and I can't be around you. I can't … I've gotta get out of here. I'm sorry, I just can't … I've gotta go." Before I have a chance to say a word, Natalie spins and runs out the door.

There's total silence, and I realize everybody's staring at me. "What the fuck was that about?" Ghost growls.

"I have no idea."

"Did I do something wrong? I-I-I didn't mean to. I thought I was being … friendly," Izzy stammers.

"You didn't do anything wrong," I answer in a hoarse whisper. What just happened here?

"What the hell is your girlfriend's problem, man? Treatin' my woman like that? That's bullshit, man," Ghost snaps.

"I don't know what just happened, but I'm gonna find out," I say and dart toward the door. I can't believe Natalie would act like that. What's her problem? Izzy is a good person.

When I clear the doorway, she's twenty-five feet away and burning mileage toward her car. "Hey! Hey, hang on a god damn second! Stop!"

When she spins to face me, her face is a mass of tears. "I've gotta go."

"What the fuck is wrong with you? Why'd you treat Izzy like that? She hasn't done a damn thing to you! You owe her an apology!" There's a slow fury boiling in my gut, and I need an answer. "What's your problem?"

That's when I realize she's shaking all over. "I can't be around her, Dennis. Nowhere around her. I can't see her, can't talk to her, and I sure can't shake her hand or eat in the same room with her."

"Why? What did she do wrong?"

"Nothing. Those jury selections I told you I was presiding over?" I nod. "They're for the trials of those guys who allegedly shot her helicopter down."

Well, fuck me. It never occurred to me that she'd be involved in that. "Oh my god, Natalie, I'm sorry. I had no idea."

"I was going to tell you about them tonight after dinner when we had a chance to talk. Those were their arraignments I did on Monday, and Wednesday I approved the attorneys' questions for the prospective jurors, and I saw the witness lists. She's on them. We seated the juries today. The trials start in a couple of weeks. In the meantime, I can't talk to Isolde Bruce, or see her, or even hint that I know her. I can't. It could throw the whole trial process, and I don't want that to happen."

"Neither do we. We want those bastards buried in prison for the rest of their lives."

"So do I, if it's proven that they did it."

"Oh, they did it."

"No. We can't talk about it. I can't tell you anything about it, and you can't tell me anything about what you know. Nothing, Dennis. It has to be that way. Do you understand?" She's actually crying now, and I feel terrible.

"Yeah, yeah. I understand. I get it. Listen, go back to my cottage. You can—"

"I should just go on home."

"No! It'll be fine. We can keep doing what we've been doing. Some of the guys and their girlfriends can come over and eat with us in the cottage. It's okay. And I'll explain to Ghost and Izzy what's going on."

"Oh, god, Dennis, they're going to be so mad at me for

the way I just acted!" she cries out, tears pouring down her face.

"No. I'll make them understand. Now, you go on over to the cottage and I'll bring our dinner like before, okay? It'll be fine. You'll see. Go on, baby. Get yourself calmed down and I'll be there in a minute."

"O-o-o-okay. Thanks." I watch her walk away, her head down, shoulders shaking with sobs, and I feel terrible, but I couldn't have known. It just never occurred to me.

When I step into the kitchen again, all eyes turn toward me. "Want to tell us what the fuck that was about?" Ghost snarls.

"Yes." I turn to the woman standing beside him. "Izzy, Natalie can't be around you. She's the judge hearing the cases on the guys who are accused of shooting you down."

Her jaw drops, and I can see the same reaction from virtually everybody else in the room. "Are you serious?"

"Dead serious. She can't even appear to know you or it could throw the case. So for now, she has to stay away from you. We all want these assholes put away, and she does too. Her being here with you could jeopardize two of the cases, and I'm pretty sure there'll be more to come."

"Oh, god, no. I don't want that. I want those bastards to pay for what they did to Dean and me. Tell her it's okay, please? I don't want her to feel bad. We'll have time to get to know each other after that's over, but for right now, it's gotta be that way, and I completely understand." Being a trooper, I'm sure she does.

"Hell yeah. We don't want to do anything that could jeopardize that. Tell Natalie it's all fine. We understand. And we're looking forward to a time when that's all over and we can all get to know each other," Ghost says. Before I can answer, he gives me a bro hug.

I instantly feel better. "Thanks. Thanks to all of you. We don't like it, but it has to be that way. And if anybody would like to come as a couple or a single and have dinner with us some night in my cottage, we'd welcome that. She wants to get to know all of you, but right now, Izzy and even Ghost are off-limits. Has to be this way."

"Hey, Paddy?" a voice calls out, and I turn toward Hollywood. "Let us fix some plates and Audrey and I will come over there in a minute. You just go on to be with her. It'll be fine."

"Thanks. I really appreciate that."

"Can I come too?" a little voice asks, and I turn to smile at Taylor.

"You're always welcome, buddy."

"Yay! I get to meet the lady! Okay. I'll help Mom and Dad and we'll be there in a minute, Uncle Paddy."

"Okay. See you in a few minutes." When I head toward the door, Patch is standing right beside it. I stop and wait to hear what he's going to say.

"You guys do what you have to. Penny and I will support you however you need us to. This was a big step, including her in dinner, and I'm sorry it turned out this way, but it won't always be like this. In the meantime, we'll all do everything we can to help you."

I nod, and then his arms wrap around me and I realize all of my brothers are with me. "Thanks, man. Thanks for everything. I really appreciate it."

"I love ya, man. It's gonna be okay," he whispers to me.

"Love you too. See you guys tomorrow." He slaps my shoulder as I step out, and I feel like it's going to be all right. We're going to be fine.

And now all I've got to do is convince Natalie of the same.

I STEPPED INTO THE COTTAGE TO FIND NATALIE SOBBING, BUT we got that under control very quickly. In a few minutes Hollywood and Audrey showed up, Taylor in tow, and we had a pleasant dinner.

After she hears all about it, Natalie makes me promise to take her to the park where Audrey's house was, and Hollywood is so gentle and kind to her that I could kiss him. Taylor brought a book, and he begs her to read it to him. Watching her sit there with the little boy fills my chest with warmth. She looks like she's really enjoying spending time with him, and it gives me hope for the future.

Hollywood, Audrey, and I are all still sitting at the table while Natalie and Taylor curl up on the sofa, and Hollywood asks, "When are you going to tell her?"

"When am I … Oh. Yeah. I'm going to tell her later when we're alone."

"Good. She needs to know. She'll be proud of herself for helping you make that decision. Hell, *I'm* proud of you for making that decision," he says and pats my shoulder.

"Me too. I think it's high time you start to reclaim some of the life you had before," Audrey says, a smile on her lips and a twinkle in her eye. They're such good people. I hope they're always as happy as they are right now.

We continue to chat while Natalie reads the book a second time, but in a few minutes, I hear a whispered voice say, "Dennis?" When I glance up, she's smiling at me, and Taylor is leaning against her left arm, sound asleep.

"Looks like somebody decided the party's over," I say with a grin and point toward the sleeping child.

"Yep. Any excitement wears him out," Audrey says with a motherly glow on her face.

"We should probably take him home and let you guys have some alone time. I think you've got a lot to talk about," Hollywood says and rises. "Want us to take the dishes too?"

I just chuckle. "Nah. I'll wash them later and bring them back in the morning. You guys go on. Maybe you'll get a little time to yourselves if you can keep him asleep."

It only takes a minute, and they've collected him and headed out the door. Standing in the doorway to watch until they reach the kitchen, I feel warmth behind me and two arms wrap around my waist from behind. "Did you have a good time?" I ask and press a hand to her joined ones.

"Yeah. They're really nice. I'm glad they came over."

I watch the kitchen door open and close, and then I turn back to her. "And we've got a lot to talk about," I say as I step back inside and close the door behind me.

"Yeah. We do." Something about the way she says it tells me there's something else I don't know. I grab her hand on the way past and pull her toward the sofa with me. When we reach it, I plop down, then pull her down beside me. "Who goes first?"

"How much do you have to tell me?"

She rolls her eyes. "A lot."

"Okay. I'll go first." I sit up a little straighter. "I called Lisa today. She's coming and bringing the boys next weekend."

Her eyes go wide and her mouth gapes, then she grins. "Oh, Dennis! That's great! I'm so happy that you decided to do that!"

"Yeah. I thought about it this week after you and I had talked about it a few times, and I figured I should try to get to know them. They were babies when I left. They're young men now. Our relationship will be different, but it'll still be a relationship. I assured her I'm not trying to take her husband's place. I just want to get to know them so they know if they ever need me, I'm here for them."

"That's perfect! I'm so happy for you! I really think this is the right move."

"You know, I feel better now that I've done it. I do."

"Good."

"Now, what do you need to tell me?" She's not looking at me and she's not speaking, and I'm starting to get very, very nervous. "Look, I already know you're handling the cases against the guys who shot down Izzy's bird."

Her eyes rotate upward until they meet my gaze. "We're just getting started. There are two of them right now, but after that, there are more. But there's a … complication." I just wait. I'm not going to make this easy. She needs to tell me, and I'm not going to beg. There's a long, long silence before she finally says, "The first day, at the arraignment, there were a bunch of guys in the back of the courtroom, and two of them were really obvious. They looked completely out of place, and I was suspicious. My bailiffs were too, so they backed me when I asked the sheriff's office to run facial recognition on them, and it turns out they're part of the cartel the first two on my docket worked for."

"What were they doing there?"

"We didn't know. After we found out who they are, Sheriff Copeland recommended that I call my superior and ask for some security."

"Which you did."

"Um, I haven't yet."

"Natalie! You've got to—"

"I didn't finish."

"What else is there to say?" I bellow.

"That they were waiting by my car this evening when I left the building."

"They *WHAT*? You've got to be kidding me! What happened?"

"Quentin Asher, the commonwealth attorney, saw them going out after I had and he followed them. Before he came out the door, he hit the panic button, and Darrell and Cliff, my bailiffs, came out the door just a few seconds later. They ordered the guys off the property."

"Are you shitting me? Natalie, do you—"

"I know, I know. I've got to call Judge Martelle. He's our chief judge for the district. Sheriff Lasher said she'd go along with Sheriff Copeland and recommend that I get some security."

"Who would do that?"

"I'm federal, so they'd assign an FBI agent to me."

"Won't hurt my feelings," I blurt out.

"I don't want somebody babysitting me, but …" And she stops.

"But what?"

There's a look in her eyes that I haven't seen before when she says, "I'm afraid."

"No. I don't want you living your life in fear. Get somebody else to hear the cases."

"I can't do that! These will be my first big cases in this district, and I can't pass them off to somebody else because I'm scared. I just can't."

"Natalie—"

"No! I can't!" A fresh bout of crying begins, and her hands have started to shake again.

Instead of scolding her or demanding anything of her, I just pull her to me and hold her, hoping to help at least a little. Sure enough, she stops shaking, but she's still crying softly, so I stroke her hair and squeeze her a little bit tighter. "Babe, we'll get through it, whatever it takes. But you've *got* to call that judge, whatever his name is, and get somebody to be your bodyguard."

"I know. I will. I hate to, but I will. It makes me look so weak, and the male judges would never do it, but—"

"Oh, yes they would. They have wives and families, and they'd do it in a heartbeat if it meant they and their families would stay safe. They'd be scared too. These guys aren't a joke. They mean business, bad business."

A couple of little sniffles sneak out before she says, "I feel safe here with you."

"You have no idea how happy that makes me. I mean, I'm not happy for the reason, but I'm happy that you trust me."

"I do."

"Good. Did you bring your stuff to stay the night?"

"Actually, I brought enough stuff to stay the weekend, but now that Izzy's here and we know—"

"You let me handle that. We'll work it out. But right now, I think you need some sleep. You've had a really stressful day."

One eyebrow pops upward. "I thought maybe we were going to …" And she winks.

"Maybe in the morning, but not tonight. Tonight you just need to sleep. Tomorrow isn't a workday, so it's not like we won't have time."

"Okay. I've just gotta go out and get my stuff from the car. Won't take—"

I grab her hand as she stands. "Oh, no. You're not going out there. I'll go get it all."

"Why?"

"Because they could be out there."

That grimace tells me she's pissed. "They didn't follow me."

"How do you know?"

"Because Darrell followed me to the county line, and there was no one following me when he backed off, so no one followed me. I'm sure of it."

"Doesn't matter. Just in case." I stand and head that direction. "What's in the car? What do you need?"

A long, irritated sigh slips from her lips. "My floral print bag and my briefcase. I need my laptop. Plus there's a bag on the floorboard that has shoes in it."

"Be right back." When I step out and close the door behind me, I'm struck by how dark it really is out here, and it occurs to me that maybe I should talk to Patch about putting in some security lights.

"You guys okay over there?" a voice asks, and I turn to see Priest on his porch.

"Yeah, we're good. Night."

"Night, brother," he calls back and disappears inside.

That's when I stop and look around. I mean, I take a really, really good inventory of my surroundings. It takes me two seconds to realize we're too vulnerable here, but I'm not sure what we could do about it. I guess hypervigilance is our best bet.

I come back inside to find Natalie washing the dinner dishes, so I set about helping her. Thirty minutes later, we're snuggled up in my big bed, her cheek resting on my chest and my arms around her. She may be in danger, but in this moment, we're both safe and together. That's when I decide I need to be honest with myself.

Regardless how she feels about me, I'm falling in love with this woman. Sure, we've got a lot to talk about, a lot to learn about each other, a lot of things we need to share, but her being a federal judge means that whatever she tells me about herself, I'm pretty damn sure she's telling the truth. And me being an ex-con, I'm guessing she figures I'm honest because I have nothing else to lose. She'd be right about that.

And like always, my thoughts go back to Michael. Things we did together when we were growing up, places we went, accomplishments, fun times, they all cycle like they always do, and they always end with that picture in my head of what I found when I got to the ground that day. It's a horror that won't go away. No one can understand how I'd feel if I suddenly could find those forms and prove that we'd done those safety checks. Every night as I drift off to sleep, he comes to me and tells me he's forgiven me, that it's okay. But it doesn't work. Instead, I'm left with the same feeling I always have.

That it was all my fault.

CHAPTER 6

Natalie

My nightmares were horrible. The two men from the back of the courtroom were chasing me, and no one could get to me, not Darrell and Cliff, not Dennis, nobody. I ran and ran and woke up in a cold sweat. When my eyes open, I realize it's Saturday morning and Dennis is right beside me, sound asleep. A glance at my phone tells me it's not even six thirty, so I snuggle up to him again and try to go back to sleep. Even in his unconscious state, his arms envelop me, and I feel safe and lo … cared for.

I was about to think that I feel loved, and I know it's too soon to use that term, but I do. This man has gone out of his way to do anything and everything he can think of to make me feel comfortable, accepted, and safe. Lying here, the warmth of his body against mine soothing me, I'm thankful for a quiet moment like this while he's asleep so I can think and feel.

Sleep is slipping up on me again when I feel his lips

against my neck, and I roll to face him. "Hey. Good morning," he whispers and drops a tiny kiss on my lips.

"Good morning to you."

"Sleep well?"

"Yeah," I lie. I did—kinda. It would've been a helluva lot more restful if not for the nightmares.

"Good. What do you want today to look like?"

Nobody's ever asked me that before, so I have to think for a minute. Then I say, "I dunno. Just hanging out and relaxing, I guess. What do *you* want today to look like?"

He's lying back, arm resting on his pillow with his elbow bent and his hand behind his head, the expression on his face as serious as I've ever seen. "I want to get the day started right. Go do whatever you need to in the bathroom and get back here. Without the pajamas."

I grin. "So you're ready to rumble, huh?"

"No. We're gonna rumble. It's not up to you. It's up to me, so get on it. I'm hardening up just thinking about it and I really don't want to wait."

"Uh, okay." I'm not sure what I was expecting, but he's being just a little harsh. I've managed to empty my bladder and started brushing my teeth when I realize something: *This is what you wanted, Natalie—a man who'll take charge.* Something in that thought excites me beyond my wildest imagination. That's what he's doing, trying to give me what I asked for, and I'm going to make him happy that he's doing so.

Careful to open the bathroom door slowly, I take my time crossing the room and crawling back under the covers, but before I can get all the way in, he hops up out of bed and heads for the bathroom. Holy shit, his flag is at full mast. I can barely wait until he gets back!

And when he does, he surprises me. Instead of sliding up

against me, kissing me, stroking my hair, or any of that stuff, he glares at me. "You need to grab hold of the headboard rungs and hang on."

That's a little alarming. "What exactly are you planning to do?"

"Why are you questioning me? I'm going to drive you crazy. And you're gonna like it. Now do as I said." I slip my fingers between the rungs and tighten them around the wood.

There's an evil gleam in his eyes as he spreads my legs and kneels between them, and it makes my breath vacate my lungs. He's not planning to make love with me or have sex with me. He's planning to use me, and I'm thinking I'm going to love the hell outta this. Without another word, he drops to all fours, stretches out on the mattress, and plants his face squarely into my cunt. His breath is warm on my skin, and I can feel his tongue snaking down from the cleft at the top, down the hood of my clit, and then upward under—

Holy shit. A white-hot bolt of sexual current shoots up through my body, hardens my nipples, and whips the breath right out of my lungs. The second lap of his tongue is as powerful as the first, and by the third, I'm right on the edge.

I wasn't kidding when I said I'm sensitive.

I can feel myself slipping toward the edge when he stops. "Whaaaa—"

"Shhhh. We're doing this my way." I can't really see what he's doing, but I feel two fingers slip into my pussy and then curl. He strokes my G-spot like a maniac, and I feel totally out of control. "Don't you dare come," he whispers through clenched teeth.

"Oh, shit. Oh, Dennis. I'm not sure—"

"I told you no," he repeats and abruptly withdraws his fingers. In a split second, I feel his breath on my flesh again, and then that tongue strokes right up my clit.

"Oh! Oh, damn. I think … I can't take a lot of that. I mean …" Three more strokes, and I can feel my body readying.

And he stops again.

Fuck me. I know what this game is now, and I'm miserable. The fingers return, and I can't help but writhe a little. "You don't get to come, sweet pea. Not until I say it's okay." My entire body feels like it's on fire, and it's hard to breathe. I reach down to touch his hair, and he growls, "I told you to hang onto the headboard. Don't turn loose."

"O-o-o-okay," I answer on a gasp, barely able to speak. He starts the whole process over, and everything inside me is churning, my belly heavy and my hips thrusting ever so slightly. "Oh, god, babe, please … Dennis, please? Please?"

His fingers are pumping into me like crazy, and I hear him chuckle. "Okay, sweet pea, this time I'm going to let you come, but I want you to let go. However loud you need to be, however crazy you need to be, it's okay. Just let go. You hear me?"

I wheeze more than speak. "Uh-huh, yeah … I do … Okay."

"Okay. Hang on." In my mind, I imagine his fingers making a *POP!* sound as he pulls them out, and his warm breath is on my skin again. His tongue is like an electric probe as he drags it up my tiny little swollen bud, and I'm trying so hard to stave it off, but I can't. I feel it building, goosebumps rising on my skin, that chill sweeping through me, and then …

It hits like a cannonball. My back bows, every muscle in my body stiffens, and I can't think or speak. I can't even breathe. It rips through me, tearing down every wall and throwing open every window and door, and some kind of weird sound comes from my throat, but I'm powerless to stop it. It's this guttural, primal … almost a roar. That's what it is, like a roar. I'm trying to shut up, but I can't, and it goes on forever and ever, and then, just when I think I'll die from it, he stops.

There's this sensation like a vacuum, like I'm being sucked back into my own body, and the buzzing in my ears is starting to subside. I hear his voice, but it sounds far away: "Natalie? Babe, you okay? Talk to me, Natalie. Hey, come on. Say something."

"Uhhhhh … I'm not dead." That's what comes out of my mouth. I feel like an idiot, but I really can't talk.

I hear him chuckle. "No, you're not dead. Not at all. But we're not finished yet."

What the hell? "What? Are we doing that again?"

That makes him outright laugh. "No. I need you so bad, babe, so you need to buckle up and hang on."

It sounds ridiculous, and I know it's not the first time we've been together, but it might as well have been. He rocks into me, and I feel every cell in my body come to life. Something about this man speaks to my very soul, the raw masculinity, the gracefulness, the passion. He's the perfect blend of everything I could possibly want in a man. Less than a minute after he's buried himself in me, I hear him whisper into my neck, "Baby, you can take your hands down. I need to feel them on me."

My arms are long enough that my fingers dip upward as my hands slide down his back and up the slope of his ass. When I drag them upward, I can feel the muscles bunching under his skin as he pumps into me. "Jesus, Dennis, you feel so good," I groan.

"You too, babe. You're amazing. Tell me what you need to get there."

Well, that's something no man has ever said to me. "Um, probably more upward movement maybe?"

"Uh-huh. Gotcha." Even though I felt like I probably didn't do a good job of telling him what I mean, he understands. In a few seconds, he's settling on his knees, lifting my hips, and powering into me, the head of his cock raking that little ridged spot inside me.

Oh holy shit. I can reach him just well enough to trail my fingers down his pecs, through the hair on his chest, and on down. When I look up into his face, his gaze is on me. Just me. He's watching me intently, my movements, my expressions, concentrating on me, thinking only of me. My hands grip his forearms as he cups my ass, still grinding in and out of me, and I'm overwhelmed with all of the sensations. Our bodies together are a powerful thing, more powerful than anything I've ever experienced. Something is growing inside me, a hunger, and I whisper, "Oh, god, I need it so bad."

That's the moment when he bends down and kisses me, still stroking into me, and I can feel his hand between us. I'm not sure what's happening until it does.

The minute his finger touches my clit, everything below my waist contracts and in a split second, it explodes. My hips are pumping toward him, begging him for more, and he hunches into me, going deeper and faster until I dig my fingernails into his shoulder blades to hang on. As soon as I throw my head back, his lips are on my neck, kissing up and down, around the side, up to my ear, whispering into it, "Oh, god, Natalie, you're perfect, babe. Just perfect. Thatta girl. Ride it. Yeah, babe, yeah, just like that. Damn, baby. Mmmm."

His weight is comfortable when he drops onto me, and I wrap my arms around his ribcage. I don't want to leave this room, to leave him, to have his arms leave me. I want to pull him inside me, absorb him, and never be without him. We only lie there for a few seconds before he rolls us to our sides, takes my face in his hands, and kisses me. It's a kiss I've lived for, the one I've wanted since the first time that kid kissed me at summer camp in seventh grade, the kiss I wanted from my high school boyfriend and never really got. It's the kiss that sustains my soul. My hands are in his hair, my fingers winding through it, and my heart begging him to never stop kissing me.

When he does finally come up for air, he smiles into my face. But what he says next makes me believe I've found The One. "I never want to be without you, Natalie. I'm falling in love with you, and I don't know if we have forever, but I'll take whatever I can get, for however long you'll give me."

"I'll give you however long I can until you get sick of me," I answer with a grin.

"Not happenin'. I mean, I know that socially and educationally, career-wise, we're not equals. I get that. I just hope that I won't be too much of an embarrassment to you when—"

I press a finger to his lips—hard—to stop him. "You listen to me. I will never, *never*, be embarrassed to be seen with you, to go anywhere with you, to be with you." *Say it, Natalie!* a little voice yells in my brain. "I love you. I know we're just getting started, but I want this to work."

"Then it will. I'll see to it. We're going to get to spend a lot more time together starting this coming week while I'm in school, so get ready. *You'll* get sick of *me* long before I can get sick of you."

With the tiniest of shoves, I roll him to his back, then curl into his side. "I'll never get sick of you. Never. But if we don't get something to eat pretty soon, I'll get sick from hunger."

"I hear ya. But … Can we just lie here for a little while together? That's what I really want most."

I stretch upward and plant a little kiss on his cheek before I cuddle back up against him. "Nothing would make me happier."

Paddy

It's so quiet. I can hear the clock ticking on the far wall, a bird somewhere outside, and the soft, even breathing of the woman lying next to me. I cannot believe how happy that makes me.

This morning was perfect. The sex was incredible. If two people were ever made to be together physically, I think it's the two of us. She responded exactly the way I'd hoped, and I was able to be just demanding enough to give her the vibe she wants. That was my goal, and I think I knocked it out of the park. I'd been a little concerned about that, especially since we don't know each other that well yet, and I didn't want to come off as an asshole or a wimp. I think I actually managed to get it pretty much exactly right.

She's sound asleep—she's bound to be exhausted because I wore her ass out—so I slip on my jeans and a tee, slide my feet into the moccasins I keep by the door, and head to the kitchen. It's still early enough that there should be some kind of food around, and I'm not disappointed. I fill two plates with biscuits, gravy, sausage, bacon, and scrambled eggs, and head back to the cottage. As soon as the door closes behind me, I can hear water running in the shower, so I put the plates on the table, shuffle into the bedroom, and stick my head in the bathroom door. "Baby, I've got breakfast out here, so don't take up residence in there."

"I'll be done in just a minute. Don't wait for me."

"Yep. Waiting. Take your time. Just wanted you to know it's out here." That gives me time to get the coffee maker started up, and by the time I hear her come out of the bathroom, there's a cup of fresh, hot brew ready for her and I'm making my own.

She's wearing her robe and her hair is wrapped in a towel when she steps into the kitchen. "Oh, wow! This looks great! Did Audrey cook it?"

"Not this morning. Penny and Izzy actually cooked this. They try to keep Audrey out of the kitchen on the weekends if they can. And Tinsley doesn't help them because this early in the morning, the smell of food makes her sick."

"I can understand that."

What takes place in the next thirty minutes is probably the most normal breakfast I've had in over ten years, just me and a woman I'm crazy about, sitting at a table together, eating a home-cooked meal and chatting. We talk about everything. Upcoming presidential primaries—looks like we're very well-aligned in the political sense. A case she heard over a violation of a trans student's rights at school—yep, aligned there too. I ask if she's heard about a lawsuit being brought in Louisville over religious liberties—and once again, our thinking is the same. It's pretty amazing, really, that we were raised so differently and in totally different areas, but our thinking is so similar. Encouraging, really, as far as the relationship goes.

"So do you have things you need to do today?" she asks.

"Actually, I'm supposed to be helping Reboot with his boat, but I don't have to do that if—"

"No, he's your friend, and you committed to helping him.

And I'm okay with that. I was just thinking how if I can't be around Izzy, and you're going to be at my place several times a week over the next few months, I should probably go home, clean some stuff up, maybe do some grocery shopping."

I nod. "Yeah. That would work. Then back here for dinner tonight?"

She nods back. "That was my thinking."

"Okay, so I'll help Reboot and you can—"

The almost-deafening tone sounds before the speaker kicks in. "App STAR base, this is central dispatch. Respond, over."

The reply is fast—Patch. "Roger, central dispatch. This is App STAR base. Over."

"Roger, App STAR base. Report of two missing hunters north of east branch of Wolfpen Creek. KCSO and Knott County Fire en route. Staging area at the old Pearson home. Requesting assistance. Over."

"Roger that, dispatch. ETA of approximately twenty minutes. Over."

"Roger, App STAR base. Out."

I'd been listening intently and hadn't turned to look at Natalie. When I do, her eyes are wide. "So you have to go?"

"Yep. Gotta go." I hop up, strip off, drag on a pair of underwear and socks, then my brush pants and a tee, and finally grab my coat and my go-bag. She sits here and watches the whole process before I finally turn to her. "My boots are by the door. I have no idea when I'll be back, but I'll call you, okay?"

"Okay. Be careful, please?"

"I will. Everybody's numbers are on the fridge. Just call Penny and she'll come get the dishes and—"

"I'll wash them and ask her to come get them before I leave. Don't worry. It'll be fine. But please be careful."

She's followed me to the door, talking the whole time while I'm pulling on my boots, and it's my turn. "That's good. And I meant what I said, Natalie. I'm in love with you. I'll be careful. I have more to be careful for now than I did two weeks ago. I'll get back as fast as I can."

"I love you too. Tell all the guys hi for me."

"I will." I head out the door toward the Jeeps, noticing that most everybody is already there, then turn and walk backward. "Won't be long before you can tell them yourself." Then I turn and run.

These MPs aren't gonna find themselves. If they could've, they already would've. Now that's our job.

I just hope it doesn't take all day.

Natalie

Wow. Abrupt. I wasn't expecting that. Of course, neither was he, but it's still jarring to be carrying on a conversation, eating a meal, and then two minutes later, he's gone. The nature of the beast, I suppose.

I've gotten the dishes washed and I'm drying them when there's a knock on the door. I open it to a smiling brunette. "Hey! Heard you've got some dishes for me."

"I was going to call you and—"

"Dennis called me from the Jeep."

That makes me laugh. "Should've known! They're washed. I'm just drying them."

"Let me grab a towel and I'll help you."

What ensues is a fun, lively conversation, and I can say that I really enjoy Penny's company. She's funny and sweet, and she knows all the dirt on the guys. "And then Bulldog says, 'What the fuck are you doing with your hand in that jar?' And Reboot says, 'I'd been chasing that pickle with a fork for ten minutes and I thought, fuck that, I'll just reach in and get it. And now I can't get my hand out.'"

I'm screaming with laughter. "It was really stuck?"

"Yeah. Really stuck. Then Priest says, 'Make your hand into like a duck bill. You know, like you're gonna shove it up into …'"

"Oh my god! He didn't!"

"He just stopped because everybody was staring at him, and he finished with, '… Um, through a chain link fence.' And then everybody was laughing so hard."

"How'd you get his hand out?"

"Audrey poured vegetable oil all over it. Thought for a minute there we were going to have to break the jar, which would've been pretty scary. When Patch said that, Reboot said, 'Well, that's a little dangerous, don't you think?' And Ghost said, 'You've got two nurses standing here. We can fix slices and dices.' He started bitching and Bear said, 'Beats the hell outta trying to salute somebody and knocking yourself in the head with a pickle jar, dumb motherfucker.'"

"Oh my god! Wish I'd been there!"

"Yeah, it was pretty damn funny. I told Mavis about it and she teases him all the time about it. Says she's going to start putting pickles in weird places and daring him to stick his hand in to get them out. I believe it. She's a little hard to get to know, but once you get Mavis to open up, she's a hoot."

That makes me sigh out loud. "Guess I'll have to wait to find out."

"No. You won't. I hear Audrey and Hollywood came over and had dinner with you guys. Invite Reboot and Mavis! Invite Bulldog and Tinsley! Invite the single guys too. They all want to get to know you, but they understand what's happening." She drops her towel on the counter. "Well, that's all done. I'll load these up in the tub and carry them back," she says as she starts stacking the clean dishes and carrying them to a big plastic tote she brought in. "Hanging around today?"

"Before he left, I told him since he was helping Reboot with the boat, I was going home to do some things around there and I'd be back this evening. Did you hear? His kids are coming next weekend! Isn't that great?"

"It is. I'm glad. Patch still fights every day to have some kind of relationship with Fiona, and she makes it so hard." She's finished putting the dishes in the tote, and she turns and smiles. "I'll explain that some other time. I'm going to get these back to the kitchen and I guess I'll see you later. I promised Tinsley I'd help her launder and put away all the baby things this morning, so I need to get going. But you have a good day, sweetie, and know that Patch and I are glad you're here."

"Thanks. That means a lot. See you later."

"You bet." I hold the door for her to go out, then close it behind her and start picking up my things. Fifteen minutes later, I'm ready to go.

I'm not exactly sure where the team had to go to start the search, but I drive around a little and don't see trucks or anything anywhere, so I just head on to Hazard. It's a pretty day, with the sun bright and warm, and I figure if they've got to search for somebody, this is the right kind of day to do it. My car rolls on past Food Kingdom, our grocery store, and I start to think about what I'm going to need for next week. I'll make that list at home and come back later.

After I check the mailbox—hasn't come yet—I head on inside. As soon as I get the washer started, I pull the already-dry towels out of the dryer, fold them, and put them away. There's a corked bottle of wine on the counter, so I yank out the cork, pour myself half a glass, and take a few sips before I unload the dishwasher and reload it. Once it's humming along, I set about changing the sheets on the bed. With that done, they're ready to wash, so I carry them into the laundry room. I've barely gotten in there when I hear a knock at the door, so I head that direction.

And there's no one there, at least not through the peep hole. I start to turn away, but then I think, what if somebody sent me something? So I open the door a crack and, sure enough, there's a package on the porch. A quick glance tells me there's nobody around, so I step out and reach down to pick it up.

And my heart stops. The only thing written on the package …

Judge Anderson

No address, no return address, no postage, nothing. It's just a wrapped box, nothing but brown paper, with that written on the top.

I've never slammed a door that hard and fast in my life. Never. I whip my phone out and dial nine-one-one. A voice answers, "Perry County Emergency Nine-One-One. Can I assist you?"

"Yes. This is Judge Natalie Anderson, Eastern District of Kentucky. There's a suspicious package on my front porch. Twelve oh three Jessamine Drive. Hazard. Please send somebody. Please?"

"Yes, ma'am. Hold just one second." I can hear her in the background: "Perry County Sheriff's Office, this is Perry County central dispatch. Respond, over."

Another voice comes over the radio. "Roger, central dispatch. PCSO unit two, over."

"Unit two, I have a Judge Natalie Anderson on the phone. Says there's a suspicious package on her front porch, requesting that somebody come look at it. Over."

Immediately, a voice pipes up. "Central dispatch, this is PCSO unit eight. I'm en route to Judge Anderson's home. ETA two minutes. Tell her not to touch that package. Over."

"Roger that, unit eight. Over." There's the sound of movement and her voice is back. "Ma'am, did you hear that?"

"Yes. I did. Thank you so much. I'll wait for them."

"Yes, ma'am. Stay safe. Bye."

That two minutes feels like two years. Finally, a Perry County Sheriff's Office cruiser pulls up and stops in front of my house. I open the door, but he shakes his head. "Don't come out the door. I'll go around to your back door."

"Okay. Thanks." By the time I run to the back door, he's already rounding the corner of the house. "Thank you for getting here so fast."

"I was just two blocks away when I heard the call. So did you come home and find it?"

"No, sir. I've been here for maybe thirty minutes or so? Somebody knocked on the door, and that's how I found it. But I didn't see anybody anywhere."

"And did you touch it?"

"No, sir. I was too scared."

"Good. You should be."

That's a weird thing for him to say. "What makes you—"

He interrupts me. "Didn't you find it strange that I got here so quickly?"

Now I'm just scared. "I didn't think about it, but—"

My fear must be written all over my face because he stops me cold. "It's okay. Don't panic. We got a call from the Laurel County Sheriff's Office telling us about what's going on with you and asking us to keep an eye on you. I'm going to stay here with you, but I'm calling in reinforcements."

An hour later, there are five cruisers here, as well as a bomb squad from Knott County. Doesn't matter. I have no idea what's going on because I'm sitting in the kitchen at the table, shaking. There's at least one officer with me at all times, and to say I'm scared doesn't even scratch the surface. Finally, another comes in and says, "They x-rayed the package."

"And?" I ask, hoping for something good.

"It looks like there's nothing in it but an old-fashioned alarm clock, one of those with the bells on top."

That's weird. "Yeah?"

"They're going to use a robot to put a scope inside it and see if there's anything else in there."

"Okay." There's nothing I can do even if I wanted to, and I don't want to. All I really want right now is to see Dennis and run straight into his arms. I fold my arms on the tabletop and bury my face in them.

I don't know how much time passes before someone says, "Judge Anderson?"

My head pops up. "Yes?"

"There's nothing in the box except the alarm clock and a piece of paper. We're opening the box now," a young man tells me. Based on his clothes, I'm guessing he's a detective.

"Thank you." A bigger man, older and better dressed, steps into the kitchen. "Did you open it?"

He nods. "Yep. This is what we found." In his hand is a small plastic bag, and he hands it to me. It's a piece of paper, and on it is printed, in the same hand as my name on the outside of the package …

Tick tock. The clock is running.

That's it. Not another word. Which is fine, because I get

the message loud and clear. I know I've got to make that call to Judge Martelle, and I'm thinking about it when I hear a voice above the rest, the only voice I've been wishing I could hear.

"What the hell is going on? Where is she? No, don't touch me! I'm going in there!"

My knight in shining armor has arrived.

PADDY

IDIOTS. THAT'S WHAT THESE TWO GUYS ARE. THEY'RE hunters, but I use that term loosely. Nobody seems to be able to tell us what they were hunting, so whatever it was, I'm sure it was something that's definitely out of season or that they didn't have a tag for. The guys have been stomping around on the ground for hours and we've been in the air for three, and nobody's seen a trace of them.

Until I hear Bulldog yell, "What's that? Down there. Out your window, Ghost." The rest of us turn to look and, sure enough, just a short distance away, in a partial clearing, there's a guy waving at us like he's on an aircraft carrier and we're homed in on the deck.

Patch shakes his head in that exasperated way that anybody within fifty yards could read. "That's gotta be them. Radio it in, Ghost." In under a minute, we can see the guys on the ground making their way into the clearing, and I wonder what they're going to find.

"App STAR air, this is App STAR ground. Got a tree on top of this guy. He's not hurt, but his leg's pinned. You got Buster up there with you? Over," I hear Priest radio.

"Roger that, App STAR ground. Sending it down. Over." Patch's head swivels toward me. "Send Buster down to them." That's our nickname for the old chainsaw Bear found at a yard sale and I got back in working order. I slide the door open, ready the hoist, belt the chainsaw on, and send it down into the clearing.

"Do I need to send Bulldog down too?" I ask.

"Go ahead," our chief says, and in a couple of minutes, Bulldog's on his way down to the site.

"Hey, App STAR ground, aren't you guys out past a fence line? Over," Patch asks.

"Oh, you mean the one with the 'no trespassing' signs all over it? Roger that, air. Over," Hollywood replies.

Patch keys up his mic again. "Get the coordinates for where you are right now. We're gonna need 'em. Over." I know what that's about. We'll report to the sheriff's office where they were, and that'll get them for trespassing on top of whatever hunting laws they've violated. And it'll keep our guys from being charged with trespassing for just being there.

I've got the hoist secured and the door closed when I hear a transmission that takes me by surprise. "App STAR air, this is Sheriff Stafford. When you get to the ground, I need to talk to Paddy. Over."

"Roger that, sheriff. Over," Patch radios back. I know who he's talking to when he says, "What did you do?"

"I didn't do anything! I have no idea what he wants, but you can bet I'll be finding out as soon as my feet hit terra firma."

"Okay. I believe you. Let me know what's going on."

"Don't worry. Everybody will know." I get called out over the radio where the whole fucking emergency services countywide can hear and you can bet folks will know why, because I'll sure tell them.

By the time we set down, I'm a mess, wondering what the hell is going on. I just dial central dispatch and ask them to put me through to Sheriff Stafford. He answers with, "Paddy, before you hyperventilate, just give me a chance to finish."

That's a weird greeting that I somehow find oddly calming. "Uh, okay."

"You're seeing Judge Anderson over in Perry County, right?"

Fuck calm. That's out the window as my heartbeat triples. "Yeah."

"You need to get to her place. When you get there, tell them who you are and that I sent you. She specifically asked for you." He tells me her address, and I couldn't forget it if I tried.

"What's going on?"

"It's better that you find out when you get there, but be safe. She is. There's enough police presence there that the whole Iranian army couldn't get to her even if they wanted to."

"Thanks, sheriff. I'll be careful, I promise."

"Thatta boy. Thanks."

My feet are already moving. Patch calls after me, "What's going on?"

I can't stop running. "Something with Natalie."

"Then I'm coming with you!" he yells from behind me, and I know I have to wait for him. He won't have it any other way.

Three minutes later, we're in his truck and barreling down the highway—at a safe speed, of course. He's driving. That's most likely the reason why he wanted to go with me, to keep me from wrapping myself around a tree somewhere. "Tell me where I'm going," he says when we get into Perry County.

Five minutes later, we come to a screeching halt at a

police line a block from her house and I'm running as soon as my feet hit the pavement. When I make it to the house, five cops block my path, and one reaches for me. "Sorry, sir, but you can't go in there," one of them says.

"What the hell is going on? Where is she? No, don't touch me! I'm going in there!"

"Relax, guys. I know him. Come on," a voice says, and I turn to find Preston Ramage, our fire chief's son who's a city police officer in Hazard. "She's been waiting for you," Preston says as he leads the way. We bound up the front steps, dart through the front door, and Preston calls out, "He's here!"

No bigger than she is, she hits me with such force that I almost topple over, and she throws her arms around me and burrows into me. "Oh, god, I was so scared!"

I just grab her and hang on while she shakes in my arms. "Babe, what happened?"

"Strange package on her porch. Wasn't a bomb, but we took all the necessary precautions," Justin Lark tells me. He's one of Preston's coworkers and somebody I've come to trust and respect.

"Thank you. What was it?"

"Old-fashioned alarm clock with the two bells on top and a note."

"And the note says?" I ask.

"It says, 'Tick tock, the clock is running.'"

I push Natalie back enough to look in her face. "You know what this is about, right?" She gives me a sad little nod. "Did you make the call?" That gets me a little head shake, and she buries her face in my chest.

"What call?" Preston asks.

"She's supposed to call Judge Martelle and ask for some security, but she hasn't yet."

"Oh, she won't have to. I'll do it for her right now. Justin, can you get me his number?"

Justin nods to Preston. "I'll do you one better. I'll call him myself."

"She'll have her security detail by tonight or we'll provide one for her," Preston assures me.

So why don't I feel one bit better?

CHAPTER 7

Paddy

It took me forty-five minutes to convince them that she'd be better off out at the farm with me and the guys. I don't know if that's true or not, but I'd like to believe it is.

And I guess it really doesn't matter. As soon as we get to my cottage, I give her two shots of bourbon, make her change into one of my tee shirts, and put her to bed. I figure if she can nap for a couple of hours, maybe she'll wake up and feel better about everything. She's been asleep for about twenty minutes when I hear an unfamiliar car and glance out to see a black Dodge Charger sling gravel as it comes to a halt outside the kitchen. I don't even have to look. I know who that is.

Shoes in hand, I let myself out the door quietly and slide on my slippers on the porch. I'm on my way across the lawn when I look up to see Hollywood coming out of the kitchen, and he greets the person standing beside the car. When I get a little closer, I finally get a look at them, and I get a big surprise.

As soon as I round the rear end of the car, I'm face-to-face with one of the tallest women I've ever seen in person. She's probably every bit of five feet and eleven inches tall, and she looks like she spends four hours a day in the gym. Every inch of her is sculpted under her tight clothes, and her dark, auburn-streaked hair is pulled up in a bun so tight that her eyes are pulled into slanted slits. "I take it you're Dennis O'Brien?"

"I am," I answer.

She sticks out a hand and when I take it, I'm shocked at its strength, even though I probably shouldn't be, based on her body build. "I'm FBI Agent Sela Baldwin. I'm the private detail for Judge Anderson. Could I see her, please?"

"I'm sorry. She's asleep right now, but you're welcome to wait in the kitchen until—"

"I don't think you understand how this works, sir. I need to go to wherever she is *now*. I can't wait. If she's asleep, I'll gladly sit in the next room, but wherever she is, that's where I'm going to be. So take me to her or I'll find her myself," she says. It's not hateful or disrespectful. She's very matter of fact about it, and very clear that she won't take no for an answer. Honestly, I like it. I like her. The confidence she exudes is comforting.

"Sure. Right this way. Thanks, Hollywood," I toss back to my friend.

"No problem. Thanks for coming, Agent Baldwin," Hollywood adds.

"You're welcome. Have a good afternoon," she calls back from right beside me. I mean, she's not a foot from me. I have a feeling that could become very annoying if I were the person she was following around, but since it'll be Natalie and I'm terrified for her safety, that's fine with me. "So you and Judge Anderson are seeing each other?"

"Yes, ma'am."

"You don't have to call me ma'am. That's not necessary."

"It is. It's a term of respect, and I respect that you're willing to put your life on the line for Natalie."

"And how long have the two of you been seeing each other?"

"A week or so, but it's obvious it's going to be a long-term thing. We really hit it off. I mean, for real. Like, I never believed in love at first sight before, but I think this is about as close as you can get, and I'm crazy about her. And she says she's crazy about me."

There's no apology in her voice when she says, "Then I hope you won't mind if I look into your background."

That makes me snort. "Lady, go right ahead. My life is a matter of public record."

"That's an odd thing to say," she says, and I realize she has no idea who I am or why I'm here.

"Yeah? I'm an ex-con. Does it make sense now?" I open the cottage door and sweep my hand inward, not checking to see what expression she's wearing because, frankly, I don't care. "Please. Make yourself at home. But don't wake her." As soon as the door closes behind her, I ask in barely over a whisper, "Would you like some coffee?"

"That would be nice. Thanks."

I just have a little coffeemaker that uses pods, so I fix her a cup first and then one for me. While it's brewing, I stand and stare at it instead of sitting down to face her. I know I'll eventually have to explain myself, but I don't want to do that right now. All I really care about at this moment is Natalie. When I do finally sit down, I take a sip of coffee, then lift my head to look at her. "Any questions?"

"Questions that I can answer myself with a little bit of

research don't hold any interest for me. What interests me is how the two of you got together."

"Through mutual friends."

"I see. And what would make an ex-felon bladesmith and a federal judge think they're compatible?"

"Well, first off, I'm not a bladesmith. I actually work with leather. I make the sheaths and scabbards for the blades the other guys make, and I work with Priest to help him with tack repair. In case you're wondering, tack is—"

"I know what tack is. I grew up with horses." Well then, *touché*, I reckon. "Back to the original question." She's a nosy bitch, I'll give her that.

"Let's just say we have some of the same … desires … and leave it at that." I take another sip of my coffee, congratulating myself on answering that question about as delicately as anybody could manage.

"I see." It's her turn to take another sip, and then she fiddles with the handle of her coffee mug as she sits there, staring at the tabletop. "Sorry. I thought maybe you had some interests in common, like collecting something, or some kind of sport."

"Nope. And that's okay. I realize you're just doing your job. I suppose the better you know her, the better you can protect her."

"That much is true. And I have her home address, so why is she here?"

"I brought her here because I figured we could keep a better eye on her than leaving her alone in town with just me. I wasn't sure how fast they'd get somebody on her detail. You were pretty quick."

"There was a kidnapping case in Virginia, and I just finished up with that one. I'd been on that for a week, so fortunately, I have clothes and personal items with me because of that. I may run out of something, but right now, I'm well-equipped."

"Anything you need, we can get for you. Just say the word. And now I guess we need to figure out where you're going to sleep."

She stares at me for a second before she asks, "She's not going back to her place?"

"Uh, that wasn't the plan, no. But I guess she can." This is getting complicated fast. "Here's the thing. I can't go. I have to stay here because—"

"Monitoring?"

"No!" Why does everybody always assume that? "I finished my sentence. Not that at all. It's because I'm part of the search and rescue team, so I have to be here if a call goes out."

"Search and rescue? So that's what the logo is about!"

"Yeah. Appalachian Search, Train, Assess, and Rescue. And there are only eight of us, so I have to be here."

"But Knott County has its own search and rescue, doesn't it?"

"We're the only ones with medical capabilities—two nurses and an EMT, and I start school Monday to be a second EMT for the team. We're also the only ones in several counties with a helicopter for recovery."

"You have a *helicopter*?"

"Yep. Right out there past the tree line. Sure do. Big ol' AW139."

"Wow. Somebody's got deep pockets," she says, and I know she's fishing for info on how we got the bird.

"Yeah. We have some generous benefactors who believe in what we're doing out here. Matter of fact, they're paying for me to go to school to get my EMT certification, so we're really thankful for them."

"Sounds like you should be. Anybody I know?"

"Name's Walters. Out of Shelbyville and Louisville." The look on her face tells me she knows who they are. I hear a sound and stop to listen for a second before I say, "Excuse me. I think she's awake." Instead of waiting for Sela to reply, I just get up and head that direction.

Natalie's lying on her side, facing the door, and her eyes are open. "Hey, babe. You okay?" I whisper and drop to my knees beside the bed so I can look into her eyes.

"Yeah. Just … I dunno. Rattled, I guess."

"There's somebody here you need to meet. Come on." I wait while she puts on her slippers, then take her hand and lead her out into the living area.

Sela stands. "You must be Judge Anderson. I'm FBI Agent Sela Baldwin, and they sent me to be your security detail. Do you have any questions?"

"Yeah. What are you doing to stop these assholes?" Natalie asks, and her tone is pure acid as she takes a seat on the sofa.

"I don't know what's happening on that front. That's not my assignment. My assignment is to be right beside you at all times so you're safe."

"What now? What do I do?"

"You let me do my job, which is to protect you. That means I've got hard questions to ask."

Natalie cocks her head to one side. "Like?"

"Like are you going to stay here? Is he going to stay with you?" she asks and points toward me. "What's going on here? How does this work?"

Instead of answering, Natalie looks to me, so I answer,

"As far as I'm concerned, we stay the course. She comes here on the weekends. I stay there on the nights I have school."

Sela fixes her gaze on me. "Which are?"

"Monday, Wednesday, and Thursday. Get up the following morning and come back here to work. Spend the weekends together." Then I remember something. "Except for next weekend. My kids are coming for a visit."

Sela shakes her head. "No. We can't be around them right now. Harder to keep you safe," she says to Natalie, "and dangerous for them."

"Can't have that," Natalie answers, but there's a defeated tone in her voice that cuts me to the quick.

I reach over and take her hand when I say, "It'll all be fine. We'll work it out."

"And what's this I hear about one of the plaintiffs in the fed's case living here?"

Natalie nods. "Yeah. Isolde Bruce. She's Ghost's girlfriend. Being around her could jeopardize the case, and I don't want to do that. That means I can't be around them."

"So going to the larger buildings if there's a threat is out," Sela states, and Natalie and I both nod.

"As long as Ghost and Izzy aren't there, it's fine. Hey, wait." Something is rolling around in my brain. "My kids are coming next weekend. I was planning to stay in the lodge with them, since this place isn't big enough. Natalie could stay there with us. It would be as easy for you to guard her there as it is here."

"Who said it's easy here?" Sela's voice isn't accusatory, but I'm wondering what she means. "Very isolated, lots of wooded areas, wide open space right in the middle … It's a hitman's dream location."

That makes me shudder. "Wish you hadn't said that."

“It’s true. And there’s only one of me, so—”

“Oh! I’ve got an idea!” Natalie shuffles off to the bedroom and comes back with her phone. I watch as she pokes around on it, and then hits the speaker.

It’s ringing, and then a gruff voice answers. “Hey, you.”

“Hey! Can I ask you something?”

“Sure.”

“You know what happened earlier, right?”

There’s silence for a few seconds before the voice says, “Uh, no. I guess not. Should I? Haven’t heard.”

“Somebody left a package on my doorstep. I’m being threatened by the cartel that allegedly shot down Izzy.”

“Holy fucking shit, Natalie! Are you serious? Why didn’t you call me? God damn it! I’ll get some people there to keep an eye on you!”

“I wondered if you could do that.”

That’s when I realize who she’s talking to—Steve. He’s got a security company in Louisville. “I most certainly can, and I most certainly will. Hell, if I didn’t, Tony would. You’re seeing Dennis, Paddy, whatever, right?”

“Yeah, she is, and I’m sitting right here,” I call out.

“I swear to god, if anything happens to her, I’m coming after you, buddy. You’d better—”

“Sir, I don’t know who you are,” Sela interrupts, “but this is FBI Agent Sela Baldwin, and I’ve been assigned as Judge Anderson’s personal security detail.”

“I’ll tell you who I am. I’m the guy who’s sending you some help. I’ll be dispatching at least four Citadel Security agents as soon as I can get them rounded up and headed that direction. And Natalie?”

“Yes, sir?” I see Sela’s left eyebrow hike up when Natalie addresses Steve.

"You do what you're told. Do *not* risk your life over this. Do you hear me?" Then he mutters under his breath, "Son of a bitch, it's something all the god damn time." That's followed with a barked order: "Don't argue with them, understand?"

"Yes, sir."

"Good. Glad we got that straightened out up front. And Paddy?"

"Yep?"

"If she doesn't do what she's told, spank that ass. I mean it. I don't care if that's part of your dynamic or not. I want her safe. If anything happens to her, my submissive will kill me in my sleep with a Le Creuset skillet to the skull. And yes. Before anybody says anything, yes—I know all about Le Creuset now. In Provence. Which is a color like lavender. Shut up. I don't wanna hear it. It's like being lectured on how Cathedral Glass is the trending color in business spaces because of one of those stupid TV shows, or fat ties aren't a power statement anymore, or … Never mind. Just be glad you don't have any damn idea what I'm talking about and behave yourselves. You'll have four security agents there as fast as they can get there. And Natalie?"

"Yes, sir?"

"We love you, girl. Don't do anything that will get you killed, okay?"

Natalie chuckles. "Yes, sir. I promise."

"Okay. Good. I'll talk to you soon. Bye." And the phone goes silent.

"Wow. He's a character," Sela mumbles.

That makes me laugh and I answer, "You don't know the half of it."

Instantly, her eyes narrow and she focuses on me. "Submissive. Spanking. Sir. Now I understand your earlier comment."

Natalie's eyes dart back and forth between us. "What comment?"

I snicker. "She asked me why we thought we were compatible, because our backgrounds are so different."

"Oh. Oh! Yeah. Okay. Now I get it too." And she starts to laugh.

For the first time since she's been here, Sela smiles. It's a cautious smile, but it's a smile nonetheless. I'm not alone in this. I have help, and more help coming, and I'm starting to feel a little more hopeful.

Because all I really want to do is keep this woman safe, and for the first time, I realize if they kill her, they might as well kill me too. A world without her isn't a place I want to be.

I LEAVE NATALIE AND SELA IN MY COTTAGE WHILE I GO OUT to help Reboot with the boat. It's slow going, but at least we're doing something with it. We've been at it for about two hours when Mavis brings everybody something to drink, and the way Reboot looks at her … wow. He's totally smitten with her. She *is* beautiful. Just not as beautiful as Natalie.

We've been working along steadily for another hour when Patch appears. I figure he's going to help, but instead, he walks straight up to me. "You at a stopping point?"

"Uh, not right this minute, but I will be in about five minutes."

"Good. I need to talk to you. Office." And he walks away.

"What the fuck did you do?" Bulldog asks as he pulls another bolt out of the seat mounting bracket.

"Nothing. I didn't do anything."

Bear chuckles. "Maybe that's the problem—you didn't do anything. What were you *supposed* to do?"

"Nothing in particular that I know of." I give it another tug and the shaft comes right out. "Okay. If I don't come back before you guys knock off, please, somebody, put this shaft in the shed?"

"Yeah. We've got it," Reboot answers, and I wipe my hands on a rag before I head to the lodge.

My hand inside my shirt tail opens the door so I don't leave any grease on the knob, and I stop in the restroom and wash my hands really well before I head down the hallway to the office. Patch is sitting at his desk, deep in thought. "Hey, chief, what's up?"

"Close the door and sit down." I do as I'm told, then take a seat in the chair in front of his desk. "Natalie called Steve?"

"Yeah. He's sending her some reinforcements."

"He called me. He's concerned about you."

That's a surprise. "What about me?"

"The fact that getting to you could be the easiest way to get to her, or at least to get her to do what they want."

"I hadn't thought of that."

"Of course not. You hadn't had a chance, but that's how Steve thinks, how he's paid to think, and I'm glad he called me and said something. He's sending more guys to be here for you."

"We can't afford that, Patch. I mean, I can't begin to pay you back for—"

"It's not costing us anything." I know what that means—the Walters are paying for it, and I hate that they feel they need to do that. "But he also told me he's contacting the FBI to tell them you need somebody too."

"Oh, no. I don't want somebody hanging all over me like Sela is Natalie. I can't—"

"You can, and you will. We all need to be on alert. Ghost and Izzy too. Imagine if they could shut Izzy up. They'd love the hell out of that." That had never occurred to me. "We've all got to be on our toes until this is over."

"What about school? I start Monday."

"Yeah. We'll have somebody for you by then. In the meantime, stay on guard. We'll all talk this evening."

I just nod. Things are deteriorating quickly, and I really don't know what to think. I'm working on a boat, Natalie and Sela are in my cottage, and it's like this relationship I want so badly is slipping away from me and I'm powerless to do anything about it. I keep telling myself it's just temporary, that the case will eventually be over, but right now, I'm dying a little on the inside. It sounds like someone else's voice when I say, "Yeah, okay. Sure. Can I go now?" I'm not waiting for him to answer, but when I open the door, his voice stops me.

"Paddy? We're gonna get through this. Don't give up hope. You hear me? Stick with Natalie and everything will be okay."

Instead of answering him, I just wave him off as I go. The air around me feels thick and grainy, and I want to crawl under a rock somewhere and wait until the storm passes, the storm I know is coming. Reboot yells something to me as I cross the lawn, but I'm headed straight to my cottage, and I can't stop to see what he needs. That isn't important right now. All that matters is Natalie and me and whatever we're about to decide.

The door creaks as it opens and Sela looks up at me. "Where's Natalie?" She points toward the bedroom, so I don't knock, just open the door and step in.

"Yes, sir. I know. But I really want to see it through." A pause. I have no idea who she's talking to. "Yes, sir. I understand. And I will. The security firm is sending more people, so I'll be fine, I'm sure. I'll give you a call Monday afternoon to let you know how it's going. Yes, sir. Thank you. Goodbye." As soon as she drops the phone, she turns to me. "Judge Martelle, checking on me."

"I'm glad." There's a presence behind me, and without turning around, I say, "Sela, I'm sorry, but I need to talk to Natalie. Alone." The door closes behind her as she walks away, and I see some kind of uncertainty on Natalie's face. Once I'm sure Sela's gone, I take Natalie's hand. "We need to talk."

"Dennis, really, I—"

"Shhhh." When she quiets, I give her a smile that I hope reassures her. "Listen to me. No matter what, I'm committed to making this work, but I need to know how you feel."

A tear rolls down her cheek. "I don't want to stop seeing you, but I don't know what to do. I don't know how we're gonna work this out, babe. It's getting complicated, and maybe dangerous, and there are so many people having to help us, and—"

"We're getting help."

"Maybe you should just walk away. It would be safer for you, and not so much of a hassle, and it—"

"No! I absolutely will *not* walk away! You listen to me, sweet pea. I spent a lot of years alone, a lot of years believing no woman would ever want me because of the things that have happened to me. Meeting you … Natalie, you just don't understand. When I look at you, I don't just see a woman I love. I see *hope*. Pure hope. Something I haven't had. I've tortured myself every day for years over Michael's death, over losing Lisa and the boys, over the way I've felt about myself, what a failure I'd become, how the doors to a decent future for me had all closed. There were days when I didn't want to keep living. When I came to this place, I saw a glimmer of hope for the first time, but babe, you … That first time? When you kissed me? I remember thinking that somebody was playing a joke on me, that it was my imagination, that you were just messing with me because you couldn't possibly want me, especially for more than one night. Walk away? Wild horses couldn't drag me away, babe. Not a chance in hell. If you go down, I'm going down with you, but neither of us are going down. It's not happening. We've got the guys here, and Sela, and Steve's sending people, and we're gonna make it. And you're gonna sit back and watch while a jury puts those assholes away forever. You hear me? There's no walking away."

I can feel tears trickling down my own face as she falls into me, sobbing. This is it. I've made my stand. Nobody's going to hurt her, not while I have breath. It's a defining moment for this relationship as we cry together, both of us scared and unsure, but no matter what happens, she won't face it alone. Not happening.

She finally comes up for air and looks up into my face. Those eyes, sapphire blue and teary, rip a hole in my heart. "I don't want anything to happen to you."

"Nothing's going to happen to me, sweetheart. Nothing. You just worry about you and getting yourself back and forth to that courthouse. Worry about doing your job and doing what Sela tells you to do. That's all you need to worry about." I wait a second, then ask, "So we're good?"

She nods. "Yeah. We're good."

"Good. We've got visitors coming in a few hours, so we need to be ready. And it looks like we need to move over to the lodge so we're all together."

"But Ghost and Izzy—"

"They'll give you a wide berth. It'll be fine." And it will be. "I'll ask Patch to ask them to stay in Ghost's cottage."

The head shake she gives me surprises me. "This isn't going to work. It's too complicated for too many people. We should just put this on the back burner until these trials are over."

I bend down to her level and look into her eyes. "Is that what you want?"

"No."

"So let's stick to the plan. We can do this, Nat. We can. I know we can." Then there's a rap at the door.

As soon as I step out, she's standing there, hands on her hips. "Four cars just pulled up. Two men each. Patch came out and greeted them, so they must be our reinforcements."

"We should go see what they have to say, I suppose." Natalie has stepped up behind me, and that means she's ready. "Let's go see what the experts have to say."

Eight men are waiting for us when we step inside the lodge. Thankfully, I know at least one of them. As soon as our eyes meet, I can see that he remembers me. "Hey, Paddy!" In a second, his hand is reaching for mine, and we shake heartily. "Good to see you, although not under these circumstances."

"Same here, bud. Glad to see you." Marshall Smith is one of Steve's best men, and he helped when we rescued Penny. I remember that he was military, and possibly Green Beret, with a lot of other specialized training. Working for Steve must feel like a vacation for him, and I couldn't be happier that his boss sent him. "How'd you draw this duty?"

"Actually, Steve's been thinking of opening an office in this end of the state, and this is a good chance for me to scope out the territory again, really get a feel for things, and tell him what I think."

"Would you be heading up the office?"

"I'd like to think so." Honestly, I don't think he has anything to worry about. Steve would be a fool to choose someone else. He claps his hands together, looks at me, Sela, Natalie, and Patch, and says, "Okay. Brief us and let's see what we need to do."

I watch their faces, all eight men, as Patch, Natalie, and I fill them in. Then Sela jumps in, and I can see the respect they have for her. She knows what she's doing, I'll give her that. "So we've actually got nine now," she says as she looks around. "Our field office is sending more, so we'll have a few agents to help out as well."

"Any idea how many?" a guy named Drummond asks.

"Not yet, but I'm thinking four or five. They'll most likely be assigned to the judge herself, but they'll coordinate with you. We never mind having help."

"That's what we're here for," Marshall assures her.

"Great." I can practically hear the gears turning when she says, "Let's sit down with their schedules and decide what we need to do."

It takes me a whole ten seconds to figure out that Natalie and I have no say in any of this. They're planning exactly how this is going to go, and we're along for the ride. It's starting to be a little irritating when I suddenly realize something important. The real goal here, the only goal, is for us to get through this trial and come out the other side alive. Without their help and expertise, there's a good chance that it won't happen. Natalie might have other ideas, but I'd really like to live to see another year, and I get the distinct impression that without them, the chances of that greatly diminish.

When all is said and done, they decide that we're going to

keep the schedules we'd already set up. Natalie will keep going just like she has been. I'll start school on Monday, stay the night at her place, come home on Tuesday morning, go to school on Wednesday evening, and come back here on Friday morning. But for next weekend, she won't be here. She'll stay home, and the boys will come here to see me. Since we'll be here with all of the guys and I'll have security, it should be fine.

Friday morning. That's the last time I'll see her until the following Monday evening. A month ago, I didn't even know she existed. Now, kissing her goodbye on a Friday morning and not seeing her until the following Monday night seems like an eternity, and I'm not sure how I'll survive it.

Natalie

The stroll back to his cottage has been quiet until I finally speak. "You shouldn't wait. You should call them. Video chat or something."

"Why?"

"What if something happens to you? Wouldn't it be best if they'd already talked to you at least?"

"I dunno. I kinda hate to think that the first time they see me after all these years is on a video chat. That seems like a cop-out somehow."

I'm so thankful when Sela hops into the conversation. "Why? I mean, if they lived in Tokyo, you couldn't just hop on a plane and go, so that would be your solution. And maybe it would help because it's not like they'd be standing right in front of you. If they feel awkward or don't want to talk, they won't have to."

"Those are really good points," I say in agreement.

"Yeah, okay. I'll call Lisa and ask her, and we can set something up if they're game," he says. There's a certain measure of disappointment in his voice, but I feel hopeful. Maybe this will work out okay after all.

We've been in the cottage for a whole five minutes when he says, "I'm gonna go in here in the bedroom and call her. Need some privacy. I'm gonna tell her about you, and if she throws some kind of fit, I don't want you to have to hear that."

"You think she's gonna throw a fit?"

"No, but it's possible."

What can I do? It's not up to me. "Okay. I'll be out here."

"You'd better be. Be right back." And the bedroom door closes.

Who sang that song, "One is the Loneliest Number?" Three Dog Night? Because that's how this feels, sitting out here, knowing they're talking about me. It's weird and I'm about to totally freak out. When the bedroom door opens and he steps into the room, I feel like I'm going to jump out of my skin. "Well?"

"We're going to do a video chat tonight at seven thirty."

"With the boys?"

"Yep."

"And you told her about me?"

"Yep."

"What did she say?"

There's an odd, wistful look on his face. "Surprised me. Said she's happy for me, and you sound like a great person."

"That's nice." I don't know what else to say, but I'd sure love to know what he told her. Did he tell her about what's going on here? With the security and all? I'm guessing he didn't. "Maybe someday I'll get to meet her."

"You will tonight. I want you to."

It's too soon. Isn't it too soon? I'm not even sure. "Are you positive you want to do that?"

"I do." When he reaches for my hand, there's a pain in my chest that's pure fear. "You don't have anything to worry about. It'll be fine."

"What if it's not? What if she hates me?"

"Why would she hate you? Honestly, I think you'll like Lisa. She's a good person. There was no animosity between us. What she did to me was because she felt backed into a corner, and I don't fault her for that. I was bitter about it for a good while, but now I understand, and I'm okay with it. She and the boys have had a good life with Luke. She did the right thing."

If he can forgive her, I guess I can too. She hasn't done anything to me, but the way she hurt him hurts me, even though he seems to be fine with it all. I guess the question is, who am I to say? "Okay. If you're sure."

"I am." With a check of his watch, he sighs. "It's just four thirty. Let's figure out what we want to do for dinner."

That idea makes me very sad. "You mean figure out what we *can* do for dinner."

"Nat …"

"Most couples in our situation are going on their third date. Maybe kissing for the first time."

"Most couples in our situation are in their twenties and we're not. We're not kids, Nat. I'm forty-four. You're forty-one. You have no kids, and if you want one, your time is dwindling."

Ouch. "Thanks for reminding me."

"It's not that. My point is that yeah, we cut a few corners, and yeah, we've moved really fast, but I'll tell you right now, if I know something's right, I'm too old to just sit around and see what's going to happen. And this relationship? Nat, it's right. You know it. I know it. And right now, we're inconvenienced. It's an unusual reason, but people are inconvenienced by all kinds of things all the time. We'll make it through this, and we can eat whatever the fuck we want, whenever the fuck we want. Right now, we're going to do the best we can, stay safe, and love each other. When we get past this, we'll come out the other side stronger, wiser, and even more in love, not to mention the trust we'll build."

That breaks me, and I can't stop the tears. I don't want to keep going; I just want to curl up in a ball and cry. This man, he's the one I've waited all my life for, the one person I want to spend the rest of my life with, and now it looks like the rest of my life might not be that long. I expect him to tell me not to cry, but he doesn't. His arms wrap around me, and I hear him whisper, "We've got this, sweet pea. I've got you."

If I could just freeze this moment in time and live in it forever … I hate that my calling on this earth has dragged this good man into a mess that may kill him. If anything happens to him, my life will be over. Living with him, loving him, being loved by him, is all I want. It's all I'll ever need. And it feels like it's slipping away a minute at a time. My heart is crushed as I answer, "Leave me. Save yourself."

"Not a chance in hell. We're in this together. Don't you *dare* try to chase me off, because it won't work. I'm stuck to you like glue, beautiful. And now …" he says, pressing a strand of my hair behind my ear, "we're going to find something to eat, and then you're going to meet two of the finest young men ever born. I hear one of them looks exactly like me." Then he snickers. "And I hear the other one is good-looking."

"If one of them looks just like you, he's the handsome one." I squeeze his waist tightly and press my cheek to his chest. "I love you, Dennis."

"I love you too, sweet pea. But I'm hungry, and it's Saturday night, and I think we should invest in something that used to moo. How does that sound?"

"Sounds great." Guess that's settled. There's a steak in my future.

CHAPTER 8

Paddy

Well, that was interesting—the two of us at a table in the corner, while nine other people sit scattered throughout the restaurant, all taking turns staring at us. I don't know if anybody else in the restaurant notices, and honestly, I don't care. All I really care about is the woman across the table from me and making sure she's okay and having a good time. I can tell she's not, but I keep trying to make her laugh. It's almost impossible.

But when the door to the cottage closes, I'm in full-blown panic mode. I run around, trying to figure out which is the best place to sit, then start sounding like a twenty-something about to go on TV. "Do I look okay? Is this shirt okay? Is my hair okay?"

"Dennis, you look fine," Natalie says, smoothing my hair. "Although you could use a haircut."

"Is Tinsley home, I wonder? Because she could cut it real quick and—"

"Babe, your boys aren't going to care about your hair."

"What if they do?"

"They won't. It looks fine. And sitting at the desk is fine. The light is fine there."

"But you won't have anywhere to sit."

"I'm only going to make a brief appearance. You should be the one talking to them, interacting with them. They're calling you, not me."

"But I—"

"Dennis." She grips my upper arms and stares into my face. "Nobody cares. You look fine. Try to relax and enjoy talking to them. Keep it light. Make them laugh. Ask them questions. Just show them that you're interested in them. That's all they really want."

"Relax. Talk. Light. Laugh. Questions. Interested. Got it."

"Oh, lord. You're a basket case. Are you calling them, or are they calling you?"

I feel my chest tighten. "Oh, shit. I don't know. Should I send Lisa a text and ask … Or should I just call her, or—" My ruminations are cut short by a weird sound coming from my computer. "What the hell is that?" A box pops up in the upper right-hand corner with a blue circle and a red circle.

"It's the call coming through. Click on the blue circle." I freeze. "Dennis! Click the circle!"

"Oh, yeah. Right." I slide the cursor up to the blue circle and click it. The screen flashes dark for just a second, and then I see a face I haven't seen in years except in pictures—Lisa. It takes me a few seconds before I finally say, "Hey!"

"Hey yourself! How's it going?"

"Um, going good. Just had a steak." Fuck. That sounds dumb.

"You've always liked a good steak. We had spaghetti for dinner."

"I love spaghetti." A voice in my head barks, *What are you, twelve?* I sound like an idiot. Why am I so nervous? "Um, so yeah, a good day. What's everybody up to?"

"Tegan's in the bathroom. Borden's upstairs, and he said he'll be down in a minute. I think he's a little nervous."

"Nervous? Why would—"

From somewhere outside my field of view, I hear a voice ask, "Is he on there? Can he see me?"

"You'll have to come over here by me, honey. He can't see you over there." From the left side of the screen, somebody comes into view, and he bends down a little to look into the screen.

Holy shit, it's a younger me.

"Hey! How's it going?" I ask. That's lame as fuck, but I don't know what to say.

"Um, good. You're my dad, right?"

"Yep. I am. Haven't seen you since you were a tiny little baby."

"Because you were in jail."

"Tegan Lynn!" I hear Lisa shriek.

"No, no. It's okay. Actually, I was in a detention center. It wasn't like a prison, with cells, but I couldn't leave, so it was like a prison in that way. But now I never have to go back there, so …" I don't know how to end that sentence.

"Yeah. That's what Mom said. She and Dad said you shouldn't have gone there, that you didn't deserve that." There's a split second of fright on his face before he stutters, "Um, I mean, I know you're my dad, but Dad, um, Luke, um—"

"Hey, look, don't sweat it. You can call me Dennis. I

mean, we really don't know each other, right? So just call me Dennis. It's fine."

"Uh, okay. Dennis. That's your name." Then he laughs.

It makes me laugh too. "That's what it says on my driver's license!"

There's more movement and I hear a voice say, "Move over, squirt."

"Don't call me squirt!" Tegan yells as I watch him being shoved out of the picture.

"My turn." A face that looks a lot like Lisa's fills the screen. "So you're my biological material contributor."

It shocks me so much that I fumble for a few seconds. "Uh, okay, yeah. I guess you could say that."

"Because you're sure as hell not my dad," the totally pissed off young man says.

"Borden! You apologize right this instant!" Lisa barks.

"Nope. Get dragged away to prison and then waltz right back in? Why should I make this easy for you?"

"Borden! You can't—"

"Lisa!" I see her in the background. "He's got a right to be angry. I get it. Really, I do. Borden, look, I don't expect you to call me Dad or feel all warm and fuzzy toward me. That would be unrealistic because we really don't know each other. How 'bout this? How 'bout you tell me what your favorite thing is to do?"

"Make out with my girlfriend." Okay then. He's a smartass, and his focus is sex. It appears we have more in common than he thinks.

"Borden!" Lisa yells.

"That's okay. Really. You're fifteen. That's what I was doing when I was fifteen."

"Oh, yeah? You had a girlfriend when you were fifteen?"

"I had two girlfriends when I was fifteen, and I was busy trying to keep one from knowing about the other."

From beside me I hear Natalie whisper, "Scoundrel."

"Yeah, well, bet you don't have a girlfriend now," Borden says with a smirk.

I reach for her, grab her hand, and pull her into my side. "I'd like you to meet Natalie. She's my girlfriend."

"Hi, guys," Natalie says, but her voice is weak.

"Wow, you must be desperate if you'd settle for an ex-con," Borden says, staring at Natalie.

"Nope. I met him through mutual friends who know what a great guy he is, and we really hit it off."

Borden shoots her an evil grin. "So, whaddya do? Sling plates at the Pancake Hut?"

I don't get a chance to answer before Natalie says, "Nope. I'm a federal judge. Eastern District of Kentucky. And right now I'm presiding over the pretrial for a couple of big trials of guys from a cartel who allegedly shot down a Kentucky State Police helicopter."

His eyes go wide. "Cool. Seriously?"

Natalie nods. "Yep. Seriously."

"How in the world did you catch *her*?" he asks me.

"My good looks, wit, and charm," I answer back with plenty of snark.

"Uh-huh. Okay then." And he sits back in his chair, then folds his arms across his chest.

Then there's a flash and Tegan's back, leaning over in front of Borden. "Hey, you wanna see what I made?"

"The only thing you make is turds, and nobody wants to see that," Borden tells his little brother.

"Mom!" Tegan yells.

"Borden, could you *please* act like a normal human being?" Lisa snaps.

"How boring is that? So you live on a farm?" Borden asks.

"Yeah. We make knives and swords and—"

He sits bolt upright. "You mean like on that show, *Hollywood Forging*?"

"Yeah. Only our shop isn't as nice."

"Yeah, but making swords and stuff? That's cool!"

"No, it's really, really hot. Trust me on that. I don't actually make the swords. I'm a leatherworker, and I make the scabbards and holsters and things like that."

He sighs loudly. "Of course. Nothing as cool as swords."

"I'll learn how soon, I'm sure."

Something shows up in front of the screen, and then Tegan's face comes into view behind it. "I made it in art class. It's a bowl." As he speaks, he pulls it back toward him, and I can finally see it clearly—it was too close before. It's dark blue, shiny, and fairly good-sized.

"Did you throw it on the wheel?" I ask.

His eyes go wide. "Yeah. You know about ceramics?"

"Of course I know about ceramics! I did some throwing and slab building myself when I was in high school and then college."

"Cool!"

"And we have a guy out here who blows glass."

"Oh my gosh! Could I see sometime?"

"Actually, I was going to ask you guys if you want to come and visit," I say, and I can feel Natalie's hand on my back.

"I want to! When can I come?"

"Your mom and I will work it out. Borden, would you want to come too?"

"To a farm?" my older son asks.

It's time for my ace in the hole. "We have a helicopter."

"You what? You have a helicopter? What?"

"A helicopter? A *real* helicopter?" Tegan screams.

"Yeah. I'm part of a search and rescue team, and we have a helicopter we do rescues with. You know, lifting people out of bad places, letting our guys down to help rescue people. Stuff like that."

"Your own helicopter?" Borden asks, and I can tell he's shocked.

"It belongs to the team, but yeah. It's ours. Big red and yellow Agusta Westland. Pretty thing. I'll send you a picture."

"So about this visit … We could really come?" Borden asks, and I know I've got him.

"Sure! Talk to your mom, and she and I will talk, and we'll work something out. Okay? Not a problem."

"Yeah, okay. Yeah!" Tegan crows.

"Sounds good," Borden says, trying hard to not sound too enthusiastic.

"Okay. Listen, I'll talk to your mom and we'll work it out. But I want you to know that it was really, really good talking to you, and I'm here for you if you need me for anything, okay? Anything at all."

"Yeah. Okay. Later." Borden disappears from view.

"Okay. Hope it's soon. I want to see that helicopter. Bye!" And Tegan is gone.

Lisa's face fills the screen. "So that went well, I think."

"Lots better than I thought it would."

"Hey, Natalie?"

She leans into my shoulder and smiles. "Yeah! I'm here."

"I just wanted to say hi and thanks for supporting him in this. I've wanted him to see the boys for years, but he's always said no. I have to believe I have you to thank for this."

We both laugh before she answers, "Let's just say I encouraged it greatly."

"Well, however much of a part you played in it, small or large, I appreciate it. And Dennis, thank you. I always wanted them to know you."

"I know. I just didn't want them to see me institutionalized. I wanted to wait until I was out. Seeing me in there could've really hurt their self-esteem, and I didn't want that."

"I get it. I do. You've just missed out on a lot of years you can't get back, and I wish that hadn't happened."

"Me too, but it did, and there's nothing we can do about it except try to make up for lost time."

"I agree."

"And if it helps, Luke is welcome too."

"No. I think that would make the boys uncomfortable. You know, trying to get to know you while maintaining loyalty to him. That's additional pressure they don't need. You don't need it either." Gotta give her credit, she's a smart woman.

"I get that. Makes sense."

"Good. Well, we'll talk about next weekend during the week after I've had a good chance to keep up a dialogue with them. Nice to meet you, Natalie."

"You too, Lisa. Thanks for this."

"You're very welcome. Talk to you soon, Denny."

"Yep. Thanks. Bye." I click the little red circle, and the screen wallpaper pops up.

And I just sit there. I really don't know what to say or think. Those were my *kids*. My *boys*. The children I haven't seen for twelve years. They look so different, and yet I still see the faces of the babies I held when they were born.

A soft voice asks, "Are you okay, babe?"

"Yeah. Just trying to process it."

"I get it. Take your time. But Dennis?"

When I turn to look into her face, I'm blown away by the compassion there. "Yeah?"

"I'm so, so proud of you. So proud. You have no idea. You're going to have great relationships with them. I just know it."

My hand grips hers, and I feel my eyes filling. "Thank you. Thank you for being here for me, for giving me the courage, for believing in me."

"I do. It's all going to be fine. Really."

That's when I realize that just a few hours earlier, I was saying those same words to her, how it's all going to be fine. We're here together, and we're good for each other. I see that now. "We're a team," I whisper as I kiss her forehead.

"Together or apart, we're a team." We have each other. Next weekend, I'll have my boys. I have the guys and their girlfriends and wives. I have a family. I have friends. We have plenty of help.

We just might make it.

NATALIE

"NOW. BEFORE IT GETS DARK." SELA'S ORDERING US around, and I kinda hate it, but I also like that she's here, so I'll take the bad with the good. And she's got a point. Dragging bags across the lawn to the lodge in near darkness doesn't sound like a good idea.

I finally get to spend time with everybody except Ghost and Izzy. They're all so friendly and welcoming, and it's hard to believe that any of these guys were ever in prison. Well, except for Bear. Honestly, he kinda scares me a little, but everybody seems to love him, so I'll just have to get over it.

Mavis' Aunt Sarah has a room in the lodge, so we choose one up and across the hallway. I'd hate to wake her up if we're fooling around. Sela takes one on the other side of the wall from us. I know why, but I still wish she was in another building. The eight men who've come in here to stay with us are bunking two to a room, so the place is packed. That'll all change Monday when half of them go with me. Where the hell they're going to sleep at my house, I have no idea. Sela will be there too, so it's going to get complicated real fast.

By the time we get settled, it's getting late, so we take turns getting ready for bed, then climb in and prop ourselves up against the headboard. That only lasts a couple of minutes before we're naked and all over each other. We've been kissing and touching and groping and sighing for ten minutes when he sits up, leans back in the pillows, and stares me in the face. "And?" I ask, wondering what he's thinking.

"Suck me. Do it with your ass in the air." I'm about to say something when he says, "And take it all the way down. Deep."

I intentionally bat my eyelashes at him. "Yes, sir." The smile that creeps across his face makes me warm all over.

I kneel between his legs and wrap my hands around his shaft. It's not huge, but it's plenty big enough and completely rigid. For years, I thought the times I'd scened with Steve had forever colored my desires, but with Dennis, I've come to realize what was missing from those encounters—emotions. Yeah, Steve liked me, still likes me, loves me as a friend, but it wasn't the same. It was just pure desire, nothing more. With Dennis, I want to please him because I know he loves me, and damn, the sex is amazing.

As soon as I take him in my mouth, he lets out a long, low

hiss. With a *pop*, I let go and look up at him. "Remember, we're not alone. There are people on the other side of the wall and across the hallway," I remind him.

"Oh, god, it's gonna be so hard to be quiet," he mutters.

"Yeah. I know. But we have to." This time when I pull him into my mouth, he lets loose with a deep, quiet sigh, and I know he's enjoying it. I suck hard; I don't suck at all, just move; I use my tongue to tease the tip, to slide up and down while I'm sucking. Every couple of minutes, I change it up a little to keep it interesting, plus I like to hear and feel his reactions. They tell me what he likes and doesn't, and so far, it seems he likes everything I'm doing, based on the little bit of precum I taste.

"Fuck, sweet pea. Fuck, fuck, fuck. Damn, that's good," he whispers, his fingers winding into my hair. I think I know what he's about to do when he says, "Don't panic. Hear me? You know I won't hurt you." Using my hair, he pulls my head down, and I'm forced to take his hardness deeper. The panic is momentary, but I will myself to stay in the moment. "Ohhhh, good girl. Damn." The pressure disappears, and I can take a breath. "Okay?"

"Yeah," I answer, my voice strangled.

"You'll learn. Felt amazing. Keep going, babe."

He does the same thing twice more, and the third time, he holds me still and thrusts into my throat. It takes everything I have not to press myself upward, hands on his thighs, but I manage, and I hear him groan out, "Ohhhhh, yeah." It's clotting my throat, and my mouth is full of it. When he turns loose of my hair, I'm gasping. "You okay?"

It's running down my chin, and I'm still swallowing. "Uh, yeah. Yeah."

"Here." Softness hits my face, and I realize he's wiping it

with a tissue. “Let’s clean that off.” In a second, there’s another one, a clean, dry one, wiping my eyes. “Better?”

“Yeah.” It’s still a little hard to catch my breath, but I’m trying. “Yeah, better.”

His hands wrap under my armpits and he drags me up to him, then locks his lips to mine. I know exactly what he’s doing—he can taste himself on me. Pulling back just a little, he whispers against my lips, “Fuck, I’m hard again. It’s time for me to take you. I want you bad, girl. Real bad. You ready for me?” His hand is creeping down my side, and then he slips it forward and his fingers stroke into me. “Oh, yeah. You’re soaked. On your knees, ass to me.”

As I press my face into the pillow, I smile. Dennis looks so meek and mild, but there’s an animal inside that hard body, and I like that I can bring it out for my pleasure. I’m expecting what I always do when I feel something cold and wet hit my … what the hell? “What are you doing?”

“I’ll press it in and you’re gonna take it.”

“What …” Whatever it is, it’s hard. “What is that?”

“Butt plug. You ever had one before?”

“No.”

“Well, tonight’s your lucky night.” He presses hard, and nothing happens. “Open up, Nat. It’s going in there.”

“But—”

“Exactly. Butt. That’s where it’s going.” It disappears, and something else takes its place. “Gettin’ you ready.” Shit. It’s his finger. “Come on, girl. Let me in. Bear down.” Bear down? What does he mean by … Oh. I get it. “Yeah. There ya go. That’s better.” It’s a little uncomfortable, but not painful. Then it disappears.

And it’s replaced with something cold and hard again. This time, I do the same thing, and I feel it press me open. “Damn!”

"You okay?"

"It burns!"

"Yeah, it takes a little getting used to. But once it's in, it's in. It won't come out until I take it out, and by then, your body will have adjusted to it."

"So it's not like … You won't be pulling it in and out …"

"No. It's a plug, babe, not a dildo. Different."

"Oh, yeah. I know what you mean." First time for everything. I don't really understand the purpose of this, but okay. I guess he likes the look.

"Get ready. This will feel a lot different." I feel the tip of his cock in my slit, and in a split second, the world explodes for me.

I'm almost panting. "Holy shit."

"Yeah. Like that? Because I sure as hell do," he mumbles.

"Oh, god." It feels like he's as big as a fence post, and now I understand why he likes the plug. Less room, more stretch. "Oh, damn. God, Dennis. Burns." And that burn is a spark. "Oh, damn. Fuck me. Please, god, fuck me."

"Oh, you're gettin' a fuckin', girl. A hard one."

What happens next is transcendental. Twelve strokes in and I have this orgasm that snatches the breath right out of my lungs. Good thing my face is in the pillow or they'd hear me shriek a mile away. And he just keeps going. I don't know how much of this I can take. My legs feel like spaghetti and my arms are trembling so violently that I'm having trouble staying in position. They finally give out and I'm just buried from my tits up into the bed. He's just going to town on my pussy, thrusting into me so hard that he's pushing me up toward the headboard, and I don't even care. I hear him whisper, "Damn, girl, your pussy is amazing. I'm gonna fuck you all night, Nat. You won't be able to walk in the morning. And look at that ass. Oh, baby, I'll be plowing into that in a couple of weeks. I'm gonna fuck you every way I've ever dreamed of and probably make up a couple of new ways. Yeah. That's it. Come again for me."

And I do. I can't help it.

"Ohhhh, fuck, Nat." There's a sudden heat and wetness, and I know that's it. At least I think it is. Instead, he pulls out, picks me up, practically tosses me over, and looks down at me. "Open your mouth."

"Huh?" I mumble, exhausted.

"I said open your mouth." In two seconds, the head of his cock is in there, and I wallow it around with my tongue. "Yeah. That's what I need." He's hardening again, and I know what that means. *He's going to ravage me again!* my inner slut squeals.

Next thing I know, he's propped on one hand above me, his cock slamming into me again, and this time, he uses his other hand to tweak, twist, and pull my nipples. Horniness like this is something I'm not accustomed to, and yet if he wanted to drag me out onto the lawn and fuck me in front of the whole damn place, I'd let him. I want him so badly that I can't even think. "Use your hand to get yourself off, girl. I want to hear you scream."

"But the other side of—"

"I don't give a damn who's on the other side of the wall. Let them hear how damn awesome fucking you is, because, baby, I've never been this hard in my whole damn life. You come around me and I'm probably going to pass out. Not kidding."

So I do what he says, and in a few seconds, I can feel it building. "Ohhhh, Dennis. Oh, god, no. I can't—"

"Yes, you can. You can take it. You're the finest fuck in fifty states, and you can definitely take it. You're gonna take everything I give you and you're gonna love it, understand? I own your body, Natalie. It's mine to do with as I please, and what pleases me is to drive you crazy with my cock."

When it hits, I don't scream. I can't. My whole body goes rigid and as much as I want to make my finger stop, it doesn't. It's still stroking, and everything below my waist is convulsing and pulsing. The butt plug is forgotten. I just feel the spasms and that cock forcing me open over and over.

My arm drops from exhaustion, and it takes the orgasm with it. It's gone, and I hear him say, "Oh, shit." Another wave of wetness and warmth blooms inside me, and then he stills on top of me.

The only sound is our breathing, labored and desperate. My own voice seems detached to my ears when I whisper, "I've never been fucked like that in my life."

I hear a low chuckle. "Oh yeah? I hope you mean that in a good way."

"I mean that in an incredible, unbelievable, amazing way."

"Good. I don't want you running off with somebody else."

How could he say that, even in jest? "I'm not going anywhere without you. You're mine."

He rolls to lie beside me and his arms wrap around me. "And you're mine. I want you with me always."

"Same."

"Let's rest for a bit, and then I want to do this again."

Is he kidding? "Jesus, Dennis! I don't think I can! And can you please take this thing out of—"

"Oh, yeah. Hang on." He rolls me onto my side with my back to him, and in a second, I feel the plug pop out. "Taking this thing to the bathroom. I'll clean it up in the morning."

"Good plan. Grab me a towel while you're in there, please."

"You got it, babe." I hear him moving around in the other room, then smile into the darkness when he comes padding back in with the towel. "Here ya—"

In a split second, he shoves me off the bed, and I hit the floor with an *oomph*. "What the—"

"Shhhh!" His hand comes up and covers my mouth. What the fuck is going on? "You stay here. Right here. Don't move." He fishes around on the floor, and I think he picks up his underwear, but I'm not sure. I lie there as he crawls around the foot of the bed and darts out the door. I can hear some whispering out in the hallway, and then he's back. But instead of the bed, he heads straight to the closet, slings the door open, and kneels behind it. "Get in here. Right now."

"But what is—"

"In. Quiet. Hurry." I just do as I'm told, and once I'm inside it, he whispers, "I'm closing it. Don't come out until somebody comes for you." And the door closes.

I have no idea what's going on, but I'm scared. I sit there in the dark, alone, for about ten minutes, before the door opens, and I'm terrified. But it's Dennis' face I see. "It's okay. You can come out."

"What the hell?" I let him take my hand and help me to standing. That's when I remember that I'm stark naked.

"I saw somebody outside the window."

I can feel the blood draining from my face. "This window?" I say and point.

"Yes, babe. But Sela saw them too, and she was already on the move. Couple of the guys too, the ones on this side of the building."

There's a rap on the door, and he reaches for the knob. "Grab the sheet," he orders, so I snatch it from the bed and wrap it around myself. "Yeah?"

It's Sela. "Whoever it was, they're gone."

"How many of them?" I ask.

"Three. The guys got a glimpse of them through the trees, but it appears they stashed a car somewhere down the road. Bartlett said they heard a car start, so the assholes got away."

"But how did they find me?"

Dennis cuts his eyes toward me. "We haven't exactly been covering our tracks. They followed us from your house, I'm sure."

"Yeah, that's most likely what they did," Sela says in agreement, and I want to curl up in a ball and cry. These guys are now actively pursuing me. They know where I'm staying. They shot down a helicopter, for fuck's sake.

I'm in deep shit.

Paddy

Right this minute, I'm thankful for Steve sending these guys. I'm thankful for Sela. I'm thankful we're still alive. Shit's getting real, and I don't like it one bit.

But I look at my baby, and my heart is broken. She's terrified and sad, and I'm powerless. I feel like I need to do something, but I'm not sure what that would be. All I can do is hold her and let her cry, and she's been crying for hours now. I've been through a lot of shit, and I've never felt as helpless as I do right now.

She finally cries herself to sleep, and I find myself wanting to stay awake, to watch over her, but I know I need some sleep too. I mean, I know Sela is doing that, and the other guys. Then I wonder … Does Sela ever sleep? Because when I stepped out into the hallway, she was dressed and had her weapon in her hand. That was pretty damn quick. I'll have to ask her sometime. But right now, I do need some rest. I'm supposed to help Reboot with the boat tomorrow for a little while, and I won't be able to do that if I'm dragging ass. When Michael comes to me tonight, he really doesn't say much, just smiles and gives me a goofy little wave.

The next thing I know, there's sun shining in through the slats in the blinds, and I look over to find Natalie still sound asleep, but even unconscious, there are deep worry creases in her forehead, and that tears me apart. God, I love her so fucking much. I didn't know it was possible to love somebody this much, but apparently it is. When I kiss her forehead, she stirs a little, then one eye cracks open. "Hey. Good morning."

"Good morning. I didn't really want to wake you, but we need to go get something to eat before whoever cooked cleans it all up."

"Yeah, I guess so." She pushes herself up and pivots to throw her legs off the side of the bed, but when she stands and takes a step, she moans. "Ohhhh, god."

There's no stopping the chuckle. "Sore, huh?"

"Yes, motherfucker, I am. Thanks a lot." She's mincing her way along toward the bathroom and I'm still laughing. "You can stop laughing at me now."

"You liked it!" I say, almost crowing.

"Yeah, I did. But it's a good thing I'll be going home late this afternoon and won't see you again until tomorrow night."

That makes me stop laughing. "You don't mean that."

Her face is sad when she turns. "No. I really don't. I mean, my pussy does, but I don't."

All I can do is nod. "I get it."

She rolls her eyes at me. "And to think you wanted to do it again."

"No. I didn't just want to do it again. I wanted to do it again and make love to you. That's how I wanted the evening to end. But …" And I stop. Anything else I say will only make her feel worse.

"Yeah. I ruined that." I watch as a single tear trickles down her cheek, and I just can't take it.

My legs are long enough that it only takes me three strides to reach her, and I reach out and pull her into my arms. "No. You did not. Somebody else did. That's not your fault, so don't say that. Nothing was ruined. It wasn't how I wanted the night to end, but it's okay. We had fun, right?"

"Yeah," she whispers and nods against my chest.

"And I feel closer to you this morning than I did yesterday afternoon. That's the whole point, right?"

Her head tips back and she looks up into my face. "Uh, yeah."

"Then nothing was ruined, sweet pea. Mission accomplished. Every time we touch each other, our bond is stronger than it was before that touch. Remember that. As long as we keep that connection, we can hang on. Right?"

"Right." For a few seconds, we just stare into each other's eyes. That's all. And it's powerful. Then she sighs. "I'm going to the bathroom, and then we can go eat."

"Okay. I'll pull on some clothes. I'll just plan on showering this afternoon after I've helped Reboot for a while." There's a drooping of her shoulders and her head is hung as she walks away from me, and I want to scream. I want to ask the universe why, after all this time, I find someone so perfect for me, and all this shit has to go sideways. I want to know what I did to make one disaster after another follow me around, starting with Michael.

And then I think of Mavis. That poor woman … Her life was absolute shit. Parents who abused her and let other people abuse her. One lost job after another. A grown woman, living with her aunt because she couldn't hold a job. Afraid of everything and everybody. And when the chips were down, Mavis fought back. She fought back hard, she did something heroic in the process, and she won in the end. Now she and her aunt have a huge family of people who love them and will protect them, she has a great job, and she's happy with Reboot, plus she has the satisfaction of knowing that she's getting justice. Her life has completely turned around.

If Mavis can do it, I can too. I'll persevere, and I'll prevail. I won't let anything happen to a woman I love more than life itself. Natalie is mine, I'm hers, and we're together. It's going to stay that way.

And those Mexican bastards can kiss my fucking ass.

CHAPTER 9

Natalie

All my adult life, I've wished I could find somebody who'd fill that empty place inside me, the one person who understood me and loved me like no one else. My soulmate. I've finally found him, and now this.

Everybody moves *en masse* outside to head toward the kitchen, but just as we step out the door, I stop. "I forgot my phone. Be right back." I've already decided that while he's helping Reboot today, I need to call my parents and talk to them. My phone is plugged in to charge on the nightstand, so I run in, grab it, and head back out.

And run straight into Bear's huge chest. It's like slamming into a concrete block wall.

"Oh, my god, I'm sorry!" I blurt out, as startled as I've ever been.

"Oh. Damn. Sorry, Natalie. Didn't mean to step right into you."

"Uh, it's okay. I just, I didn't know you were over there,

and …" That's when it hits me: What the hell was he doing in the room across the hallway? That's weird. "I'm sorry."

"It's okay. I'm sorry. Apologies all around. You goin' to get something to eat?"

"Yep. That's the plan."

"Be careful. Paddy can't lose you. You don't understand the difference you've made in his life. He loves you, Natalie. Don't do anything stupid that'll put you in harm's way."

"I won't. I promise. Thanks. Uh, see you later." This is really strange. I mean, really strange. What was he doing over there?

Everybody's waiting for me just outside the door. The guys are in a circle around us, moving with us, and Sela's right behind me. But I manage to lean over to Dennis and whisper, "Bear was in the room across the hall."

I'm probably the only one who catches his tiny head shake. "Later." What does that mean?

When we get to the kitchen, Penny, Audrey, and Mavis are all working like crazy. Sarah's sitting at a table, and it looks like she's breaking green beans. I suppose those are for dinner tonight. Now I feel really bad. It was my understanding that everybody is supposed to kind of do their own thing so nobody has to work, but there are nine extra mouths to feed, so somebody has to do it. "Why didn't you guys come get me? I'd be glad to help," I say to Penny when she comes over and hugs me.

"We wanted you to be able to sleep. I know last night was stressful."

"I'm sorry I took Patch away from you." She gives me this funny look, like she doesn't understand me. "I mean, when everybody went looking for the men who were prowling around."

"No. Patch wasn't with them. None of the other guys were. We're leaving that to Steve's guys and the FBI agents."

"Oh. I thought everybody got up."

"No. We didn't find out until we got up this morning. Marshall came over and briefed Patch. That's when I got everybody else up and we started making breakfast so you'd have a decent meal." I can feel tears welling up in my eyes. "Oh, honey, don't cry! You're one of us now! We love you and we want to take care of you. It's okay, really. Now, you just sit here and relax with Dennis and we'll have breakfast ready in a few minutes." She pats me on the shoulder and heads back to work, and I can't help it—I sob.

Dennis stands, reaches for my hand, and when I slip it into his, he helps me stand and leads me over to the corner where there's a small sofa and a couple of chairs. We sink into the soft furniture, and I lean my head over onto his chest while his arm wraps around me. "Don't cry, precious. It's gonna be okay."

"I feel so bad that everybody's having to do all of this."

"They don't have to. They want to. So let them. It's just a temporary situation, Nat, and when it's all over, you'll have plenty of time and ways to thank them for everything."

Everybody else is at the tables, talking and laughing, and then I think of something. "Hey, what was Bear doing across the hallway in that room?"

Dennis drops his head to the side so he can whisper, "When I got up to go get Sela, he was in her room."

My head whips toward him and I can feel the air hitting my eyeballs because they're open so wide, my eyebrows up in my hairline. "In Sela's room?"

"Yeah. Actually, in her bed."

"What? Are you serious?"

"I was shocked too."

"Do they know each other from somewhere else?"

"I don't think so. I mean, I haven't even seen them talking to each other."

"Wow." My brain is fishing for something else to say, but it's not coming up with anything. "Wow."

"Yeah. Wow. I'm pretty sure they don't realize that I saw him, so he moved across the hallway to the other room so nobody would catch him in there. I wondered how he got out of there without anybody seeing him, and then you ran into him."

"I did—I literally ran straight into him. Bounced off his chest. What the hell were they doing?"

He shakes his head as he rolls his eyes at me. "They sure as hell weren't playing checkers, babe."

"Wow." I hear him chuckle. "Well, I will say, at least she's tall enough to be a good match for him."

"Yeah, but can you imagine the shitstorm that would ensue if anybody from the agency knew she'd done that? They'd can her ass."

"Yes they would. So it's our secret. Right?"

Dennis nods. "Right. I mean, if the guy's gettin' some, I sure don't want to mess it up for him."

I couldn't be more shocked. Really. It's not like I think it's a bad thing. It's just a … surprise. A big one. As I sit there trying to fathom it, I hear one of the women yell, "Breakfast is ready!" Dennis stands and reaches down, takes my hand, and helps me up. He's right.

If Sela's managing to get some while she follows my stupid ass around, who am I to mess that up for her?

PADDY

. . .

I WORK ON THE BOAT MOTOR FOR A COUPLE OF HOURS, THEN check on Natalie. She assures me she's fine, sitting in the kitchen talking to the rest of the women, and I can see that being there with them, relaxing and chatting, is helping her feel normal. With a kiss on her cheek, I head back out to work on the boat.

Bear's running the grinder, taking the paint off the trailer, as I work on the motor. Bulldog and Reboot head toward the shop for some tools, and Priest has started carefully taking apart the upholstery so the guy at the upholstery shop can use the pieces as patterns. That requires him to take the pieces to our leather shop, take pictures of them with numbers on every piece, and then take them apart. Ghost is working on some of the wiring, and he carries some of it off into the shop because he has to solder on it and needs electricity. As soon as they all disappear, it's just me and Bear, and when he turns off the grinder for a minute, I quietly say, "I saw you."

He pivots just a little and stares at me. "You saw me?"

"Yeah. I saw you. Last night. In Sela's room."

"You must've seen somebody else because—"

"Cut the crap. I know it was you. And your secret is safe with me." I think he's about to say something when I add, "And Natalie told me about you coming out of the room across the hallway." He stands there silently, like he doesn't know what to do or say, so I repeat, "Bear, your secret is safe with me. I don't understand it, but it's none of my business, and—"

"Then why did you bring it up?"

"Because I wanted you to know that, first off, you're not as slick as you think, so you need to be a little smarter. And second, if you need somebody to talk to, you can talk to me."

His nod is slight, but I can see it. "If I needed to talk to anybody, it would be you."

That shocks me. "Yeah?"

"Yeah. You're the only other guy here who I trust as much as Patch."

Now I'm really puzzled. "Why?"

"Because you don't talk a lot. And that means whatever I tell you, you don't repeat it. And that makes me feel safe. So yeah. If I need somebody to talk to, it would be you or Patch. Or Baxter."

"Yeah. Baxter's a cool dude." If I can encourage him to talk to Baxter, I will.

"Yeah. I trust him. And the two of you. So don't fuck that up. Because I don't trust a lot of people, but I trust you, and I'd like to keep it that way."

"You can trust me. I'd never betray your trust," I assure him, and I wouldn't.

"And could you ask Natalie if she—"

"She's not going to say anything, Bear. I promise. She's a judge. She knows how important confidences are, and she'd never break yours."

"Tell her I said thanks, wouldja?"

I nod and smile. "I will. So you and Sela—"

He shrugs. "I really don't know. It's new, ya know?"

"I get it. I do." About that time, Reboot and Bulldog wander back out, so I shoot Bear a smile and get back to work.

By lunchtime, Natalie seems to be in better spirits, and that's encouraging. But she's also packing, and that makes me sad. "What time you planning to leave?"

"I'm thinking five. Gotta get everybody to my house and figure out where they're going to sleep. It's going to be really crowded around there."

When I showed up at her house yesterday, I had been so scared and stressed that, honestly, I didn't even look around. I have no idea how big the place is or how it's laid out. I do remember that the neighborhood isn't a bunch of big, fancy houses, so it's probably not that huge. "They won't all be sleeping at the same time. They'll take shifts, I'm sure."

"Oh. Yeah. You're probably right. Hadn't thought of that. So … What do you want to do for the rest of the afternoon?"

"Truth?" She nods. "I'd like to take a shower, then curl up on the bed with you and take a nap. Just a nap. No monkey business."

Her eyes narrow and her lips stretch into a tiny grin. "None?"

"No. None. Just us, close, holding each other, comfortable and safe. That's all. Is that something you'd be interested in?" I ask, taking her hand.

"Yes. Absolutely. Let's go get you a shower. While you're showering, I'm going to call my parents. They have no idea what's going on, and I think I owe them that."

"Okay. I agree." I'm going to shower, put on clean clothes, and cuddle up with her on the bed. I won't see her again until tomorrow night, so I have to make every moment count.

Natalie

As soon as he turns on the water, I dial the number. When my dad answers, I tell him to put me on speaker, and I explain to them what's happening and why. My mom is really upset; my dad is angry because I didn't call him and give him a chance to call in a bunch of favors, none of which would do me any good anyway. We talk for twenty minutes and when I hear the shower cut off, I say goodbye and wait for Dennis.

Those boxer briefs don't really hide much of anything and, damn, that's a fine-looking man. "You getting dressed?"

He shakes his head. "Figured I'd just nap in these. My clothes won't get wrinkled that way. You got a tee or something?"

"Yeah. Think I'll just put on a cami instead. It's a little warm in here."

"I can turn the air down," he offers.

"Would you? I think I'm perimenopausal." He shoots me a funny look. "Why do you look surprised? You know how old I am."

"I thought that was for older … I mean, not that you're old or—"

"*Peri*menopause, babe. It's what happens before menopause. Little signs, but not full-blown. Hot flash here, weight gain there, exhausted one day next week."

"Oh. I don't know anything about any of that stuff."

I just laugh. "You'll learn quickly enough! At some point, I'll bite your head off and you'll be bewildered. And then you'll figure it out."

"So forewarned is forearmed, huh?" he asks and laughs.

"Something like that. I have an appointment with my scoot-down doctor tomorrow, so she'll probably run some bloodwork and stuff and I'll see where I am with it."

Without another word, he hops up, heads to the thermostat, turns it down, and comes back to pull me down on the bed. "There. That should do it."

"Thank you."

"You're welcome. Now, cuddle up and let's take a little nap."

I feel him moving around and peer back over my shoulder to see him pulling the comforter up and over him. "You cold?"

A little chuckle erupts in his throat. "Freezing. But it's okay. I'll be warm as long as you're here." I just scoot backward, my back against his chest, and his arms wrap around me. "Oh, yeah. Much better."

"I'm sorry."

His arms squeeze me a little tighter and he sighs. "Listen, it may be my job to make you do what I want in bed, but it's also my job to make you feel comfortable and safe."

I know he can't see me, but I smile. "And I do."

"Then my work here is done." He wiggles just a little, like he's trying to settle in, and then he kisses the back of my neck. "Mmmm. Sleep, baby."

I'm going to sleep, and I hope I dream about him, about us. My heart is so full. I love this man so much, and I can't stand the thought that I'm going home and won't see him until tomorrow night. How the hell will I get through next weekend? It'll be the longest weekend of my life, I'm sure.

But when I think about the possibility of bringing these creeps to his kids, I know staying away next weekend is the right thing. I can't put them at risk. No way. They'll be safe here with all the guys, and we're grownups. We can miss a weekend. But it's going to be so hard—

"Why are you tensing up? What's going on, sweet pea?"

I let out a long sigh. "I'm just thinking about next weekend and how hard it's going to be to not be with you."

"Nat, a million things can happen between now and next weekend. Don't borrow trouble. Just relax and take it one day at a time, okay?"

All I can do is sigh. "I hate this."

I hear him chuckle. "Lying here with me?"

"No, silly! Of course not! I'd rather be here with you than anywhere else."

"You know what Tony told me one time?" When I shake my head, he says, "He said that one of their favorite things to do together is nap. Not sex, just a nap in the middle of the day, especially if it's raining. He said he worked so hard for so many years that a nap seemed like something he just couldn't manage. Now they curl up together, and he said he's never felt safer or more loved than when they're just snuggled up in bed together, hiding away from the world."

"I hope I get to meet them."

"You will. I promise. I would imagine Steve has told them to stay away for the time being. Hell, they already have to have bodyguards."

"Why?"

He snorts. "Nat, they're worth about forty billion dollars."

I think I heard him wrong. "Did you say forty million?"

"No. Forty *billion*. They got a tip that there was a kidnapping being planned. To take Nikki. This was a year or so ago. Steve insists that they have bodyguards now. Most of their family does. He says it's just not safe. I'm sure he's right. Last thing they need is to be here in the middle of this."

"That's true." I'm starting to get warm, comfortable, and drowsy. "I think I can actually sleep now."

"Then sleep, babe. I'll be right here, and Sela's just outside the door. You're safe here."

Safe. For the moment, I do feel safe, but I wonder how long that will last.

PADDY

. . .

I DON'T TAKE NAPS, SO TWO HOURS IN THE MIDDLE OF THE day seemed like some kind of vacation. But now comes the hard part.

"You about ready?" I hear Sela ask as she sticks her head in the front door.

"Yeah. Just a few more things. Ten minutes tops," Natalie answers, and a sharp pain shoots through my chest. She's leaving. I know it's not because she wants to but, damn, it still hurts.

"Anything I can go ahead and take out?" I ask.

"Yeah. The blue bag and the floral one over there."

On my way back from putting them in the trunk, Sela stops me. "You know she's going to be fine, right?"

All I can do is shrug. "I'm trying to tell myself that."

"She will be. There will be five of us with her at all times, sometimes watching the doors, sometimes escorting her, but she'll never be alone. Never."

"I get it, Sela. I do. But somehow that doesn't make me feel a bit better."

For the first time since she's been here, I see a little fissure in the professional façade of Sela Baldwin when she places a soft hand on my shoulder. "I understand. But we're going to do everything we can to keep her safe. It's our job, and we all take it seriously, the other agents *and* Steve's guys. Marshall will be on our detail, and I really don't think I've ever met a tougher motherfucker, so she couldn't have better people with her. We'll get her through this. Try not to worry, okay?"

"I'm trying. Really, I am, but it's hard." For a split second, I think I might ask her about Bear, but I decide against it. If the FBI found out about that, they could consider it a terrible lapse in judgment on her part, and I really don't want to be responsible for outing the woman who's keeping my woman safe.

Ten minutes later, everything is loaded and we're standing at the cars. "So you'll stay in touch, right?" I ask as she stands there. Her attempts at putting on a brave face aren't working. She looks terrified.

"Of course. I'll call you as soon as I get home and get settled."

"Good. I'll be waiting. Natalie …" For a brief moment, I think about all the people standing around us, and suddenly, I realize I don't give a shit. Fuck 'em. "Babe, you know I love you. I'll still be here when all of this is over." We're clinging to each other like we're drowning, and my heart is breaking because I'm so scared. "It's thirty minutes to your house. Thirty miles. But it might as well be next door, because that's where our hearts are—side by side. We'll do what we have to do to keep you alive, and when we're past that, we'll live our lives. I promise."

Her hand is soft on my cheek when she pulls back and looks up into my eyes. "I love you, Dennis. I'll be careful, I promise. I'd better get going. Sela is going to pee her pants if we're not at my house before dark."

"Gotta do my sweep," the tall woman announces, her eyes scanning all around. That's when I spot him.

Bear is standing just outside the kitchen door, leaning against the wall, watching all of us. But I know he's not watching all of us. He's watching Sela. There really *is* something going on between them. Nobody will find out from me.

"Yeah. Go do your sweep, and thank you," I say without turning to look at the FBI agent.

"Yessir. Doin' my job. Come on, Natalie. We need to get moving."

"Okay. Bye, babe. See you tomorrow evening." She starts

away, and our hands stay clasped until they've reached their limit, her fingers sliding from mine. It takes everything I have to keep from running to her, climbing in the car, and letting them take me too, regardless of my responsibilities here, but I can't. She's got work tomorrow, and so do I. We've got to keep trying to have a regular life. It's hard, but we have to.

The cars start to move and in under a minute, they're gone from sight, with Natalie waving out the back window. I'm standing there, lost in thought, when I feel a presence beside me. I don't even have to look; I know who it is. His big voice is nothing more than a whisper when he says, "She'll be okay."

"Yeah. Sela will keep her safe."

"She absolutely will."

Without turning my head, I cut my eyes toward him. "So what's—"

"Nope. I know you saw. Not answering any questions."

"But—"

"Can't answer your questions because I don't know the answers to them myself. When I do, you'll know. That's if there's anything to know. And there might not be."

"Do you *want* there to be answers to those questions?" I turn to look at him.

Without looking my direction, he shrugs. "I don't know that either." Then he turns to meet my gaze. "But I'd appreciate it if you'd keep your mouth shut."

"Wouldn't dream of saying a word."

"Thanks. You're a good guy, Paddy. I hope this all works out for you."

"Thanks. I hope it all works out for you too."

He lets out a deep sigh and shoves his hands in his pockets as he starts to amble off, but before he's out of earshot, he says, "That would take a miracle."

After all those years in prison, I have a girlfriend who's a federal judge, and my sons are coming to see me next week. I'm not sure if he's noticed, but miracles do happen. I'm living proof.

Natalie

As soon as I get home and I've called Dennis, I start on laundry and dishes. They're still sitting there from when I left, and they've got to be done. When all of that is straightened out, I start working on getting everybody settled in rooms. It's a three-bedroom house, so I've got two bedrooms with a Citadel guy and an FBI guy to a room, and Sela says she won't mind bunking with me, if I can stand it. I assure her that's not a problem. One of Steve's guys and one of the FBI agents will take the first indoor shift and one of each will stay awake inside, so Sela and I will get some sleep. A few hours later, the other guys will get up and let the first four sleep, and they'll rotate around. We left the other four Citadel guys at the farm, which makes me feel a little better.

At bedtime, I pull out my phone, and as soon as she sees me with it, Sela mumbles something about needing a snack and disappears into the hallway. She knows I'm calling Dennis, and she doesn't want to eavesdrop. It only rings once on my end before he answers with, "Hey, sweet pea."

"Hi. You doin' okay?"

"Yeah. How 'bout you?"

"Eh. Okay. Getting ready for bed. I've got a long day tomorrow."

"You're going to London, right?"

"Yep. Pretrial. I'm sure they'll be there," I throw in.

"I'm sure they will be. You just hang tough and don't let them see you afraid. Make sure you're confident."

"I can fake it 'til I make it," I assure him.

"Okay. Get some sleep. I'm turning in myself. And I love you, Natalie. Don't forget that."

"I won't. Don't forget that I love you too."

"I won't. Night, baby."

"Night." Even after he hangs up, I hold the phone to my ear, praying for another minute's conversation. But I really do need some sleep.

I don't know if Sela was listening outside the door, but she steps back into the room almost instantly when I put the phone on the charger. "Everything good?" she asks.

"Yeah. It is." I think about it for a second before I say, "Hey, can I ask you something? If it's too personal—"

"I just won't answer it," she snaps.

"Good enough. So Dennis said when he went out into the hallway, he thought he saw—"

"Too personal."

"Uh-huh. Okay. Never mind."

"Look." She turns toward me before she starts to speak. "I like you. You're a nice person. But getting too personal with the people I'm serving can make me sloppy. It's not that I don't care about your life. I'm absolutely obsessed with your life. Not the minutiae. The *alive* part of your life. As for the personal part, I won't be around long enough to know much about that. When the bureau deems your threat dissipated, then I have to go. So it's nothing personal. My goal here is not to get to know you. It's to make sure that you live a long, healthy, happy life insofar as I can help you do that. Otherwise, not my place."

"Got it." Yeah. I've got it, all right. She wants to use Bear to get her happy on, and then she'll walk away like he never existed. If he knows that, it's okay. That's part of John Stuart Mill's philosophy, the difference between a means and a mere means. Asking somebody to lunch to get information on a job opening and pretending to be their friend is a mere means to an end, and it's wrong. But asking somebody to lunch to get information on a job opening and making it clear that that's the only purpose of the lunch, not friendship, is a means to an end, and as long as they understand that and consent by going to lunch with you, it's fine. It's never okay to use someone as a mere means to an end without their knowledge or consent. If that's what she's doing to Bear, I'll never forgive her for it. I think before this is all over, we'll be having that conversation. Matter of fact, I know we will.

THANK GOD SELA DOESN'T SNORE, AND WHEN I WAKE UP AT five thirty and head to the kitchen, she's already got coffee going. Then I realize something. What if the reason she didn't snore was because she didn't sleep all night? Now I'm wondering if she ever sleeps.

Before too long, I'm ready and we're heading out the door. Two of the guys ride in front, and Sela and I ride in the back. The other six men bring up the rear in two other cars. The drive to the courthouse is uneventful, and I'm in my chambers fifteen minutes before the pretrial conference is due to start.

When I step into the courtroom, everyone is already there—including the two guys, who are once again sitting in the back. There's a third man with them today, and I try not to stare while also trying to memorize his face. I can't say a word about what happened. Anything I might say about that could taint someone's opinion of the defendants and cause a mistrial, so I have to stay quiet, but I'm pretty sure Quentin Asher knows about all of it. One of the bailiffs surely told him. Albert Collins? No. The defense attorney doesn't have any idea unless whoever hired him for the defendants told him. If they did that, he's as guilty as they are. It occurs to me that he may have told them their only option is to kill me because they stand such a poor chance of getting off from these charges, but I have to hope that's not the case.

"You may be seated," the bailiff says after I've taken my seat.

"Good morning. I hope everyone is ready to proceed. Mr. Collins, we've all received copies of your discovery and evidence. I trust you have, Mr. Asher?"

"Yes, Your Honor."

"And you've submitted your own?"

"Yes, Your Honor."

"Mr. Collins, is there anything else you need to submit?"

"No, Your Honor. You have everything we have."

"Gentlemen, are there any witnesses who will need special accommodations for any kind of physical or emotional difficulties?" I have two dozen questions I have to ask before we can move on, so I'm trying to be efficient. I also have to run through their witness list with them, and that's pretty easy too.

We finish all of it before lunchtime, so I can take a deep breath and head back to chambers. They've beefed up security at the courthouse, so one of the agents and one of the bailiffs are together in my chambers when I step in. Sela is, of course, right inside the doorway, and she has been the entire time I was on the bench, watching covertly through the barely-open door. Another bailiff goes out to pick up lunch for us, and we sit in my chambers and eat quietly.

As soon as lunch is over, I have an arraignment on a big embezzlement case, but that doesn't take long. I have that doctor appointment at three forty-five, and I want to get finished before then so I can run by the house, freshen up a bit, and go on. I don't know what we're going to do about dinner. Dennis will be in class tonight, and he'll come over when he's finished. I can barely wait.

I'm out the door by ten before three, and the cars head toward my house. While they're driving, I press the contact and wait. "Hey, babe!"

I smile when I hear his voice. "Hey. Having a good day?"

"Yeah. Got two scabbards finished. Got a third one cut out, and I got my leather dies, so I'm tapping the designs in. It's kinda fun. Your day okay?"

"Yeah. They had the third guy with them today, but nothing happened. I'm headed home now to freshen up a little before I go to the doctor."

He laughs. "Oh, yeah. Don't want swamp crotch in the gyno's office."

"Nooo. That would be *soooo* embarrassing! So call me when you're on your way after school?"

"I will. And you be careful. I love you."

"Love you too. I'll talk to you in a bit. Bye."

"Bye, babe."

I hit END and smile. "Everything okay out at the farm?" Sela asks.

"Yeah. So far, so good."

"Good. Everything's gonna be fine, Natalie." I hope she's right.

I make it to the doctor's office at three twenty-five and fill out all the paperwork. They call me back at three thirty-five, and five minutes later, I'm in a paper dress and stirrups. "She doesn't want to talk to me first?"

"We'll save that for afterward," the nurse says, and that seems strange to me, but whatever.

The doctor comes hustling in five minutes later. "Hi, Natalie! I'm Dr. Perkins. How are you?"

"I'm good, thanks. A little chilly but—"

She laughs, and I like the way it sounds. "Everybody says that! Sorry. The rest of us have clothes on, you know."

"Yeah. Actually, I'm a little surprised that I'm chilly. I think I've been having hot flashes."

"Let's see. You're forty-one … You could be peri-menopausal."

"That's one of the things I wanted to talk to you about."

"So let's see what we've got down here and then we'll have a nice long conversation," she says, standing between my legs at the end of the table. "Now I'm going to …"

She's probably the gentlest doctor I've ever been to. I really like her. I always liked Dr. Lourdes, and I was pretty sure when I came here that I'd have a hard time finding a doctor I liked, but so far, she's a peach. When she's finished with the pelvic, she does a rectal. After that, she scrubs her arms all the way up to the elbow, puts on another pair of gloves, and does a breast exam on me. "You've got really dense breast tissue. Have you had a mammogram?"

"No."

"I think it's time for your first one. I'll order it. Here. Let me help you sit up and we can talk."

What takes place next is the best conversation I've ever had with a doctor. She asks me questions and actually listens to my answers. Finally, she says, "Yeah. I'd say you're peri-menopausal. Of course, it's all the more reason for you to stay on birth control, because you could certainly get pregnant, and if you do, you'll be a high-risk pregnancy. Not something you want to have happen accidentally. If you decide you want to get pregnant, we'll need to talk more, plan carefully, expect extra monitoring. Okay?"

"No plans to, but okay."

"In the meantime, I'm going to order the mammogram and some bloodwork. That will tell us if you need some kind of intervention hormonally, but otherwise, you seem very healthy. The nurse in check-out will give you the information for the tests. And it was really nice to meet you, Natalie. Let me know if you have any more questions or anything comes up, okay?"

"Okay. I will. And thank you so much."

"You're so very welcome. Have a lovely evening and just head on out when you're dressed and ready."

The first person I see when I step out of the room is Sela. She's been standing in the hallway the whole time. My tone is intentionally snarky when I ask, "Why didn't you just come on in?"

"Because I don't like going to my crotch-watcher. I sure didn't need to be in the room while you were with yours."

"What, you don't think she had an emergency exit she could've dragged me out of?"

"They don't have those in gynos' offices. If they did, I would've already found one," she answers with a sneer.

I stop at the desk, and the lady there tells me where to go for the mammogram and bloodwork. The physician's office is in the hospital, and so are the imaging and lab offices, so at least it'll be easy to get to. She says I can go on down for the bloodwork, and imaging will schedule my mammogram if I'll go by their office. "Got a couple of stops to make before we leave the building."

"Okay. Right behind you." We make our way out of the office, and once we're in the hallway, I stop. "What?"

"I don't know exactly how to get to those offices. I've

never been in this building before. There's got to be a directory around here somewhere." We head toward the elevators where I can see two of our guys standing by, waiting, but down the other hallway, I see something on the wall. "I think that's one right down there."

Sure enough, it's another bank of elevators, and there's a directory right beside them. There's a sign above them that reads STAFF ONLY. Why did they put the directory by the staff elevator? I swear, for a building full of Ph.D.s, they sure aren't the smartest. "Let's see. The lab is—" That's when I hear it. A click. And I turn.

There's a man behind Sela, his arm around her neck and a gun pointed at her head, and I feel something cold on the back of my own head. An arm snakes around my neck, and I hear him whisper, "Ahhh, *bonitas tetas*, we meet again. Quiet or we'll kill you both." The guy holding Sela kicks the door behind him and it swings wide—the stairwell. Shit. The guys don't know where we are. "Let's go, *perra*," he growls and shoves me toward the door.

As soon as we're through that doorway, he shoves me up against a wall face-first. "Stand there. Don't move." I hear movement, and then he's back. I'm pretty sure he just disarmed Sela, because she looks pissed as hell. "Okay. Let's go. Quiet. I guess if you must be shot, the hospital is a good place to die. If they find you in time, maybe you live. But just maybe," he says with an ominous chuckle, and my heart freezes. What do they think they're going to do with us? He can't keep me until the trial is over. That would be months.

Oh, god. They're planning to kill us.

CHAPTER 10

Paddy

As soon as work is over, I clean up, eat dinner, and head to the school. My mind is racing. I'm terrified I won't be able to cut it and I'll fail. That would let Nikki down, and I can't do that. And I'm worrying about Natalie too, although I shouldn't. Sela and the guys are with her. She'll be fine.

I'd thought about buying a car. I mean, I'm going to be driving back and forth, and I can't keep using Patch's truck, but they let me know quickly that I won't have to. Everywhere I go, they'll be taking me, so having a car isn't necessary, at least right now. Once this thing is over, I can buy one, and I'll need to get one big enough for the boys to be comfortable in. I'm sure we'll be going places and doing things.

The class is larger than I thought it would be, but it's still only about twenty people. I was expecting only about twelve, but honestly, with employment being what it is in this area, I shouldn't be surprised. I hear the vocational-technical portion of the school is really busy these days, more so than the community college and its core classes. People are looking for quick training that'll give them high-dollar positions, and the trades will do that. The instructor seems nice, and when he finds out I'm part of the App STAR team, he asks me to come up and talk about what we do. I didn't realize until that moment how proud I am to serve with the team, and I hope that pride comes through when I speak about them.

When we take our break, there are a lot of other people taking breaks too. There are plumbing students, and electrical, and auto body, some culinary arts people, and even people taking courses to be security guards. There's a really nice lady in her fifties or so who's in the tailoring classes, and when she realizes I'm with the team, she comes over to thank me for helping to find her neighbor who was lost while he was out hunting morel mushrooms. We strike up a conversation, and I find out that she knows Tinsley and Audrey too. It's a small world. The whole time I'm out there, I'm aware of my bodyguards standing here and there inconspicuously, and I don't acknowledge them. I know they wouldn't want me to. They're almost invisible, and that's how they want it.

Just as we're walking back in, I try to call Natalie, but she doesn't answer, and I figure she's in the shower or something. No biggie. I'll call her when I leave.

The rest of the evening is concentrated on watching videos to see how squeamish we are. A couple of people have to leave the room. They're not going to make it. After seeing what happened to Michael, nothing seems that bad to me, even people who've been ripped up by bears or had half their head blown off with a shotgun. Nothing compares to Michael's death—nothing.

We're finished at nine, so I meet up with what I've decided I'll dub my "crew" and stroll out to the parking lot. Two of them are already out there, one at each car, and the other two are with me, and I notice that they're looking at each other oddly. "Is something going on?"

"No," one of them answers abruptly.

I ride in the front car with two guys named Alex and Tim, and Rick and Greg are in the car behind us. Everyone is oddly silent. Alex is driving, and just as we get onto Natalie's street, I see Tim poking the screen on his phone. "Stop the car," he barks, and Alex comes to a dead halt, the car behind us doing the same. "Greg and Rick are going ahead of us. We're staying here." I watch as the big black sedan passes us and parks two blocks down. I can see the doors open, but that's about it. It's pretty dark. In a few seconds, Tim says, "All clear."

We pull up in front of Natalie's house and my heart stops. It's totally dark. I see a light snap on in the living room. "What's going on?"

"Stay put." Tim hops out and leaves me in the car with Alex, windows up and doors locked behind him. In ten seconds, he's back. "Get him inside."

There's a mad dash as Alex runs to my door, snatches me out by the arm, and runs up the front steps with me. Rick and Greg are both on their phones. "Yeah, when? Uh-huh. Okay. Yeah. In forty-five. Bye," Greg says as he cuts his call. "Sit down. We need to talk." The other three guys are still on their phones, and they're speaking in very hushed tones. I don't like this at all.

"What's going on?"

Greg sits down in the chair across from where I've taken a spot on the sofa. "Natalie and Sela are missing."

"What? What the hell do you mean, they're missing?" I see Alex step out the front door, which makes me want to hear his conversation even more. "How can they be missing? There were eight agents with them. Eight. Four of whom are FBI. They can't be missing."

"She finished at the doctor's office. The office told Marshall that they checked her out, gave her instructions for going to the lab and imaging, and she and Sela left. But Marshall and Carlton were at the elevators on that floor, and Phillip and Yates were at the elevators on the ground floor, and they never came down. Police are there. They've done a sweep of the building and they haven't found a trace of them. They never made it to the lab or the imaging center, so somebody took them from the floor the doctor's office is on."

No. This can't be happening. It just can't be. This wasn't supposed to happen. I whip out my phone and hit the contact, then wait for it to ring. "Hey, bud."

It's hard to keep from being completely hysterical, but they can't help me if I can't tell Patch what's going on. "Do you know what's happened?"

After a few seconds of silence, he says. "No."

I start to tell him, and I can feel myself slipping. It's pouring out of me, the few details I know, and I'm talking so fast that I can't breathe. When I finish, I wail, "God, Patch, what do I do? I've got to find her!"

His voice is measured and quiet. "Come home, Paddy. I'll call Sheriff Stafford and Sela's boss, and I'll call Izzy and Steve too. We'll find them, I promise, but … Hey, Steve's calling me right now. Get them to bring you home. You need to be here with us. Okay? Come on home."

Home. I want to be there, but I want it to be with Natalie. "Okay. Yeah. I'll get them to bring me. I'll be there in a bit."

"Okay. Gotta get this call. We love you, buddy. Come home." And the phone goes dead.

Terror fills every cell in my body. She's out there somewhere. I don't know where. I don't know how to find her. I don't even know where to start. Maybe in the meantime Patch will figure out what to do.

All I can do right now is do what he said.

I need to go home.

Natalie

The trunk is tiny, and Sela and I are squished in here like tuna in a can. They've bound our hands and feet, and there's tape over our mouths. I can feel Sela doing something, though. In a couple of minutes, I hear her gasp. "Well, that's a little better. I've got the tape off my mouth. Listen to me. Don't panic. We're going to get out of this. I need you to roll as far away from me as you can. Can you do that?" I make a noise behind the tape and try to roll, but it's hard. I have no way of pushing. All I can do is try to throw my weight forward. That lands me with the trunk latch pressing against my shoulder, but that's okay. She's still wiggling, but suddenly, I hear her say, "There we go! I got the rope off my hands."

There's a tearing sensation across my face, and I can breathe easier with the tape off. "How the hell did you do that?"

"There's something back here in the trunk, I think maybe a jack, and I rubbed the rope on it until it broke. Let me get yours untied since your back is to me right now." I can feel her gently working the ropes and in a couple of seconds, they loosen. "Almost got it. Yeah!" My hands are now free, and I rub my wrists to get the blood circulating again. "It's going to be hard to get our ankles untied, but I think we can do it."

It takes some finagling, but we both manage. "Now what?"

"Now we wait until they stop and open the trunk. As soon as they do, we've got to make a break for it. I want you to run. Don't worry about me. Just run like your ass is on fire. We've got to put the tape back on our mouths. They won't be able to see our hands and feet, so we make like they're still tied until we're out and then we hit it. Do you understand?"

"Yeah. Run."

"Yeah. Like Bigfoot is chasing you. Like a chupacabra is on your tail. Like—"

"Fuck, Sela, I get it! Shit."

"Good. You're in a bitchy mood. It'll serve you well."

"Aren't you in a bitchy mood too? You should be." I huff.

"No. I get paid to not be in a bitchy mood because if I'm in a bitchy mood, I'm not thinking as clearly, and one of us has to be thinking clearly."

"So now I'm addlebrained?"

"Wow. You really *are* in a bitchy mood!"

Ten minutes later, I'm even bitchier. They've turned off the main road and we're bouncing along some kind of rutted wagon path, or at least that's what it feels like. I'll have a concussion just from my head banging around. And then the car stops.

Sela hisses, "Remember the plan." I do. I'd run anyway, even if that wasn't the plan. I want the hell outta here and away from these assholes.

There's talking, but it's in Spanish, and although I can hold my own in the language, with the trunk lid closed, it's impossible to tell what they're saying. The exhaust fumes dissipate and I can smell mud, wet leaves, and just general outdoors-type smells. Matter of fact, there's a little whiff of skunk in there somewhere. There's a sound that I can only assume is them pissing on the ground, and then the very muffled sound of footsteps. I was right. We're not on a gravel road. Matter of fact, I'm wondering if we've stopped because wherever we are, ahead is impassable.

I catch the phrase, "Too open. Up in the trees somewhere." They're planning to take us up in the trees and kill us. I hear a *pop!*, and there's daylight.

One of them grabs me first and drags me out by the hair, so it's really hard to keep my hands together behind my back, but I manage. The other one grabs Sela, and as soon as I know her feet are on the ground, my knee comes up and both thumbs head straight for his eyes. He lets out a scream of pain, and the one who has Sela does the same. I don't know where she is and right now, I don't care. My feet are already moving, and I'm tearing through the brush and undergrowth like a demon, both men shrieking and screaming obscenities. I can hear Sela's footsteps right behind me, so I know I'm not alone. The tape is back on our mouths, and I realize there was another reason she did that—I can't talk to her and she can't talk to me. We're running silently through the forest, no sound except our crashing footsteps, and the men are behind us, yelling and bitching, so we know exactly where they are. And we just keep running.

There's a small clearing with more open space beyond it, and I run toward it, but when I step out, I leap back. It's a bluff, a high one, maybe fifty feet. Sela almost knocks me over the edge. In one smooth move, she rips the tape from her mouth and glares at me. "Back to the abyss. When they come, fight. Fight with everything you have, and while you're struggling, grab the guy, spin him with his back to the drop, and push. You'll go over too, but he'll cushion you. Got it?"

Frankly, that sounds like suicide, but whatever. We're trapped. Both men, their faces scratched and bloodied from the whip-like branches we've all run through, come bursting into the clearing, and they don't see what we already know is there. I try to sidestep the one coming for me, but he grabs me, and I do exactly what Sela said to do. I feel us falling, and the only thing I see as I go down is the asshole's face, his eyes wide with terror, looking up into mine. The ground is rushing up, and we …

My arm hurts. My leg hurts. I don't know how long I've been in this position, but it's dark now, so it's been a while. I'm lying on something soft, and I feel around with the arm that doesn't hurt. Whatever it is, it's got hair attached to it, and then I start to remember. It's the guy who was chasing me. He's under me. Sela said that's what would happen, and it did. Sela. Where's Sela?

It's so dark that it's hard to see, and it hurts to move my head. It's turned to the right, and I don't see her there, so she must be on the other side. I need to get up and go to her, make sure she's okay, but I can't. I don't think I can move. Everything hurts.

I've been lying there for I don't know how long when I hear a groan, and it's not deep enough to be the man, so it must be Sela. "Sela? Sela, you okay?" Another groan, and then silence. Where are we? We were in the trunk, so I have no idea where we are. I can't see anything. It's too dark. They took my phone, so I don't have that. There's no way to get help.

I'm so tired. Letting myself just fall asleep seems like the right thing. Nobody's going to find us. They don't even have the vaguest notion where to start looking. Even if I had a way to communicate, I wouldn't know what to tell them. All I can do is wait.

It occurs to me that I may never see Dennis again on this side of eternity. A good life. That's what I want for him, to have a good life, to reunite with his boys, to find a woman who'll love him the way I do. I couldn't have known a month ago that I'd meet my soulmate. And I couldn't have known a week ago that I'd leave him behind. But he'll be okay. He's got the guys, and the Walters family, and his own family. And I won't hurt anymore. Right now, that's all I really want.

My eyes are closing when I see a man just a few feet away from me. Who is he? "Help. Me," I try to say, but no words come out.

"You're going to be fine, Natalie. It'll be okay." Even though I'm willing my arm to reach out to him, it won't, and I feel a desperation I've never felt before. "Trust me. Dennis will find you."

As I watch through one cracked eyelid, he disappears and I'm alone in the dark. Why didn't he help me? He was right there! But now I'm alone.

All I can do is close my eyes and hope for a miracle.

Paddy

Our car pulls in at the farm, and I'm stunned. There have to be fifty cars there, most of which are sleek, black sedans or big SUVs. Feds. An agent is missing, and they've come to find their own.

The first person who notices me when I step into the kitchen is Penny, and she rushes me and wraps her arms around me tightly. "Oh, Paddy, honey, we're gonna find them. Please know that."

"I don't know anything right now. I'm so scared." A hand presses against my back, and I turn to see a man standing there, someone I don't know, but his eyes are familiar, and in a blinding flash, I realize who he is. "Mr. Anderson?"

"Dennis, I wish we didn't have to meet this way. I hope somebody can do something to find her."

"Me too." There's a small woman beside him, and she's crying so hard that she can't speak. "I'm so sorry, Mrs. Anderson."

"It's Pauline, dear, and I know. I'm so scared!" Her crying ramps up, and I understand. If I had time, I'd cry too.

"Listen up, everyone!" a tall man yells as he stands on top of one of the tables. "I'm spearheading this search. Let me tell you where we are with this. We were able to pull surveillance footage from the medical plaza and identify the car they were taken away in, and we got the plate number. It's a rental out of Florida, plate number …" As he reads it off, everyone in the building is writing it down, some on their hands. "Because it's a rental, it has a transponder in it, and we've been able to track it to an approximate location before the signal dropped, probably because of back-country terrain. Its last known location was somewhere in this area." There's a map on a big whiteboard, and he draws a circle, a far too large circle, in an area not far from here. "Is there anyone here who knows this area well?"

Sheriff Stafford speaks up. "I do, and I know Preston Ramage does too." Preston gives the agent a little salute from offside. I can see Justin Lark with him, so the Hazard Police Department is represented. There are a lot of other law enforcement people here, uniforms I don't recognize, so I'm betting Perry County is here too. I doubt there's anybody here from London. They're probably still working the scene at the medical building.

The tall man points to them. "We'll be coordinating with them. Do any of your agencies have a tracking dog?" Everybody is looking at each other and shaking their heads.

And then Patch speaks up. "One's on the way. ETA of about forty-five minutes."

Oh my god. Raiden's coming, and he's bringing Duke. I'd trust the Eagle Point men with my life, and they're coming to help. For the first time since this has started, I feel a glimmer of hope.

The tall man starts to say something, but Patch interrupts him. "I'm not finished. All of my flight guys, you need to get some rest. We'll be taking the bird up tomorrow morning at first light. Everybody else can help with the search, but we've got to have the bird. Izzy?"

"Yeah, chief," she answers from somewhere in the back of the room.

"Will Commander Grummond assign you?"

"Yes, sir, I'm pretty sure she will. I'll call her right now and get it set up."

"There's a good chance you'll need a hoist operator. Bulldog can ride with you guys as your medical liaison."

"Copy that, chief."

"My crew will be Ghost, Reboot, and Paddy."

A guy in a Perry County deputy's uniform says, "I was a field medic. I'll work as second if anybody needs me."

"I was too," another guy in a Boyle County uniform says.

"We can use you guys on the ground." Patch turns and looks at the tall man on the table. "Not trying to steal your thunder. I'm just far more accustomed to coordinating medical rescues than most of you."

"Actually, than any of us," the man says with a smile. "We don't usually do that."

"But we do, so we've got it covered."

"Patch, please," I hear myself pleading, "can't we go up tonight? Please? It's going to be cold out, and if she's, they're, hurt, they need us now."

"No. Too dark. We don't know what's waiting for us out there. That's what we got into with Izzy. The ground teams can work in the dark, but I'm not taking that bird up tonight."

"I'll take mine up. I'm not afraid," Izzy says, and her eyes are welded to Patch. "You chicken, chief?"

"No. I'm not chi … Fine. We'll take it up, but we won't be able to see anything."

"Thank you," I say, my voice sounding weird and strangled.

"But we're not going up until the dog gets here. There's no point."

The guy on the table nods. "I agree with Captain Scott. We need to find the car first, and once we do that, the dog will be able to take us to them. That's our best hope."

I hope Raiden and Duke get here soon. This can't wait until morning. We need to find them now.

Before it's too late.

Paddy

The tall man who stood on the table has a name. He's FBI Special Agent in Charge Wendell Klutz. His name obviously isn't indicative of his abilities or he wouldn't be an SAC.

"How does that work? Honestly, the experience I've had with dogs would fit on the head of a straight pin," he says with no signs of embarrassment. I like a guy who can admit when he's ignorant on a subject and is willing to learn.

"We have the last recorded position of the car, and from there, Duke will be able to pick up the scent," Patch explains.

"Even if they drove on farther?"

"Possibly. If not, we have a couple of deputies in this group who are excellent trackers. They should be able to follow the path of the vehicle and find it. And once the vehicle is found …"

He nods. "Got it. So who is this guy?"

"Former Coast Guard dog handler. Raiden Walker. Dog's name is Duke. Bloodhound. You see Raiden, you see Duke. They're a pair. They work with Eagle Point Search and Rescue out of Fallport, Virginia."

"Can't wait to meet them. How do you know them?"

"The guy who founded the Eagle Point team is Ethan Watson. Former Navy SEAL. I knew him from the service."

"So you were military?"

"Yeah. Lost this eye under fire in Afghanistan. Chief warrant officer doing MEDEVAC and CASEVAC in a Sikorsky HH-60 Pave Hawk called Early Bird. Busted glass got me."

"You guys had a tough time over there. Glad you made it back."

"Yeah. A lot of us didn't. Most of the ones who made it back carry scars, a lot of which can't be seen." I've heard Patch talk about his deployments, and it was terrifying. He's ten times the man I'll ever be.

The kitchen door flies open and Ethan "Chaos" Watson strolls in. "Whaddya say, brothers?" he calls out, and every guy from the farm heads toward him. Right behind him is Drew Koopman, and Raiden and Duke bring up the rear.

"Boy, are we glad to see you guys!" Patch calls back as we all encircle them. There are hugs and back slaps all around, and then Ethan turns his attention to me.

"I hear you've got a vested interest in this search."

I nod, trying hard to keep tears from welling in my eyes. "I do."

Ethan's smile is gentle. "I'm going to do everything I can to give you the chance to say that officially in front of somebody who can make that happen."

"Thanks."

"You're welcome. I know you guys would do it for us. Plus you're the cool kids. You've got the big helicopter!" he says with a chuckle.

"Come over here and let me introduce you to the FBI special agent in charge," Patch tells them, and in a second, he's whisked them away and headed for Klutz. I'm left standing there with my guys.

"We'd better get our shit together. They're going to be ready to head out in a few minutes," Bulldog whispers. I take a glance at Bear, and he's not looking so good.

"You okay, buddy?" I whisper to him.

"Yeah. I'm fine. I'll be fine. Let's go suit up, get our go-bags, and get ready."

We hear a feminine voice over the crowd of men. "I just spoke to Commander Grummond. It's a go. Bulldog, you're with me," Izzy barks.

"Yes, ma'am. On my way. See you guys later," he says to us as he heads toward her.

I can hear Izzy talking to him as they jet toward the door. "Laurie and Pablo are meeting us at the helipad and …"

"Guess we'd better go get ready," Bear says. Everybody

else turns away, but before I can move, his hand is on my arm, and his voice is so low that I can barely hear it when he says, "I'm scared, Paddy."

"Me too. But we have to find them. For good or bad, we have to bring them home."

He nods. "Yep. We have to bring them home."

And so we're going to go out there to bring them home. No matter what.

THANK GOD FOR THE FBI'S BUDGET. EVERY GUY IN THE group has on a headlamp. They're the brightest motherfuckers I've ever seen. I mean, it would light up a whole house. From up in the air, we can see them trailing through the woods, a group over there, one just south of them, another east of them. The woods are full of men, and we've been in the air for less than five minutes when I hear a radio transmission. "All search and rescue personnel, use channel seventeen alpha. Repeat, turn to channel seventeen alpha. Over."

As soon as Ghost spins the dial, I hear a voice. "All search personnel, we have found the vehicle. Repeat, we have found the vehicle. Over."

"This is App STAR air. Advise position, over."

"Roger that, App STAR air. Coordinates …"

I watch as Ghost punches them in, and we can see the target location. "Uh-huh. There it is. We're about six miles out." He touches his comm button. "This is App STAR air. KSP air, do you copy? Over."

"Roger that, App STAR air. This is KSP air five, over."

"What's your ETA to those coordinates? Over."

"We're about four minutes out. You? Over."

"About six minutes out. Over."

"Roger that. You should be popping up on my radar any minute now. Ummm … Yep. There you are. I've gotcha. Over."

"Roger that, KSP air five. We see you on our spinner too. Over." Now we know where Izzy is and she knows where we are. No midair collisions for this crew.

"This is just getting better and better," Marshall whispers. I have no idea why Patch insisted that he come with us, but he's here, riding in the treatment area with Reboot and me.

"This is Knott County central dispatch. Search parties, confirm your positions via coordinates. Over." Each party calls out their coordinates, and I know that back at the farm, there's an FBI agent and two deputies who know the area well, all looking at the three locations. They have topical maps, and they're looking for problem areas.

A voice comes over a hand-held radio. "All parties, this is search two. Requesting all parties converge with ours. The dog has picked up the scent. Repeat, the dog has picked up the scent. We are proceeding. Over." My heart is pounding so hard that I can hear the blood whooshing in my ears.

"Hey, Paddy, you okay back there?" Patch calls back.

"Yeah. I'm fine."

"He's good, chief," Reboot says in agreement and places his hand on my shoulder. "We're gonna find her in just a few minutes, I'm sure. Just take a deep breath and let it out. It's okay."

"Search two, this is base one. Based on your coordinates, you've got a fairly deep drop from a bluff about five hundred meters to your north. Repeat, deep bluff about five hundred meters to your north. Activate your beacon. Over."

"Roger that, base one. Thanks for the heads-up. Beacon activated, over."

It's quiet for a minute or two and then the voice says,

"Search two, this is base one. You're rapidly approaching the danger zone. Over."

"This is search two. Copy. Over." Having eyes in the dark like this is a pretty damn good thing. The last thing we need is the search party needing to be rescued.

"App STAR air, this is search two. We're at the edge of the bluff and this dog is going crazy. Are you near us? Over."

Before Patch can answer, I hear Izzy's voice. "This is KSP air five. I'm probably closer. Over."

"Can you see us down here, KSP? Over."

"Roger that. I do. Over."

"We can't see over the edge. Don't have enough fire. Can you train your spots down there? Over."

"Roger that." I see Izzy's bird up ahead, and I see the big spotlight come on. "Roger, roger. We have visual. I repeat, we have visual. Over."

"This is base one, KSP. Can you advise? Over."

"Yes. Two … No, there are four down there. Lot of arms and legs. I'm not sure exactly what I'm seeing. Over."

"KSP air, this is App STAR air. I'm almost on top of you. Do we have enough bluff face to come in there together? Over."

"Negative. You'll have to make a call on who goes down first. Over."

"You first, KSP air. Send Bulldog down. Over."

"Copy that, chief. Over." We watch as she brings the ten-ton machine to a hover, and we can see the interior lights as the door opens and somebody slides out. I see him go down and disappear past the face of the bluff.

"KSP air five, App STAR air, this is … Guess I'll call myself med one. I'm gonna need some help down here. Over."

"Med one, can you report back. Over," Patch says.

"Roger. We've got two females. Each is face down and on top of a male. The males are …" There's a pause. "Obviously deceased. I've got a pulse on each female. Over."

"Roger that, med one. KSP air five, if you'll scoot, I'll send mine down. Over," Patch says.

"Roger that, App STAR air. Over." I watch as the big bird banks away, and Patch starts the gentle approach.

"Guys, get that door open and get ready to go. Reboot, you first. Then Paddy," Patch barks at us.

I can't do that. "But I'm the hoist—"

Patch's voice is no nonsense. "Nope. That's why Marshall's here. He knows how to run that thing. You're going down there."

"But I haven't had enough—"

"Paddy, this isn't about training or expertise. This is about Natalie. You need to be down there. Got it?"

We help Reboot get into his harness, and I let him down slowly. And when I do, I get a look down at the earth below us.

No.

I absolutely can't go down there. I can't.

There's no way. It's Michael all over again. I can't do it.

"Get your harness on, Paddy," Patch yells at me over the sound of the rotors and the rush of air.

"No. I can't go."

"You have to. That's an order."

"No. I can't. You don't understand."

"I do. And you have to go."

"No. It's like Michael, and it's—"

"Paddy, you *have* to go. It's Natalie, and she needs you. Knowing you're there will help her."

"But what if—"

"Yeah. What if, and you're not there. You're already

torturing yourself every fucking day over Michael. You want to torture yourself every fucking day over her too? *Get your ass down there*. If you don't get that harness on, I'll just come back there and push you out the fucking door myself. DO IT! NOW!"

My hands are shaking so hard that I can't fasten the buckles on my harness. "Can you …" I plead with Marshall.

"I gotcha, buddy. Here. Let's get this thing taken care of." I just stand there and let him buckle and fasten everything, then hook the cable on and slide my go-bag over my shoulders. "You ready?"

"No."

"You're going anyway. Go on. I'm going to count down and when I hit one, you step out. You got this, Paddy. I believe in you." I don't know whether to punch him or kiss him, but I let him help me get into position. "Okay. Here we go. Three. Two. One." There's a gentle push on my shoulders, and my feet leave the deck.

I'm hanging in midair, and I'm terrified. I've never been so terrified in my life. I have this picture in my mind of what I'm going to find when I reach the ground, and everything starts to spin as I realize I'm about to pass out. I can't go through this again. I won't survive it. And from nowhere, in midair, I hear a voice, just like he's right there with me. "It's okay, Denny. She needs you. You can do this."

In a few seconds, I feel my feet hit something. "I've gotcha. Come on, bud. Let's get you loose." It's Reboot, and he's right in front of me.

I look around and see Bulldog bending over Sela. Reboot's standing right there beside the other person, and I recognize Natalie's shoes. Everything, all my fear, apprehension, tension, just disappears, and I fall to my knees beside her, stroking her hair. “Hey, babe. Talk to me, Nat. Come on, sweet pea. Talk to me.”

Reboot’s doing something, moving her arms or legs, and I hear her sigh. As he’s working around her, a bit of sound comes from her, some kind of attempt to talk. “What is it, baby?”

“Who was that man?”

“You mean the guys who took you?”

“No. There was a man here. A blond man.” My heart stops. “And he had a scar.”

Everything stops. Time stands still, there’s no air movement, and there’s no sound. It’s like a vacuum has sucked me in, and I’m almost stuttering when I ask, “On his jaw? Round? Like he was cut with a pipe?”

“How did you know?” she mumbles. I’m frozen, can’t move, can’t speak, can’t even blink or draw in a breath.

It was Michael.

In that precious moment, everything in my life starts to make sense. It’s like someone has wiped the window clean and I can see the sunshine for the first time in years. Michael was here, watching over Natalie. All this time I’d thought he was gone, and he was right here with me. And when she needed him most, he was right here with her too, because he knows she has my heart. “It’s okay, baby. Everything’s gonna be okay.”

“Whatcha got over there, Reboot?” I hear Bulldog ask.

“Looks like a broken arm and broken leg. Maybe broken collarbone and ribs, but with her face down, I can’t tell. Probably a concussion. Some blood coming from her left ear. No gaping wounds of any kind, so she may have internal, but from what I can palpate, there’s no hardness in her abdomen and her breathing is clear. How’s Sela?”

“Not so lucky. We’ve got to get her out of here.”

"Need help rolling her?"

"No. We're going to load them up just like they are, her on top of him. I think under the circumstances that's the safest thing to do. We don't have any way to immobilize everything, and that's our best chance." He hits his comm button. "KSP air five, we need the basket and several blankets down here. Over."

"Roger that, med one. Over." I can feel the big bird overhead again, and in a few seconds, something drops beside Bulldog.

"Reboot, I need you to help me here."

Reboot pats me on the shoulder and answers Bulldog. "I'll stay with Natalie. Paddy can help you."

It's not exactly level terrain, and I manage to carefully pick my way over to him. When I get there, I see what he means. Sela's legs, an arm, and her neck are in unnatural positions, and moving them could be really risky. Very, very carefully, we manage to get them into the basket, her still on top of the man beneath her, and strap them in. When he's got the cable latched onto the basket, he hits his comm. "KSP air five, ready to lift. Over."

"Roger that, med one. You'll follow immediately after. Over."

"Roger that." I stand with him while the basket goes up. Once it disappears, the cable comes back down, and in just a couple of seconds, Bulldog is gone. As soon as the door closes on the bird, Izzy banks it sharply and it's headed to Hazard.

I pick my way back over to Natalie and Reboot. "How is she?" I ask, afraid of the answer.

"Holding her own. Her pulse is steady, and so is her blood pressure—both low, but steady. If she had a lot of internal bleeding, it would be erratic, but that's not the case, so I think she's going to be okay. Probably need some surgery, but other than that, as long as there's no unchecked brain bleed from the concussion, she'll recover." He hits his comm button. "App STAR air, this is med two. We need our basket and several blankets. Over."

"Roger that, med two. Sending them down."

In seconds, the basket is beside me on the ground. "Do you remember how you and Bulldog got Sela and asshole number one in the basket?"

"Yeah."

"We're going to do the exact same thing. Tell me what he did and we'll recreate it here."

In a couple of minutes, we have her loaded up. I watch the basket disappear into the air, and in seconds, it vanishes through the side door. When the cable appears again, Reboot grins at me. "We're going together."

"Both of us? At the same time?"

"Yep. Our hoist is rated for that, and time is critical. Get on over here. We'll lock it and up we'll go." I've never done a double lift, and I'm not sure it's a good idea, but he radios Marshall, and in a few seconds, we're headed up, arms around each other. The big security agent's hand lands on my foot closest to the door, and before I know it, we're both inside the bird and the door is closing. "Piece of cake," Reboot crows as he unclasps the cable. "Okay. Let's get on her and do what needs to be done. Have they shown you how to do an IV line yet?"

"No. I've only been in class one night so far!"

"True. Okay. I'll show you. Watch and learn."

I hear Patch call into the radio, "Central dispatch, this is App STAR air. We're headed to Hazard. Over."

"Copy that, App STAR air. Bring 'em home. Over."

As soon as the IV line is in, Reboot calls the hospital and

relays all her vitals, and they tell him what to push through the IV and how much. I hear them say they're getting the imaging machines ready and they'll have a full triage crew waiting on a secondary helipad. That means Sela's either already there or only minutes out. I know I shouldn't, but I have to.

I pull out my phone, look up his contact, and press CALL, my finger in my other ear to try to block the rotor noise. It rings, and he answers almost instantly. "Please …"

"I think she's already there. It's not good. You really should go."

There's silence for a few seconds, and I know he's stomping through the woods with the rest of the guys, headed back to base. And then he says the magic words: "Fuck 'em all. I'm going."

"That's it, brother. I'll see you there." When I hit END, I know I did the right thing.

As soon as I turn, I find Reboot glaring at me. "Who was that?"

"Can't say."

"You know I'm going to find out, right?" he says, side-eyeing me. "When he shows up at the hospital, I'll know. It's Priest, isn't it?"

Do I? He's right. He'll know as soon as everybody gets to the hospital. "Uh, no."

"It's not Priest. So it's … No. You're shitting me."

"Nope. Not shitting you. And I didn't tell you. Say I didn't tell you."

"No. You didn't tell me. Process of elimination did."

"Well, process of elimination needs to keep its fucking mouth shut."

"What are you two yammering about?" Marshall asks.

In unison, we turn and snap, "Nothing."

"Yeah. You go with that. Jesus. Sorry I asked."

I take Natalie's hand and whisper down to her, "Everything's gonna be okay, sweet pea."

Even in the dim light of the bird's interior, I see a tiny smile on her face as she squeezes my hand ever so slightly. "Sweet pea," she whispers.

My sweet pea is back with me. My world is right.

CHAPTER 11

PADDY

THE HOSPITAL IS BUZZING WITH ACTIVITY WHEN WE GET there, and it's hard to watch them wheel her away and out of my reach. I'm terrified. Reboot keeps telling me her vitals are stable. He doesn't say they're *good*; he says they're stable. There's a difference. Even with my limited knowledge, I know that.

Her parents are there and, to my surprise, we've been there about forty-five minutes when my parents walk in. I just sort of fall into their arms. "Oh, honey, I'm so glad somebody called us."

"Who called you?"

"Someone named Penny?"

"Yeah. Patch's wife." I'll have to remember to thank her. Having them here means the world to me. In ten minutes, Mom and Mrs. Anderson are chatting, and it's nice to see that they're spending their time that way instead of crying.

Another thirty minutes goes by and the waiting room door opens. "Family of Baldwin?"

Agent Klutz stands, but so does Bear. Every head in the room swivels toward the huge man, but nobody says one damn word. "Here," Klutz says, then gives Bear a weird look, but Bear doesn't seem to even notice.

"She's in emergency surgery," the nurse says. "Punctured lungs, broken clavicle, severely broken legs, one broken arm, a concussion, possible vertebral fractures. They're also doing a nerve conduction to see if there's any paralysis. We'll know more when that's finished. We also think she may have some internal injuries."

"Thanks. Keep us posted," Klutz says. As soon as the nurse disappears again, he turns to Bear. "Wanna tell me what this is about?"

"No. I don't. And right now, under the circumstances, it's none of your business," my huge friend says. I see Patch's eyebrows shoot upward. I can almost hear his brain saying, *Holy shit*. Because that's what mine is saying.

Ten more minutes and the door opens again. "Family of Anderson?"

"We're all here," Mr. Anderson says and rises with Natalie's mother, but before he takes a step forward, he reaches for my hand, and I take his and walk with them. The nurse smiles. "She has a broken leg and broken arm, but her spine and vertebrae are intact. Slight concussion. That guy really cushioned her fall, and it helped that she's short. If she'd been taller than him, she might be in much worse shape. She's in surgery right now to repair the arm, but she should make a full recovery."

"When can we see her?" her dad asks.

"When she comes out of surgery, she'll go to post-op. As soon as they move her to recovery, you'll be able to go back and be with her. We'll keep you updated as the surgery goes on, but I'm guessing she'll be out of there in about thirty minutes and in post-op. Chin up. She's going to be fine."

"Oh, thank God," her mother whispers. "Are you okay, Dennis?"

"I won't be okay until she's out of there. Excuse me. I need to go talk to Bear." The chairs on either side of him are empty. He's sitting there alone, worried out of his mind, and no one has reached out to him, mostly because they didn't realize until about ten minutes ago that they should.

I take the chair to his left and settle in. "How ya doin'?"

"Kinda numb, I guess."

"Hang in there. She's strong."

"Yeah. She is."

"So do you all know each other very well?"

"No. Of course not. But there was something there. I mean, we didn't talk about it, but I know there was." Actually, that means there was something there for *him*. I'm not sure about Sela. She made it clear that she'd be gone as soon as the job was over, so I don't know what he thought was going to happen. And none of that matters right now. I'm just concerned about his mental wellbeing. It further drives home to me that people see a big, burly, kinda scary guy when they look at him, but he's tenderhearted and sweet, kind and gentle, and everybody totally misses that.

"I'm sure you're right. She's going to need some care when she gets out of here. Maybe you can help her."

"I want to. I definitely want to."

I sit there for a minute, then ask, "I think I'm going out to get some air. Wanna come?"

"Nah. I'll just sit here."

"Okay." The doors are only a few feet away, so I step over, wait until they open, and wander out.

The night is clear and the air is brisk, and it's the kind of midsummer night that I usually love, but tonight has been nothing but terror for me. I sit down on a bench just outside the entrance and stare up at the stars. There are so many, and I think about the heavens, how big they are, how vast. I don't hear anything until a voice says, "Mind if I sit with you?"

"Of course not." I pat the bench and Mom takes a seat beside me. "You're always welcome to sit with me."

"I'm so glad Penny called us. We want to be here for you. We love you, son. We just want you to be happy."

"I am, Mom. I really am. Natalie is the best thing that ever happened to me."

"Better than your kids? You really should see them, Dennis."

"I'm seeing them this weekend. Lisa's bringing them to the farm to spend the weekend."

"Oh, that's wonderful!" she crows and pats me on the shoulder. "How exciting."

"Except for this." Do I dare? I have to tell someone. "Mom, Natalie said something weird to me out there tonight."

"Weird? How?"

"She asked me about the man she saw. Said there was a man there with her, a blond man with …" I can't say it. It sounds insane.

My mother whispers, "With a scar on his jaw?"

"How did you know?" I ask, my eyes wide. What the hell?

"Honey, I firmly believe they never leave us. They're watching over us, and Michael was there with her tonight because he knows she loves you and you love her. He was there so she'd know she wasn't alone. And she wasn't. Because he, and your love, were with her. I know, that wouldn't be a popular viewpoint in the church. Screw them," she says and chuckles. Who is this woman, and what has she done with my mom? "My point is, he was there with her because he was waiting for you to get there. He did that for you. He loved you, Dennis. He was your best friend. And he still loves you, just like you still love him."

"I do. I always will. He was with me too, you know. As they were lowering me. I could hear his voice."

"Then smile. She's going to be fine, and your friend made sure of it. And from this point on, never, never doubt."

She doesn't have to worry. I won't.

Natalie

Ooooo-WEEEEEE.

This cloud I'm riding on is amazing. I can feel the wind blowing through my hair, and there's a bird singing somewhere. Wow. Sunshine and fresh air. And a pterodactyl. What? What the hell? What's that beeping sound? It's not like a bus backing up. What is it? "Natalie." Somebody's calling my name, but I can't open my eyes. "Natalie, it's Mom. Can you hear me?"

"Mom?" What's she doing here?

"Honey, it's me. Open your eyes." I'd like to answer her, but I can't. "Natalie, open your eyes. Dennis is here and he wants you to talk to him." Dennis? Oh. Yeah. Dennis. My boyfriend. What does he want?

"What? Dennis?"

"Yes. Open your eyes, Natalie. You can do it. Look at me. It's Mom."

It takes me a couple of minutes, and I can hear talking

going on around me. When I finally manage to get one eye partially open, the light is really bright. "Owww."

"Hey, Dennis, honey, can you reach back there and turn the lights off for a second? I think they're hurting her eyes."

When I look again, it's dark. Well, darker. Not as dark as with my eyes closed, but still pretty dark. "Better."

"Better, huh? You need to talk to us, Natalie. Do you know where you are?"

"The sky?" I have a feeling that's the wrong answer.

"No, honey. You've been in surgery and you're waking up. They told us to talk to you to get you to wake up. Do you remember anything?"

"Man."

"What man?"

"Tall man."

A deep voice asks, "A man with a scar?"

"Yes!" Wow. That was a little more enthusiastic than I intended for it to be, but whatever.

"Okay. It's time to wake up. Are you thirsty?" the male voice asks, and then I remember. Dennis!

"Is that you?"

"It's me, sweet pea."

Sweet pea. It all comes rushing back, and suddenly, I'm crying and I don't know why. "It happened, and it hurt, and I'm scared, and I want to go home now, okay? Please?"

"Babe, open your eyes. You need to open your eyes so you can see us, okay? Please?"

It's a struggle, but I finally get them open. I see my mom and my dad, and then a face I remember comes into focus. "Dennis."

"Yeah, babe. It's me. Do you remember how you got here?"

"No. Wait." There's a sound that I remember … "Helicopter?"

"Yep! That's right. You came in our helicopter. Patch keeps saying he's going to name her Chiquita because she's yellow like a banana, but the guys said no."

"Patch. I remember Patch."

"Of course you do. And Penny and Audrey and Mavis, and Tinsley."

"Tinsley's having a baby."

"Yes. She is. See, you do remember."

"I was at work. And I was at the doctor's office. And then …" It all comes rushing back like a spring flood. "Oh my god. Sela. Where's Sela? She's supposed to be with me!"

"Babe, Sela's in pretty bad shape, but she saved your life. She's a hero."

She's hurt? Wait. I fell. We both fell. Now I remember. Oh, god, I remember it all. "Dennis, where's Sela? I need to see her. Is she okay? Is she going to be okay?"

"She's just coming out of surgery, but it was rough. But she saved your life. If you had just fallen off that bluff, you'd be dead, but you fell on that asshole and he broke your fall."

The asshole. Oh, yeah. One of the guys trying to kill me. Now I remember. I was in the trunk of a car. We ran in the woods. I'm so confused. "I'm going back to sleep now. I can't think."

I hear him chuckle. "Okay. Go back to sleep. We'll still be here when you wake up. But know this. I love you, sweet pea. It'll all be okay."

"Okay. Bye." Maybe I'll feel like visiting later. Not right now. I just want to sleep.

I OPEN MY EYES AND THE ROOM IS KINDA DARKISH. THE ceiling lights aren't on. They'd be too bright, so I'm glad they're off. A machine somewhere nearby is emitting tiny little beeping sounds, but it's not bad. Somebody's sitting in the chair across the room, and it takes me a minute to focus.

It's Dennis. I try to say something, but it comes out as a hoarse whisper, and he immediately sits bolt upright. "Hey, sweet pea. Do you need something?"

My hand goes to my throat. "Dry."

"Hang on. Here." I watch as he pours some water into a cup, then holds it for me. I try to take it, but my arms are so tired. "I'll help you. Take a couple of sips, babe." The water tastes so good as I swallow it down that it might as well be wine. "Slow down, babe." Instead of gulping at top speed, I try to slow down a little. After I've managed to down pretty much the whole glass, he pulls it away. "There ya go. Now, what were you trying to say?"

"Did you tell me earlier that Sela's not good?"

"Yeah. She's out of surgery and in a room, but it's ICU. She was hurt pretty badly."

"And Bear?"

He sighs. "Yeah. Finally came out and I guess you'd say he told everybody. When the doctor came out to talk to the family about Sela, he stood with the special agent in charge. Everybody wanted to know why. He didn't tell them, so they had to draw their own conclusions, and I'm figuring they probably got it right."

"Damn it." Poor Bear. "Is he with her?"

"I'm pretty sure he is. I'd be surprised if he isn't." He's quiet for a few seconds before he says, "I sure hope she wasn't playing with him. You know … before."

"I don't think Sela has the ability to play with anybody. Everything she does is purposeful and intentional. If she was with him, it was because she knew it was right. Otherwise, she never would've touched him or let him touch her. That's just how she is."

"You've got that part right."

"I tried to ask her about him, but she shut me down."

He quirks up one corner of his mouth. "That's not surprising. I would've been more surprised if she'd told you."

"Yeah. Me too." I'm getting really tired just from talking. "So what all is wrong with me?"

"You have a broken leg and a broken arm. The arm required surgery and some pins. The leg isn't all that bad. You also have a concussion, and they're monitoring that. They think you ruptured your left eardrum, or at least damaged it, probably in the fall. You've got a couple of broken ribs, but fortunately, none of them were severe enough to puncture a lung. Right now they're just trying to keep you medicated enough that you're not in pain. You will be in a few days though."

"Great. Something to look forward to." Then I remember something. "Hey, are your kids still coming this weekend?"

"Yep. I was going to tell you that I'm going to spend all the time I can with you here, but I'll still have to work, still have school, and then the boys will be here. But it's one weekend and only a few weeks out of our lives, and then things will get back totally to normal. We'll go back home and go back to work, and everything—"

"Work. Oh, shit! The trials! I've got to get out of here and get back to—"

"Nat, there aren't going to be any trials."

"What do you mean, no trials?"

"This turned into such a mess that the two guys you had on trial are pleading guilty. So are the others who were involved. And the two who took you and Sela had a helper.

Cops found him dead last night. So either the two who took you killed him, or his bosses killed him when they realized he and his two buddies failed to get rid of you."

"Wow. A girl takes a nap and wakes up in a new world," I say, shocked at how everything took a turn.

"Yeah. Kinda like that. But just know that whatever time I can't be here, your mom and dad will be. They're staying at your house, so they'll be in and out."

"Okay."

"And my parents will be leaving in about an hour, but they really want to meet you."

"Oh, baby, I'm sure I look like shit," I say, embarrassed at the thought that I'll be meeting two of the most important people in his world looking like this.

"They came all this way out of concern for you and me, and we owe them that much."

"Okay. I'm sure they don't care what I look like anyway."

"Nah. They just want to meet you and get to know you."

Almost like he's alerted them to my consent, the door squeaks open just a crack and a face appears. "Feel like company?"

"Sure. Come on in." A tall man appears, and there's no doubt who he is. Now I know what Dennis will look like when he's that age. "Hey, sweetie. I'm Kevin, Dennis' dad. This is my wife, Dennis' mom, Freida."

His mom smiles and takes my good hand. "Hi, honey. We just wanted to come by and meet you, tell you how glad we are to have you here and safe."

"Thank you. Thank you for coming to be here with him. I know it meant a lot."

A tear trickles down her cheek, but she's smiling. "Doesn't matter how old he is, he's still my baby boy. He's had a lot of rough years lately, and I don't want that to ever happen to him again, anything like that. But he seems really happy with you."

Love is just pouring off this woman, and I know in this moment that she's somebody I really want to have in my life. "I'm happy with him. He's a good man. The best."

"Just like his daddy," she says and her other hand pats our joined ones.

"Well, we'd better get going. That marina won't run itself, and we've got a fishing tournament going on nearby this weekend, so it's gonna be busy, but we'll be checking in on you and coming to visit again as soon as we can. You do what the doctors say and get better, you hear me?" Kevin says, his smile warm and loving.

"I will. I promise."

"Okay. We'll see you soon. Walk us out, son?" Kevin says, and Paddy stands and nods.

"I'll be right back," he says, leaning over to give me a kiss on the forehead before they leave the room.

"I'll be right here," I assure him. Hell, where else would I be? I mean, a beach in the Bahamas would be nice.

But I doubt that's happening anytime soon.

Paddy

We walk in silence toward the elevator, and when we get on and the doors close, my mom finally turns to me. "She's lucky to be alive."

"Boy, you got that right." It falls quiet again, so I finally ask, "Well? Whaddya think? Like her?"

"Oh, gosh, yes! She's a lovely girl. Just lovely. Don't you think so, Kevin?"

"I do. But are you sure you're evenly yoked?" he asks, drawing on that verse from the Christian bible.

"Yes. In the ways that count. You should see her house. It's just a little three-bedroom bungalow. She drives a little Honda CRV. Nat's not into all the trappings of success. She just wants to live a quiet, productive life, loving people who love her back. She's happy about being a federal judge, but not because of the status. It's the intricacies of the cases that she enjoys dealing with, the details, the letter of the law. Being successful at this tells her that she learned her craft, and that's important to her. And using embossing tools to decorate the scabbards and holsters I make tells me I'm learning mine. We like to be good at what we do, but we don't really care about the status."

"Then you'll do fine, son." The elevator doors open and we step off—and my dad runs headlong into Bear. "Oh my gosh, I'm so sorry!" Dad sputters.

"Sorry. I'm so sorry. Wasn't watching where I was going," Bear stammers. "Oh. Paddy. Didn't see you there."

"Yeah. This is my dad, Kevin, and my mom, Freida. Mom, Dad, this is Bear. He's one of my brothers out at the farm."

My dad's hand automatically extends, and Bear shifts the bouquet of flowers he's carrying to his left hand. "Pleasure to meet you, son. I've heard good things about you."

My big friend seems shocked. "You have?"

"Well, I mean, all of you. I mean, let's just say Dennis didn't single you out and say you were a horrible person. I haven't heard anything bad about you." My dad is stammering like he thinks if he says something wrong, Bear's going to pound him into the tiled floor.

"Oh, well, guess that's good," Bear answers, seeming a bit bewildered.

"Going up to check on Sela?" I ask, trying to redirect the conversation, and my dad finally turns loose of Bear's hand.

"Uh, yeah," he answers, giving me a look that tells me he thinks my parents are a bit mental. "Figured I'd go up, try to brighten the room a little, sit for a while."

"Oh! So the two of you are together?" my mom asks, and I wish I could retract that question immediately.

"Um, we're friends?" he answers, looking to me like he's trying to get me to help him.

"Yeah. They're friends," I toss out. "They, um, both enjoy … ballet?" I'm pretty sure he's going to kill me when we all get back to the farm, and it's all I can do to keep from busting out laughing.

"Ballet? Well, that's … unusual," Mom says. "But whatever floats your boat, I guess."

"Exactly. Well, you'd better get to it," I tell Bear. If I were bacon, the look he's giving me right now would fry me to a crisp.

"Yeah. Nice meeting y'all. Hope you'll come back sometime to visit," Bear says and strides into the elevator as the doors open. "And I'll be seeing you a whole lot sooner," he snarls at me.

"I bet you will. Later, buddy," I call to him as the doors close, and I turn just in time to see him pop me a bird.

"Well, he's a nice fellow. Ballet, huh?" Mom says, still pondering it all.

"Yeah. Real ballet freak. Pirouettes and pas de deux and all that stuff. Loves it. Sela does too. So, y'all be careful going back and I'll talk to you in the next day or so."

"Okay, son. Take care of that girl," Dad says and hugs me.

Mom hugs me next. “Yes. Take care of her. The two of you make such a cute couple. We’ll talk soon.”

“Yep. We will. Love you both. Say hi to everybody for me.” I watch as they head out, and my mom turns to wave back at me just before they turn the corner outside.

When I get back to Natalie, she’s awake. “Want the TV on?”

“Nah. They get off okay?”

“Yeah. Mom says we make a cute couple.”

She reaches her good hand out to me. “That’s because we do.”

When I take it, I squeeze it. “Ran into Bear downstairs. He was heading up to see Sela.”

“Yeah? Is he okay?”

“Yeah. I think so. So … Did you know that he and Sela both love ballet?”

She screws her face up. “What?”

“Yeah. I told my parents that was what they had in common—they both love ballet.” I can’t help it. I’m chuckling as I say it.

“In front of Bear?”

Now I’m laughing. “Yeah!”

“You realize you’re in a lot of trouble, right?”

“Don’t care. You should’ve seen the look on his face!”

“Yeah, well, that look is your guarantee that he’s not going to forget, so there’s that.”

“It’ll be worth it!” It takes me a minute to get my laughter under control, but when I do, I press myself against the bed rails and lean over to give her a kiss. “You okay? Need anything?”

“All I need is you. And I’m a little hungry.”

“They should be rolling the breakfast carts down the hallway any minute now.” All I can do is stand there and look down at her. She's truly the most beautiful thing I've ever seen. "By the way, there's something I should tell you."

"Yeah?"

"The man you said you saw last night? The blond man?"

"Oh! I mentioned that? Yeah. He was there. He said it was all right, that everything would be okay, that you were coming for me. It was weird."

"With a scar on his face."

"Yeah. Exactly. How did you know?"

"Baby, that was Michael."

Her brow furrows downward. "Michael? He's dead."

"Yes. He is. But that's Michael."

"How could he—"

"He was with me too. I looked out the helo's door and saw you down there, and it took me right back to when he fell. I didn't want to go. I told Patch I wouldn't, and he threatened to throw me out of the helicopter if I didn't get harnessed up and get down there. And on the way down, I heard Michael's voice, telling me to take care of you."

"I … I don't know what to say."

"Just know that he was watching over both of us, babe. We were never alone out there last night. He was right there with us."

She lifts our joined hands and kisses the back of mine. "I love you, Dennis. Thank you for coming to get me."

"You're welcome, baby. Keeping you safe—it's my job."

Of all the jobs I have, it's definitely the most important one of all.

"Well, Natalie, if you keep improving the way you've been going, we'll let you out of here Monday. How does that sound?" a doctor named McGraw asks her as he looks over her charts.

"Sounds good. I'm … I'm a little scared, but it's okay."

"Why are you scared?" he asks.

"I'll have to have somebody to take care of me."

"Your mom said she'll come during the day while we're all working," I tell her. "And in the evenings when I don't have school, you'll have me, and if I'm at school, you'll have everybody else. You'll be fine. Reboot's an EMT, and Ghost and Bulldog are nurses. Somebody will look after you."

"Bulldog's got his hands full already."

"Not yet. They will when the baby gets here, but right now, Tinsley's still working, so it's fine. You'll have plenty of help."

Her eyes close and she sighs. "Fine, fine."

"Yes," Dr. McGraw says. "It'll all be fine." As he speaks, I see someone look through the glass on the door.

"Okay. Do I have physical therapy at some point?"

"When you get the casts off, but not until then. Until that happens, we want you to be up and moving around as much as possible to keep your strength up."

"Got it."

"Okay. I'll see you again tomorrow morning. Take care." And he disappears.

He's barely out the door when it opens, and another person steps in. "Hi, guys. Brought you something." Izzy sets a big bouquet of flowers over on the credenza, and she hands Natalie a cute little stuffed bear. "Figured you could use some company who didn't ask for anything in return."

Natalie reaches for the bear, drops it on her belly, then reaches for Izzy's hand. "Oh my god, Izzy, I hope … Please don't hold it against me that I—"

"No, no, honey! Never! You did what you had to do. It's

fine. I hear you got the assholes who shot down me and Dean to take guilty pleas."

"I didn't do that. They did it on their own. I think they saw the writing on the wall. There's no way they could get out of this now."

"That's sure true." Izzy turns and looks at me. "Hey, if you wanna take a break, I'll stay here with her. Go get some air, walk around a bit."

I grin at the two of them there together, strangers who are instant friends. "Think I will. Y'all enjoy yourselves." I've got a call I need to make, and I need some privacy.

There are super comfortable chairs all over the downstairs lobby, so I take up one of those and pull out my phone. She answers on the second ring. "Hey, hon."

"Hi. Got a minute?"

"Yeah. I'm between classes." She's a music teacher for the Mason County elementary schools in and around Point Pleasant.

"You need to know what's happened here over the last forty-eight hours." I launch into the whole story, and Lisa doesn't make a sound. I finish with, "So they think she'll get to go home next Monday."

"Oh, god, Dennis, that's horrible! She's really all right?"

"Yeah. She'll be fine. She's got a long road, but she'll be okay. And I was a little worried about bringing the boys here in all of that, but it's all resolved now, so it'll be fine."

"Who's going to sit with her at the hospital while you're with them?"

"Her parents will be in and out, and I'm sure some of my folks from the farm will be there too."

"Okay, if you're sure."

"I am."

"Then we'll see you on Friday. Hey, over the weekend,

I'll go sit with her some of the time that you're with them, if that's okay."

That makes me smile. "I think she'd like that, and I know I would."

"Great. We can get to know each other. Oh, here comes thirty-two first graders. I'll talk to you later."

"Yep. Talk to you later. Bye."

It's all settled. Lisa, Borden, and Tegan will all be here this weekend. I'll have my family back together. If only Natalie could be with us. But I'll bring the boys to the hospital to meet her at least. And it won't be long before we're back to normal. Whatever that is.

Natalie

It's way too early, and I know his phone is on Do Not Disturb, but I call and leave a message anyway. At six thirty, mine rings. "Hey, babe. What's going on?"

"You're still at my house, right?"

He chuckles. "I'm still in your bed."

"Um, can you get a bag and get some things together for me? And bring them to the hospital?"

"Uh, sure. But you're running out of room there."

"Doesn't matter. Can you just do it? And come here?"

"Yeah, yeah. Tell me what I'm getting and I'll bring it all."

"Get a piece of paper and a pencil."

There's some rustling around and then he says, "Got it."

"Okay. So, if it's in my shower, I need it. And I need at least eight pairs of underwear from my drawer, and my robe, and my slippers. And I need the contents of the first drawer on the right of my vanity, especially my hairbrush and all my hair thingies."

"This is an awful lot of stuff for the hospital, babe."

"It's not for the hospital. It's for your place. They're letting me out today."

There's silence for just a few seconds, and then he screams, "Today?"

"Yeah. Like, when you get here."

"Oh my god! Yeah! I'll get all of this stuff together and I'll be right along. Oh, god, baby, you're coming home!"

"Yep. But I have to have a ride. So don't disappoint me, big boy."

"Not a chance in hell! See you in a few minutes!"

I'm going home, and I don't even care where that is, as long as Dennis is there. Anywhere he is, that's my home.

CHAPTER 12

PADDY

THE CAR PULLS UP, AND I WAIT. I CAN FEEL MYSELF trembling. I couldn't have anticipated how afraid I could be of two teenage boys, but I really am—afraid of their rejection. It'll break me if they reject me.

Both front doors open, and one back one. Lisa crosses the short distance and wraps her arms around my neck, so I hug her back. "It's so good to see you, Dennis. You look great. Super buff!"

"Yeah, I work hard." The boys are creeping closer. Tegan looks like I did at that age, but Borden looks just like Lisa. "Hey, guys. It's good to see you."

They both stop about six feet away, and Borden nods. "Good to be here."

"Hi." That's all Tegan says.

"Okay, well, I know we don't know each other that well, but I hope we do before the weekend is over. Are you guys hungry? Want some snacks? I think the ladies have set some stuff out in the kitchen, so help yourselves and I'll get your stuff."

As they start toward the kitchen, they stop in front of Natalie as she sits there in her wheelchair. "We heard you got hurt. Are you okay?" Borden asks.

"Yeah. It'll take a while, but I'll be fine. Your dad rescued me with the helicopter, you know," she says with a smile.

"Cool," Borden chirps.

"Yeah, cool," Tegan echoes.

She grins at them. "Go get some snacks. We'll have plenty of time to talk later."

I turn back to Lisa. "Okay trip?"

She nods. "Yeah. This place wouldn't be the easiest to find, but your directions were good. They decided to let you out of jail this morning huh?" she says toward Natalie.

"Yeah. Surprise!"

Lisa steps over to her and takes her good hand. "It's a good surprise. I'm glad you're here. I feel like getting to know you should be a priority for me, since the boys will be around you."

"I understand that completely. If I were a mom, I'd feel the exact same way."

Lisa tips her head. "No kids?"

"No. Never married."

"You'll have your hands full with him," Lisa says and points back at me, a huge smirk on her face.

Natalie laughs. "I've figured that out already."

"Oh, wait. I've got something for you." Lisa heads back to the car, opens the trunk, and pulls out a box.

I take it out of her hands, and it's not particularly heavy. "What's this?"

"It's a box of stuff that came out of Michael's truck. Leslie said she wanted you to have it."

"She kept it all this time?"

"Yeah. Apparently. She called me out of the blue a couple of days ago and told me I needed to take it in case I ever saw you again. I have no idea what's in it. Didn't look. Didn't feel like it was my place."

That's some weird timing, and it's not lost on me. I set it down on the ground and get down on my knees beside it on the walkway. The flaps are folded together, so I pull them back and stare down into the box. It's just a lot of junk, all kinds of small tools, pencils, pens, a magazine, a pair of boot laces. A voltage tester. A tire pressure gauge. Down in the bottom are some papers of some kind, so I pull them out. Proof of insurance. Copy of the registration for the truck. Copy of our liability insurance waiver.

But when I look at the next two, everything around me comes to a grinding halt. I can't draw a breath, and my hands are shaking so hard that the papers fall to the ground. There's a shrieking sound, and I realize it's coming from inside my head, because I can't make a noise. I hear Lisa's voice ask, "Dennis? Dennis, what's wrong?"

"Dennis?" Natalie calls out. "Dennis! Babe, what's wrong?"

The edges of my vision are growing black, and there's a buzzing in my head. Lisa's voice says, "What the … Oh. My. God. Oh my god! Dennis! Somebody! Somebody help us! Help!"

Natalie screams, "Patch! Bulldog! Reboot! SOMEBODY! We need some help out here!" There's a lot of movement around me, and I feel myself being lifted, but I can't speak, can't fight them off, don't really understand what's happening. "What is that?" I hear Natalie's voice ask Lisa.

I know what they are. All these years. All that pain. All that time in prison. All the anger, and hurt, and sorrow, and grief. I know what they are. How could we have missed them?

The next thing I know, I'm lying down, a cold, wet cloth on my forehead, and there's a lot of chatter around me. When my eyes flutter open, the first face I see is Natalie's. "Baby, talk to me. You okay?"

"Yeah, I … Oh my god. I thought I found—"

"You did," Lisa's voice says. "You found the safety check sheets. They were in the bottom of that box the whole time. It's them. The date is right, and you and Michael signed them. The signatures are clear as day. Dennis, you found them."

I found the safety check sheets from that day, the ones we'd looked for all these years. "How did we not—"

"They were in that stack of papers, and I guess Leslie never even looked through them, just threw them in that box before the truck was sold. They've been there the whole time."

Now it's all coming back to me. We'd taken both of our trucks because he had a doctor's appointment that afternoon and needed to go straight from the tower site. I remember we signed them, and he took them. I didn't know what he'd done with them, and it was unusual for both of our trucks to be there, so I hadn't even thought about it. "My god. All those years for nothing."

Natalie smooths the backs of her knuckles down my cheek. "Not for nothing. Everything that happened led you here, babe, to this place. To these men. To me. That's how you came to be here, that one slip. If you didn't believe in fate before, I hope you do now. I know I sure do."

I just roll to my side to face away from them all and cry.

Hours, days, months, years of anger and hurt pour out. I cry for myself, for the parts of my life that I lost. I cry for Mikey, for my friend who's always been with me, the one whose death I blamed myself for all these years. Tears for my family, who've been run through the mill because of me. Tears for my sons, who don't even really know me. Tears for poor Lisa, who got dragged through all of it and abandoned. Tears for Leslie, the sister I'd found through Michael, whose heart was broken and life was shattered. My heart is broken in ways that will never, never mend, but maybe sometime in the future, it'll be better. Maybe it'll be stronger in the mended spots. I can only hope.

"Dennis?" Natalie's voice is soft, and her hand is on my shoulder. "I need to talk to you." I roll to my back and before she even speaks, she hands me two tissues, so I mop my eyes with them and then wipe my nose. "I have the sheets. I'm going to call Steve and Judge Martelle. Steve will call Tony, and Tony will call the governor. And if everybody signs off on it, I'll personally reopen your case and exonerate you. It would be my honor, not just as someone who loves you, but as a federal judge in this state, to restore all of your rights to you. It would be my *privilege*," she says and takes my hand. "I love you so much, baby. You'll be free to do whatever you want to do and go wherever you want to go."

I look around. The room is full of people, and I hadn't even realized it. I'm on the sofa in the big kitchen, and everybody is waiting, watching me, wondering what I'll say. And there's absolutely, positively no doubt what that will be.

"The only place I want to be is right here with all of you," I tell them, and I see seven men smile. They had nothing to worry about. I have no intention of ever leaving this farm.

This is home.

Natalie

"They look like they're having a good time," I say as Lisa and I sit and watch all the guys playing football. Taylor's running around like a maniac. He says he's the quarterback, and it's obvious he has no idea what a quarterback is supposed to do, but he's having fun. Tegan's been really kind and patient with the little boy all weekend, but Borden's just blown him off. His testosterone-laden gaze has been following Fiona around all weekend, but she barely gives him the time of day, which makes Dennis, Lisa, and me extremely relieved. But we weren't really worried. She's not going to pay a minute's attention to a fifteen-year-old boy.

They only have a few hours before they have to leave, and the biggest attraction is about to begin. "You guys ready?" Patch asks as he steps out of the kitchen in his flight suit. Ghost is right behind him.

"Yeah!" Tegan yells.

"Yeah!" Taylor screams.

"Whatever," Borden answers. Nothing less than I'd expect.

"Can I go too?" a voice asks, and I turn to find Fiona standing there. Will wonders never cease …

"Sure. Come on. Paddy, you going too?" Patch asks.

Dennis nods. "Oh yeah. Wouldn't miss this for the world."

As they head toward the helipad, we can hear their entire conversation, and I hear Tegan ask, "Why do they call you Paddy?"

"We all have nicknames, and that's one a lot of people use for Irish men."

"Irish?"

"Yeah. O'Brien is an Irish name," he explains.

"Yeah. It's an Irish name, idiot," Borden snaps at his brother.

"Stop calling me an idiot!" the younger boy screams.

"Hey! None of that stuff. We can't have that in the helicopter," Dennis warns.

Borden's eyes flash. "So you want me to go back?"

Dennis stops dead in his tracks and stares at the boy. "I want you to do what you want to do, but be respectful doing it." Have I mentioned how much I love this man? Because I do. He's an awesome dad.

"Yeah. Be respeckful," Taylor says and grins at Borden, who scowls at the little boy.

Once again, the older one answers, "Whatever." We're going to have a talk about that. Not appropriate.

"Lord, that's a difficult age," I mutter.

"You tell me." Lisa's shaking her head. "Some days I wonder why I'm worried about college costs, because I doubt I'll let him live long enough to get there."

"What's gonna happen when Tegan hits that age?"

"Aww hell, girl, I don't even want to think about that," she says with a sour chuckle. "I'll bring them down and leave them with y'all!"

"Dennis would definitely whip them into shape," I assure her.

"I think he would. He will. Natalie …" She stops, and I wait. "Listen, I just want you to know that I really, really like you. You're good for Dennis. I can tell. He seems so happy and content here, and I can tell you really love him."

"I do. More than I could ever say."

"Good. He didn't deserve what happened to him … Well, I mean, we all know that now."

I lean toward her just a little. "So I've set the plan in motion."

"Yeah?"

"Yeah. Talked to Steve an hour ago. Talked to Judge Martelle too, and he found a way to work it all out. Will you bring the boys and come?"

"Absolutely. I think it would be good for them to be there."

"I agree. I'll let you know as soon as we've got it set up."

"Thanks."

We sit there in companionable silence and watch as the helicopter rises from behind the tree line. For the two women sitting here, those are all of our hopes and dreams right there, sitting inside that shiny red and yellow Chiquita banana, and it makes me smile. I'm the luckiest woman in the world, and I know it. My life has been so blessed.

I can't wait to start the next chapter.

"How do I look?" When I turn toward his voice, I gasp. "Too much?"

The suit we bought for him is gorgeous, and he looks amazing. "Oh, babe, I could undress you right now and jump your bones. Love the tie."

That lopsided grin gets me every time. "Yeah, I think it looks good with this." He's got excellent taste. Charcoal suit, pale blue shirt, blue, silver, gray, and charcoal striped tie.

"It's perfect."

"You don't look so bad yourself," he says with a warm smile.

"For somebody who has to have help to shower, I clean up okay, I reckon," I say as I fuss with my earrings. It's hard to put on earrings with the hand from the opposite side of my body, but I managed. "Judge Martelle will be there with us. He said since I'm officially on leave, I can't sign the documents, but I can preside over the proceedings."

"Good. That's going to mean a lot to me."

When we get to the courtroom, I'm shocked. All of the guys are here, and their wives and girlfriends are too. My parents are here. His parents are here. Incredibly, all of the guys from the Eagle Point team are here to support him. Most importantly, Lisa and the boys are here. Quentin Asher is sitting at the prosecution's table, and he shoots me a smile. He knows his role here today. I've never met them before, but Kelly is sitting with a couple, and the guy is gorgeous. I know instantly who they are—it's Tony and Nikki Walters. Steve is sitting at the defense table, waiting for Dennis. As soon as they're together, I ask Mavis to help me, and she rolls me out of the courtroom, around the back, up the elevator, and into chambers. "There you are! You're looking well, Natalie," William Martelle says when I roll into the room, and Mavis jets out the door, heading back to sit in the gallery.

"Thanks, Your Honor. I appreciate it."

"It's just William back here. We've all been so worried about you, but it looks like they're taking good care of you."

"They are. I've got the best support any girl could ever want."

He helps drape my robe around me, then helps me zip it up the front. "There. It's not perfect, but the parts that aren't are parts nobody can see, so you're fine."

"Thank you." I suck in a big breath and let it out.

"You ready?"

"Yep. Let's do this thing," I tell him with a smile.

As soon as he rolls my chair through the doorway, I hear Cliff say, "All rise. Court is now in session. The Honorable Natalie Anderson presiding."

When I'm positioned behind the bench, I pick up a folder, open it, and calm myself. "Please be seated." Everyone sits and waits. "We are here today in the matter of The United States of America and the Occupational Health and Safety Agency versus Dennis Shane O'Brien. Counselor, it's my understanding that new evidence has come to light."

"It has, your honor," Steve says as he rises.

"Approach the bench, please."

He brings the paper toward me and hands it to me. "Your honor, since the prosecution's entire case was built around the fact that no safety check had been done on equipment the morning of the day in which the death of Michael Wilson occurred, a lapse that resulted in his death, we'd like to submit these recently-discovered documents that clearly show the safety check *was* done and what happened that morning was a simple equipment failure and not an act of negligence on the part of the deceased or his business partner, Mr. O'Brien."

I motion for Steve to return to his seat, then turn and look at Quentin. "Counselor, I trust you've seen these documents?"

"I have, Your Honor, and they're all in good order. They prove beyond doubt that the safety checks actually did take place. Mr. Wilson's signature on the documents has been verified as authentic, as well as Mr. O'Brien's. With this discovery, we'd ask that the original verdict against Mr. O'Brien be vacated, that he be exonerated, and that his record be expunged, with our apologies."

"Very well. Mr. O'Brien, would you please rise." As he stands, I see tears roll down Dennis' face, and I'm fast losing my battle to keep my composure. "Mr. O'Brien, it is the opinion of this court that the crime for which you were convicted did not occur. While this court can never restore the years you lost and the other personal losses you suffered," I say as a tear escapes my eye, "we can now take the appropriate steps to restore all freedoms to you under the laws of the Constitution of the United States of America. Mr. O'Brien, it is both my responsibility and my privilege to announce that you are exonerated from the crimes of which you were accused, and your criminal record will be expunged as though none of this ever happened. You have no parole requirements, and all rights are restored. Congratulations, Dennis Shane O'Brien. Your life as an individual is restored to its time before your trial, and may your life be long and prosperous. This court is adjourned." Thank god Judge Martelle grabs my chair and wheels me back through the doorway of my chambers. The second the door closes behind me, I'm hysterical, sobbing and gasping for breath.

His voice is soft. "Natalie, I don't know how you did that. I couldn't have held it together like you did. Hell, I'm crying and it has nothing to do with me!" William says, and one look at his face tells me he's not exaggerating—tears are rolling down his cheeks too. "How does it feel to give a man back his dignity?"

There are no words to describe how I feel in this moment. No words. If my parents ever questioned whether or not my law degree was worth the money spent on it, this is the answer to that question.

It was worth every penny.

"GOT SOMETHING I WANT TO SHOW YOU." WE'VE BEEN AT the doctor's office this morning, and now Dennis is driving me across Hazard. I have no idea where we're going.

Until we pull into the car lot. "Oh. Car, huh?"

He grins. "Yeah. I realized I have no way to drive the boys around when they're here, and I figured it was time to buy something. Plus it'll make it easier for me to get back and forth to school and all that stuff."

"You can use my car."

"Until you go back to work, and then you'll be using it. I should just get something like this and be done with it." A salesman is making his way toward us. "Hey!"

"Hi. I see you're back! We got it all cleaned up and ready for you to drive. So you want the little lady to try it out too, huh?" the man asks.

"Hi. Judge Natalie Anderson, Eastern District of Kentucky," I say and hold out my hand for him to shake.

"Nice to meet you," he says, never missing a beat. "Craig Kennemore, ride specialist." Well, there's a term I haven't heard before, so congratulations on your fancy-pants title, Craig. "Right over this way."

Oh, it's nice. Very nice. Chevy Impala, about two years old, four door, nice extras. "Whaddya think?" Dennis says, taking a seat behind the wheel.

"Can we take it for a spin?"

"Sure! Let me help you get in," he says, and Craig trails behind us. Wonder if he's a wheelchair specialist too?

Once I'm in and buckled up, Dennis takes off. It's got a nice smooth ride. "I figured this would be a good choice."

"It is. Nice car. Seems like it's been taken good care of."

"Yeah. Very much so. Only twenty thousand miles on it. Practically new." He spins into a nearby parking lot and stops. "Power windows, power locks, sunroof, heated seats.

Full screen navigation system. Backup camera, power mirrors, parking assist, lane change assist. Seems like there's something I'm forgetting. Look in the glove box."

I open it and reach for the owner's manual. There's a small box in there. "Here. Hold this," I say and hand it to him as I dig around. "Ah. Owner's manual." When it's in my hand, I close the glove box and turn to Dennis just as he opens the tiny box and spins it toward me.

It's a ring.

Oh holy shit. Oh. Holy. Shit. "Took me forever to find a way to get you alone somewhere other than bed or the shower. There are always so many people around."

"Dennis, I—"

He presses a finger to my lips. "Sweet pea, just know that I'm not asking for tomorrow or next week. It can be the longest engagement on record for all I care. But marry me, please? Sometime in the future? When it comes to making dreams come true, you've gone so far beyond that … You've set a bar so high that no woman could ever top it. I just want to know that in this new life you've given me, you're going to be with me. That's all. Someday, down the road, will you marry me?"

"Dennis, I'll marry you right now if you want."

"Wow. Don't you think that's a little fast?" he asks with a huge grin.

"I know everything about you that I need to know."

"Have we ever eaten chili together?"

I laugh. "No."

"Then you don't know everything about me that you need to know."

"I'm pretty sure that anything chili could tell me about you it could also tell you about me."

"Oh, is that right?"

"Yep."

"So if I don't have to worry if I accidentally—"

"Nope."

"Well, that's a relief. My intestines and I thank you for that."

"You may regret those words."

"Let's find out. Let's take this car back, I'll make all the arrangements, and then we'll go have chili over at Tango Tamale." Instead of answering, I just sit there. "What?"

"Are you going to put the ring on me or not?"

The sun catches the diamonds around the big center stone as he lifts it from the box. "Will you marry me, Natalie Anderson?"

"I will marry you, Dennis O'Brien." I watch as he slips it on my finger, and I can hear my heart singing. I belong with Dennis O'Brien, and he belongs with me.

Judge Natalie Anderson-O'Brien. That sounds perfect to me.

BUT WAIT! THERE'S MORE! WOULD YOU LIKE TO KNOW what happens next? It'll surprise you, I promise! Just click for more: https://deanndrawrites.com/ATormentedManBONUSCONTENT

CURIOUS ABOUT TONY, NIKKI, VIC, AND LAURA? YOU CAN FIND them all in the Bluegrass Dynasty series here.

Have you met Ethan Watson and the men of Eagle Point SAR? You can find Susan Stoker's Eagle Point SAR series here.

Want more Kentucky romance and suspense? Grab the

Bluegrass Bravery books in Susan Stoker's Operation Alpha: Police and Fire world. They're all here, and some of the guys will show up in the Appalachian STAR series too! Just click here.

So what's next? Keep reading to enjoy an unedited excerpt from the next Appalachian STAR book, A Fierce Man!

COMING NEXT ...A FIERCE MAN

AGGIE

Oh, lawd, that man is fine!

And the things he said … I never thought I'd say I respect a convicted murderer, but I do. It's obvious to anyone who takes a minute to talk to him that Darius Fowler has his act together. He's a smart man. Seems kind too. I'm real curious about him.

The class I have in this time slot doesn't have lunch for an hour—our cafeteria is so small that we have to go in shifts—so they'll be waiting for me when I get to the classroom. On the way, Deborah, one of the math teachers, stops me. "Something I think you should know," she whispers.

"Yeah?"

"That guy? The one who spoke?" I nod. "He was checking out your ass as you were walking away."

"Deborah! Oh my lawd, girl! Stop that!"

"Nope. It's true. I saw it. Cathy did too. Ask her." She grins and winks as she walks away.

I'm still a little in shock when I walk into the classroom,

and all the kids are there, waiting. “Hey, y’all. Okay, so yesterday, I gave you an assignment. You were supposed to go home, think about it, and decide if your family is a matriarchal society or a patriarchal society, then write two pages about it. Anybody want to share?” The room is silent for a minute, and then Annie raises her hand. “Yes, ma’am. Go ahead.”

The girl stands, a paper in her hand. “I was supposed to decide if my family is a matriarchal or patriarchal society. Mine is matriarchal. My mom works all day. She’s not home when I get home from school, but my older brother is. Before she leaves for work, she lays out stuff for us to fix for dinner and instructions on how to do it if it’s something we’ve never had before. We sometimes have stuff like that ’cause she could get it at the food pantry at the Methodist church. When she comes home, it’s usually just the three of us eating, ’cause Daddy’s on the sofa, drunk, and he’s been there all day. All he’s done is drink since the mine closed down, and he can’t find no job. So Mama does everything and she makes all the rules, and he just drinks and sleeps. So, really, he’s not even there. Not really. I dunno why she don’t just kick him out. So my house is definitely a matriarchal society. My mama’s daddy died when she was a little girl, and her mama had to do the same thing, so I reckon that’s how she knows what to do. She grew up in a matriarchal society too.”

I nod sadly. “I think your observations are spot-on, Annie. Matriarchal societies occur because of any combination of three things. Write this down; this will be on the test. They either come about because the women are stronger and more dominant and the men are willing to cede control to them. It’s spelled c-e-d-e—that means give in. Or they come to power because the men are either lazy or busy and don’t want to be responsible. That’s common if the men are hunting for meat, raising livestock, or raising crops. And the third is if there are no men."

Glendon's hand shoots up, and I nod to him. "How can that be? That there ain't no men? 'Cause you gotta have men to have babies."

"That's a good question, Glendon. It can happen when there's been a war and most of the men have been lost in battle. It's happened several times in ancient times, and it also happened during the Civil War. Whole communities lost virtually every man except for the old, sick, or little boys. The women learned how to take care of themselves and everybody else too. Does that make sense?"

"Yes, ma'am," he replies, and some of the other kids nod.

"Anyone else want to share?"

I spend the rest of the hour listening to kids talk about their families, and it's heartbreaking. Over half of my students are poverty-stricken and living in a home with at least one parent who's an alcoholic or addict and doesn't or can't work. I don't care if he checked out my ass or not. I'm glad Mr. Fowler came and spoke to them this morning. If what he said can change the life of just one kid, every bad thing he ever did will be redeemed.

And that's the moment I admit to myself that I desperately want to know more about this man.

Priest

"So how'd it go?" Patch asks when I get back to the shop.

"I think it went well. Some of those kids … Man, they don't have two nickels to rub together. Worn-out shoes, raggedy clothes, and skinny. So fuckin' skinny, man. You can tell by looking at them that they're not gonna make it."

"Maybe because of what you said this morning one will, and that'll be worth it, right?"

I nod. "Yeah. I mean, this one little boy, I asked if anybody knew what prison was like, and it was obvious he's talked to somebody in his family through a visitor's booth window. Just so, so sad."

"Yep. I'm glad you went there to talk to them. That's something we can do that doesn't cost us anything except a little time, helps out the community, and gives us visibility." He points toward my spot in the loft. "I think Paddy has something ready for you to work on. Blade. He went ahead and cut the strips like you like them, so it's all set." He starts to turn away, but I lay a hand on his forearm. "Yeah?"

"Hey, listen, there was this teacher … Miss Henry. You've lived here a little longer than us. Do you—"

"Know her? No. But I know somebody who probably does." I hike up my eyebrows and wait. "Tinsley. Hell, she knows everybody. Does the woman have hair?"

I laugh. "Yeah."

"Then Tins probably knows her."

"Uh, she's black."

"What? You don't think Tins can handle a sister's hair? You'd better adjust your thinking, buddy. Tins can handle *anything*." Patch is laughing as he walks away, and I make a mental note: *Ask Tinsley about Aggie Henry.* He's likely right.

If anybody around here knows her, it would be Tinsley.

Keep watching. A Fierce Man *is coming soon!*

ABOUT THE AUTHOR

Deanndra Hall is a working author living in far western Kentucky with her partner of 30+ years, crazy little dogs, and maybe a snake or two. She's written for business, industry, religious institutions, non-profits, and owned her own graphic design business, as well as working as a fiber and textile artist. When she's not writing all things romance from sweet, simple plots to explicit, erotic suspense, she can be found working out at the local gym, hiking, kayaking, reading (of course), or working on a healthy recipe. And wherever she is, chocolate is sure to be nearby.

On the Web: deanndrahall.com

Email: Deanndra@DeanndraHall.com

Amazon: amazon.com/Deanndra-Hall

Bookbub: bookbub.com/authors/deanndra-hall

Facebook: facebook.com/deanndra.hall

Goodreads: goodreads.com/deanndrahall

Instagram: instagram.com/deanndra_hall/

Newsletter: Subscribe!

Pinterest: pinterest.com/deanndrahall

Mailing address:

P.O. Box 3722

Paducah, KY 42002-3722

ALSO BY DEANNDRA HALL

Books included in Susan Stoker's

Special Forces: Operation Alpha World,

Eagle Point Search and Rescue

The Appalachian STAR Series

A Desperate Man (Book 1)

A Bitter Man (Book 2)

A Broken Man (Book 3)

A Twisted Man (Book 4)

A Furious Man (Book 5)

A Tormented Man (Book 6)

A Fierce Man (Book 7)

A Dangerous Man (Book 8)

Books included in Susan Stoker's

Police and Fire: Operation Alpha World,

Badge of Honor

Bluegrass Bravery Series

Shelter for Sharla (Book 1)

Justice for Aleta (Book 2)

Shelter for Martina (Book 3)

Justice for Daesha (Book 4)

Shelter for Jerrica (Book 5)

Justice for Landee (Book 6)

Shelter for Tanna (Book 7)

Justice for Liella (Book 8)

Justice for Maisey (Book 9)

Shelter for Nita (Book 10)

Justice for JoElla (Book 11)

Refuge for Flora (Book 12)

Refuge for Phaedra (Book 13)

Refuge for Cherilyn (Book 14)

Refuge for Ailsa (Book 15)

Justice for Samara (Book 16)

Tarpley Volunteer Fire Department Series

Fighting for Carly (Book 2)

Tarpley Volunteer Fire Department Series 2

Fighting for Lorna (Book 4)

Fighting for Amethyst: A Tarpley VFD Novel

Bluegrass Dynasty Series

Bluegrass Dynasty:

The Love Under Construction Novels

Laying a Foundation (Book 1)

Tearing Down Walls (Book 2)

Renovating a Heart (Book 3)

Planning an Addition (Book 4)

Bluegrass Dynasty:

The Citadel Novels

One Simple Mistake (Book 5)

One Broken Promise (Book 6)

One Poor Choice (Book 7)

One Wrong Glance (Book 8)

Bluegrass Dynasty:

The Legacy Novels

Atonement (Book 9)

Legacy of Pride (Book 10)

Legacy of Freedom (Book 11)

Legacy of Faithfulness (Book 12)

Legacy of Hope (Book 13)

Legacy of Memories (Book 14)

Legacy of Love (Book 15)

Bluegrass Dynasty:

The Moonlight & Moonshine Novels

Kindred Spirits (Book 16)

High Proof (Book 17)

Angel's Share (Book 18)

The Bliss Series

Adventurous Me (Book 1)

Unforgettable You (Book 2)

Incredible Us (Book 3)

Completely Mine (Book 4)

Undeniably His (Book 5)

Eternally Yours (Book 6)

Blissfully Hers (Book 7)

The Harper's Cove Series

Karen and Brett at 326 Harper's Cove (Book 1)

Becca and Greg at 314 Harper's Cove (Book 2)

Donna and Connor at 228 Harper's Cove (Book 3)

Savannah and Martin at 219 Harper's Cove (Book 4)

Cheryl and Samuel at 323 Harper's Cove (Book 5)

Tasha and Davis at 333 Harper's Cove (Book 6)

Lily and Brock at 343 Harper's Cove (Book 7)

Siobhán and Gabhain at 241 Harper's Cove (Book 8)

The Witch of Endor Series

Laid Bare (Book 1)

Ripped Open (Book 2)

Torn Apart (Book 3)

Bound Together (Book 4)

The Silent Cove Series

Awakening (Book 1)

Independent Novels

My Last Dom

The Celtic Fan

Rough Stock

There are many more books in this fan fiction world than listed here, for an up-to-date list go to www.AcesPress.com

You can also visit our Amazon page at:
http://www.amazon.com/author/operationalpha

Special Forces: Operation Alpha World

Christie Adams: Charity's Heart
Elizabella Baker: Challenging Luke
Linzi Baxter: Dangerous Rescue
Misha Blake: Flash
Anna Blakely: Rescuing Gracelynn
Julia Bright: Saving Lorelei
Cara Carnes: Protecting Mari
Kendra Mei Chailyn: Beast
Melissa Kay Clarke: Rescuing Annabeth
Gia Cobie: Saved from Revenge
Samantha Cole: Handling Haven
KaLyn Cooper: Spring Unveiled
Jordan Dane: Redemption for Avery
D.M. Earl: Claire's Guardian
Riley Edwards: Protecting Olivia
Dorothy Ewels: Knight's Queen
Lila Ferrari: Protecting Joy
Nicole Flockton: Protecting Maria
Amy Gamet: Guarded by the SEAL
Lea Griffith: Finding Ava
Desiree Holt: Protecting Maddie
Danielle M. Haas: Crossroads of Betrayal
Bree Hera: Trusting the Team
Jesse Jacobson: Protecting Honor
Rayne Lewis: Justice for Mary

Ireland Lorelei: The Detective
Kristin Lynn: Worth the Risk
JM Madden: Rescuing Olivia
A.M. Mahler: Griffin
Ellie Masters: Sybil's Protector
Trish McCallan: Hero Under Fire
Naomi McKay: Twist
Rachel McNeely: The SEAL's Surprise Baby
KD Michaels: Saving Laura
Olivia Michaels: Protecting Harper
Annie Miller: Securing Willow
MJ Nightingale: Protecting Beauty
C.K. O'Connor: Delaney's Bodyguard
Melinda Owens: Betraying Katie
Victoria Paige: Reclaiming Izabel
Danielle Pays: Defending Sarina
Lainey Reese: Protecting New York
KeKe Renée: Protecting Bria
Taryn Rivers: Savage Cove
TL Reeve and Michele Ryan: Extracting Mateo
Ariana Rose: Chasing Paige
Deanna L. Rowley: Saving Veronica
Angela Rush: Charlotte
E.M. Shue: Discovering Tyler
Rose Smith: Saving Satin
Tyler Anne Snell: Cowboy Heat
Dee Stewart: Fighting for Brielle
Lynne St. James: SEAL's Spitfire
Bella Stone: Rexar
Jen Talty: Protecting Ainsley
Reina Torres, Rescuing Hi'ilani
LJ Vickery: Circus Comes to Town
R. C. Wynne: Shadows Renewed

Delta Team Three Series

Lori Ryan: Nori's Delta
Becca Jameson: Destiny's Delta
Lynne St James, Gwen's Delta
Elle James: Ivy's Delta
Riley Edwards: Hope's Delta

Police and Fire: Operation Alpha World

Freya Barker: Burning for Autumn
B.P. Beth: Scott
Jane Blythe: Salvaging Marigold
Julia Bright: Justice for Amber
Gia Cobie: Saved from Revenge
Hadley Finn: Exton
Danielle M. Haas: Crossroads of Betrayal
Deanndra Hall: Shelter for Sharla
Jenna Harte: Dead But Not Forgotten
India Kells: Game Master
Amber Kuhlman: Protecting Paisley
Reina Torres: Justice for Sloane
Aubree Valentine, Justice for Danielle
Maddie Wade: Finding English

Tarpley VFD Series

Silver James, Fighting for Elena
Deanndra Hall, Fighting for Carly
Haven Rose, Fighting for Calliope
MJ Nightingale, Fighting for Jemma
TL Reeve, Fighting for Brittney
Nicole Flockton, Fighting for Nadia

As you know, this book included at least one character from Susan Stoker's books. To check out more, see below.

<u>SEAL Team Hawaii Series</u>

Finding Elodie
Finding Lexie
Finding Kenna
Finding Monica
Finding Carly
Finding Ashlyn
Finding Jodelle

<u>Eagle Point Search & Rescue</u>

Searching for Lilly
Searching for Elsie
Searching for Bristol
Searching for Caryn
Searching for Finley
Searching for Heather
Searching for Khloe

<u>The Refuge Series</u>

Deserving Alaska
Deserving Henley
Deserving Reese
Deserving Cora
Deserving Lara
Deserving Maisy (Oct 2024)
Deserving Ryleigh (Jan 2025)

<u>SEAL of Protection: Alliance Series</u>

Protecting Remi (July 2024)

Protecting Wren (Nov 2024)
Protecting Josie (Mar 2025)
Protecting Maggie (TBA)
Protecting Addison (TBA)
Protecting Kelli (TBA)
Protecting Bree (TBA)

Delta Team Two Series

Shielding Gillian
Shielding Kinley
Shielding Aspen
Shielding Jayme (novella)
Shielding Riley
Shielding Devyn
Shielding Ember
Shielding Sierra

SEAL of Protection: Legacy Series

Securing Caite (FREE!)
Securing Brenae (novella)
Securing Sidney
Securing Piper
Securing Zoey
Securing Avery
Securing Kalee
Securing Jane

Delta Force Heroes Series

Rescuing Rayne (FREE!)
Rescuing Aimee (novella)
Rescuing Emily
Rescuing Harley
Marrying Emily (novella)

Rescuing Kassie
Rescuing Bryn
Rescuing Casey
Rescuing Sadie (novella)
Rescuing Wendy
Rescuing Mary
Rescuing Macie (novella)
Rescuing Annie

Badge of Honor: Texas Heroes Series

Justice for Mackenzie (FREE!)
Justice for Mickie
Justice for Corrie
Justice for Laine (novella)
Shelter for Elizabeth
Justice for Boone
Shelter for Adeline
Shelter for Sophie
Justice for Erin
Justice for Milena
Shelter for Blythe
Justice for Hope
Shelter for Quinn
Shelter for Koren
Shelter for Penelope

SEAL of Protection Series

Protecting Caroline (FREE!)
Protecting Alabama
Protecting Fiona
Marrying Caroline (novella)
Protecting Summer
Protecting Cheyenne

Protecting Jessyka
Protecting Julie (novella)
Protecting Melody
Protecting the Future
Protecting Kiera (novella)
Protecting Alabama's Kids (novella)
Protecting Dakota

New York Times, *USA Today* and *Wall Street Journal* Bestselling Author Susan Stoker has a heart as big as the state of Tennessee where she lives, but this all American girl has also spent the last fourteen years living in Missouri, California, Colorado, Indiana, and Texas. She's married to a retired Army man who now gets to follow *her* around the country.

www.stokeraces.com
www.AcesPress.com
susan@stokeraces.com

Printed in Great Britain
by Amazon

42445082R00155